THE ONLY BEST PLACE

CAROLYNE AARSEN

Misty Ridge
PUBLISHING

THE ONLY BEST PLACE

FOREWORD

What other people are saying about The Only Best Place:

"Carolyne Aarsen's lonely protagonist, Leslie, may be someone you will love-or she may be someone you actually are. A confused wife, trying to see the sky, she is stranded in her husband's Eden. And the serpents would absolutely love to have a chat."

Jacquelyn Mitchard, *author of Cage of Stars and The Deep End of the Ocean*

"Okay, I'm hooked. Carolyne Aarsen writes for every woman who has said yes with her mouth but not her heart, who has led the comfort and safety of the known and stepped (mentally kicking and screaming) into the unknown." - *Neta Jackson*, *author of the Yada, Yada Prayer Group novels*

CHAPTER 1

*S*mile. *Think happy thoughts. Take a deep breath and...*

"Hello. I'm Leslie VandeKeere, and I'm a farmer's wife."

No. No. All wrong. That sounds like I'm addressing a self-help group for stressed-out urban dwellers.

I angled the rearview mirror of my car to do a sincerity check on my expression and pulled a face at my reflection. Brown eyes. Brown hair. Both the polar opposite of the VandeKeere signature blonde hair and blue eyes repeated throughout the Dutch-based community of Holmes Crossing.

During the past hour of the long drive from Vancouver to here, I'd been practicing my introduction to varied and sundry members of the vast community of which I knew about four and a half people. I'd been trying out various intros. That last one was a bust. I'd never been a farmer's wife. Would never be a farmer's wife. I'm a nurse, even though my focus the next year was supposed to be on our marriage. Not my career.

I cleared my throat and tried again. "Our year here will be interesting."

Worse yet. Most women could break that code faster than you

could say "fifteen percent off." *Interesting* was a twilight word that either veered toward the good or the dark side.

Right now my delivery was a quiet and subdued Darth Vader.

I had to keep my voice down so I wouldn't wake my two kids. After four *Veggie Tales* and a couple of off-key renditions of "The Itsy Bitsy Spider," they had finally drifted off to sleep, and I didn't want to risk waking them. The eighteen hour trip had been hard on us. They needed the rest. *I* needed the rest, but I had to drive.

I stretched out hands stiff from clutching the steering wheel of my trusty, rusty Honda, the caboose in our little convoy. My husband, Dan, headed the procession, pulling the stock trailer holding stage one of our earthly goods. Next came his brother-in-law Gerrit, pulling his own stock trailer loaded with our earthly goods stage two.

I had each bar, each bolt, each spot of rust on Gerrit's trailer indelibly imprinted on my brain. Counting the bolt heads distracted me from the dread that clawed at me whenever I saw the empty road stretching endlessly ahead of me.

A road that wound crazily through pine-covered mountains, then wide open, almost barren, plains. Now, on the last leg of our journey, we were driving through ploughed and open fields broken only by arrow-straight fence lines and meandering cottonwoods. Tender green leaves misted the bare branches of the poplars edging the road, creating a promise of spring that I hadn't counted on spending here.

I hadn't gone silently down this road. I had balked, kicked, and pleaded. I had even dared to pray that a God I didn't talk to often would intervene.

Of course I was bucking some pretty powerful intercessors. I'm sure the entire VandeKeere family was united in their prayers for their beloved brother, son, cousin, nephew, and grandchild to be enfolded once again in the bosom of the family and the farm where they thought he belonged. So it was a safe bet my flimsy request lay buried in the avalanche of petitions flowing from Holmes Crossing.

The one person I had on my side was my sister, Terra. But she only talked to God when she'd had too much to drink. Of course, in that state, she chatted up anyone who would listen.

The friends I left behind in Vancouver were sympathetic, but they all thought this trip would be an adventure. *Interesting* adventure, my friend Josie had said when I told her.

I glanced in the rearview mirror at my sleeping children. Nicholas shifted in his car seat, his sticky hands clutching a soggy Popsicle stick. The Popsicle had been a blatant bribe, and the oblong purple stain running over his coat from chin to belly would probably not wash out. A constant reminder of my giving in.

Since Edmonton, I'd been tweaking my introduction, and now that we had turned off the highway, time and miles ate up what time I had left. I had only ten minutes to convince myself that I'd sooner be heading toward the intersection of "no" and "where," otherwise known as Holmes Crossing, Alberta, than back to Vancouver.

We would still be there if it weren't for Lonnie Dansworth-- snake, scumbag, and crooked building contractor. The $90,000's worth of unpaid bills he left in the "VandeKeere Motors" inbox tipped Dan's fledgling mechanic business from barely getting by to going under. The Dansworth Debacle, in turn, wiped out the finely drawn pictures I'd created in my head of the dream life and home Dan and I had been saving for. The home that represented stability for a marriage that had wobbled on shaky ground the past year.

The second push to Holmes Crossing came when Dan's step-father, Keith Cook, booked a midlife crisis that resulted in him doing a boot-scootin' boogie out of hearth, home, Holmes Cross-ing, and the family farm, leaving a vacuum in the VandeKeere family's life that Dan decided we would temporarily fill.

Temporary had been a recurring refrain in our life so far. The first two years of our marriage, Dan had worked for a small garage in Markham while I worked in the ER at the Scarborough Hospital. When an oil company needed a maintenance mechanic, we moved to Fort McMurray, and I got a job as a camp nurse. Two years later, an opportunity to be his own boss came up in Vancouver. When we packed up and moved, Dan promised me this was our final destination. Until now.

"It's only a year," Dan assured me when he laid off the employees, pulled out of the lease on the shop, and filed away the blueprints we had been drawing up for our dream home. We could have lived off my salary while Dan got his feet under him and worked on our relationship away from the outside influences of a mother Dan still called twice a week. But Dan's restless heart wasn't in it. Being a mechanic had never been his dream. Though I'd heard plenty of negative stories about his stepfather, Keith, a wistful yearning for the farm of his youth wove through his complaints. We were torn just like the adage said: "Men mourn for what they lost, women for what they haven't got."

The final push came when a seemingly insignificant matter caught my attention. The garage's bilingual secretary, Keely. She could talk "mechanic" and "Dan," and the few times I stopped at the garage, she would chat me up in a falsely bright voice while her eyes followed Dan's movements around the shop.

When her name showed up too often on our call display, I confronted Dan. He admitted he'd been spending time with her. Told me he was lonely. He also told me that he had made a mistake. That he was trying to break things off with her. He was adamant that they'd never been physically intimate. Never even kissed her, he claimed. She was just someone he spent time with.

I tried not to take on the fault for our slow drift away from each other or the casual treatment of our relationship as kids and work and trying to put money aside for our future slowly sunk its demanding claws into our lives, slowly pulling us in separate directions.

I also reminded him that I had remained faithful, taking the righteous high road. Dan was chastened, Keely quit, and her name never came up again. But her shadowy presence still hovered between us, making Dan contrite, and me wary.

Now, with each stop that brought us closer to the farm and Holmes Crossing and the possibility of repairing our broken relationship, I'd seen Dan's smile grow deeper, softer. The lines edging his mouth smoothed away, the nervous tic in the corner of one eye disappeared.

Mine grew worse.

A soft sigh pulled my eyes toward the back seat. Anneke still lay slack jawed, her blanket curled around her fist. Nicholas stirred again, a deep V digging into his brow, his bottom lip pushed out in a glistening pout. Nicholas was a pretty child, but his transition from sleep to waking was an ugly battle he fought with intense tenacity.

I had only minutes before the troops were fully engaged.

My previous reluctance to arrive at the farm now morphed into desperation for survival. I stomped on the gas pedal, swung around the two horse trailers, and bulleted down the hill into the valley toward my home for the next year.

My cell phone trilled. I grabbed it off the dashboard, glancing sidelong at Nicholas as I did.

"What's up?" Dan's tinny voice demanded. "What's your rush?"

"The boy is waking up," I whispered, gauging how long I had before his angry wails filled the car.

"Just let him cry."

I didn't mean to sigh. Truly I didn't. But it zipped past my pressed-together lips. In that too-deep-for-words escape of my breath, Dan heard an entire conversation.

"Honestly, Leslie, you've got to learn to ignore--"

Dear Lord, forgive me. I hung up. And then I turned my phone off.

I hadn't perfected Dan's art of selective hearing. He could let Nicholas cry while he calmly read the paper. Anneke would scream and he would blithely turn the page. The phone would ring, and he wouldn't even look up.

Ignoring the phone was a genetic impossibility for me. Call display only increased my curiosity. Why had Josie phoned me at nine o'clock at night? What did the hospital want from me on my day off?

As for ignoring Nicholas? Not even an option. My little tyrant pushed and demanded until I paid attention and then, when he got it, exacted more. Ignoring Nicholas was as easy as ignoring the guilt that had been my constant companion ever since I found out I was expecting an unexpected second child.

My master plan included one child, Anneke, followed by a maternity leave wherein I suitably bonded with my daughter, then enrollment in a daycare center chosen for its forward-looking program and trained caretakers. After Anneke's arrival, I returned to work as an emergency room nurse, doing a job I loved while saving up money needed for the large down payment on the dream home Dan and I had been planning since our wedding day.

God, it seemed, had a sense of humor. Twenty months after I ushered Anneke into the world, I found out I was pregnant again.

I didn't put on maternity clothes until the very last button refused to go into its buttonhole on my largest pair of surgical scrubs. I worked until the head nurse pried my fingers off the vital-signs monitor and pushed me out the door. When Nicholas fought through twenty hours of excruciating labor, I knew it was this child's way of getting back at me. I wondered if I could truly love this child the same way I loved Anneke.

However, as soon as the nurse brought that tight little bundle of flannelette that was my son--cap of dark hair, his unfocused eyes slightly crossed--a drowning wave of love and guilt washed over me.

How could I not have wanted this beautiful child? How could I have resented this innocent being? This perfect little person with fingernails like fragile shells, eyelashes that were a mere whisper across delicate eyelids. As I touched him, felt his realness nestling in my arms, I prayed for forgiveness to a God I had acknowledged only briefly before.

But Nicholas wasn't as forgiving and quickly started making me pay for my sins. All the kisses and cuddles snatched between housework and night shifts couldn't eradicate the debt he thought I owed. Nicholas was a tiny, unrelenting loan shark, and guilt his nasty skip tracer. No matter how hard I worked, how often I played with him, sang to him, told him I loved him, the interest on the loan kept accruing.

Nicholas now jerked awake, his head twisting to one side, his hands thrust out in front of him as if denying his entrance into wakefulness. He arched his back and launched directly into a full-fledged wail, his hands grabbing at the restraint holding him in.

"Honey, it's okay," I said ineffectually, hoping my soothing voice and nonsense words would calm him down.

Silly Mommy. Declaring things to be "okay" just inspired him to prove otherwise. In a nanosecond, his cries filled all available sound space in the car, pushing away every fragment of peace and quiet. And then Anneke joined in.

I careened down the gravel road, driving too fast and not even caring. By the time I pulled into the yard, Nicholas's cries pounded against my tired head. I jumped out of the car and closed the door on my sobbing offspring. Nicholas on the verge of a pediatric coronary and Anneke sobbing her poor little heart out, and I, Lord forgive me, stepping away from the car.

I craved a few moments of silence. Of separating myself from the tentacles of motherhood and wifehood tugging me in unwelcome directions.

I stared at the old two-story farmhouse, our home for the next year, solidly anchored to the ground, its foundations softened by shrubs and plants and sheltered by a thick windbreak of planted trees.

The few times Dan and I had visited, I thought the house quaint. Now it simply looked old and tired and abandoned.

I drew in a long breath, then another, but couldn't push away the muffled cries of my children. Forcing myself out of my selfish spat, I turned back to the car. Mommy once again.

The door of the house slapped shut, echoing sharply in the silence, and as my mother-in-law stepped out of the house, inevitability laid a chilly hand on my shoulder.

"You're finally here." Wilma waved to me from the back stoop.

Note to self: Ignore the "finally." She's had a hard time. *Do not, repeat, do not look for hidden agendas.*

I had to give her credit, though, I thought as I checked out her crisp khaki Capris and pale pink shirt. She certainly didn't look like she had been recently jilted by her husband.

And my goodness, makeup and earrings?

I tried not to glance down at my own stained T-shirt and yoga pants. I had aimed for ease of movement and comfort for our trip out here, not knowing when I would have to leap a car seat in a single bound.

Wilma strode down the cracked and slanted sidewalk, looking past me. "Where's Dan?"

"He should be coming soon." I pushed down a pinch of hurt at her quick dismissal of my presence. "I got a little ahead of him and Gerrit. Nicholas and Anneke were crying, so I wanted to get here before they both burst a blood vessel." *And stop right now before she thinks you're a complete idiot instead of the incomplete version you're already projecting.* I opened the back door of the car, releasing the blast of my children's sorrow and pain into the great wide world.

Wilma's eyes snapped from the driveway behind me to my offspring. "Oh, you poor children," Wilma cooed in sympathy as she opened the door beside Nicholas. She pulled my tightly wound son out of his car seat, his back arching in anger. She held him close, stroked his damp hair away from his face, then glanced down at his coat. "Oh, my goodness. You're all sticky." She flashed me a quick patronizing smile, hitting the guilt bullseye in one shot.

"I'll take him," I murmured, holding out my hands for my son. "He probably won't settle for you."

Mothers should never, ever, utter such provocative statements. Especially around a child as contrary as Nicholas.

He gave out one more long wail, but I could hear his heart wasn't in it. Then he hiccupped a couple of times and wilted against his grandmother, making me look like some loser who would have known more about her child had she spent quality time with him instead of working evening shifts so she could keep him clothed in Baby Gap and Please Mum outfits.

Little traitor.

"Poor baby," Wilma clucked, stroking Nicholas's pale hair, a shade lighter than hers, away from his flushed and damp face. "You've had a bad trip, haven't you?"

I did too, I felt like saying, but of course mothers aren't supposed to want sympathy. I bent over and pulled out a still-sniffling Anneke.

"Hey, pumpkin. That was hard to listen to Nicholas cry, wasn't it?" I lifted her into my arms.

She nodded, sniffed again, and peeked shyly over my shoulder at Wilma.

"Hello, Anneke," Wilma said quietly.

Anneke ducked her head down and clung to me. Okay, I

confess I'm not above a little maternal smugness. Anneke's clinging warmed my heart and negated Nicholas's easy defection.

"Say hi to Grandma," I urged Anneke, ready to share her now. But Anneke only burrowed deeper into the neckline of my worn T-shirt.

"Oma," Wilma corrected as her prim smile glanced off of me, then warmed as she stroked Anneke's hair. Anneke flinched and grunted her displeasure. Wilma's smile altered into a disapproving frown.

Okay. Things were slithering right along. I needed points. Fast.

"I'm really thankful you and Judy were able to help us move." I injected a hale and hearty note into my voice.

Wilma shifted Nicholas in her arms, her brisk nod accepting my little peace offering. "We were finishing up in the kitchen," Wilma said over her shoulder as she walked toward the porch door. "I thought that should be your first priority."

Wilma gave me more credit than I deserved. Right now my first priority was a selfishly long hot bath and a good book while Dan entertained the children. Such a dreamer I am.

As we stepped onto the empty, echoing porch with its gleaming floor, I wondered if I should take my shoes off upon entering the hallowed ground of the VandeKeere home place.

I glanced around, feeling the weight of history and responsibility slowly settle on my uneasy shoulders. Dan's father had grown up in this home with his siblings, and he and his wife, Wilma, had raised their children here.

Once Dan and I moved in, we would temporarily hold the keys of the kingdom.

I heard footsteps coming down the stairs above the porch, followed by the sound of humming. In spite of the weariness fuzzing my mind and dragging at my limbs, I smiled.

Where Gloria was forceful and uptight, Judy was easygoing

and friendly. Not hard to decipher which of the sisters I felt closest to.

Judy looked up as we came into the kitchen. The same wispy blonde hair that tufted Nicholas's head drifted out her loose ponytail. Her sloppy, faded shirt and sweats couldn't camouflage her generous size--the polar opposite of her slim and put-together mother and sister. And when she smiled, I thought for the first time since we packed up the vehicles, *I can do this*.

Judy grabbed me in a quick hug and cupped my face in her hands. "Hey, Leslie. Don't you look adorable? I like the sassy haircut."

"Just got it done before we came." I threw out the comment as if the new me was something I had planned. Not done in a fit of anger when I discovered the loss of Dan's business and his unfaithfulness. The sudden splurge was supposed to make me feel lighter, cheer me up. In the end, it gave me one more bill to add to the "pay it or skip it" file.

"Suits you." Judy lowered her hands and rested them on my shoulder as her expression grew serious. "I'm so glad you and Dan and the kids are here. I know you're going to miss Vancouver and your job and all, but you can make a home here too." Judy's voice rose in a hopeful question. She touched Anneke's cheek, then slipped her arms around my shoulders, encompassing both of us. She held on for that one extra split second, turning her hug from a polite gesture into a warm, welcoming greeting.

When she pulled away, Anneke stared up at her, soft hazel eyes still puffy from crying. "Who are you?" Anneke punctuated her question with a sniff.

"Oh, c'mon, Anneke," Wilma chided. "That's your Auntie Judy."

"Do you remember me now?" Judy tilted her face to one side to catch Anneke's eyes.

Anneke shook her head.

"We have a picture of Auntie Judy and Uncle Dayton on our

bulletin board. By the phone, remember?" In light of Anneke's momentary lapse, I needed them to know I hadn't neglected the legacy that was the VandeKeeres. I took seriously the responsibility of the family pictures entrusted to me each year in Christmas cards and letters.

Judy winked at me, a small gesture that connected and forgave. "You'll remember us all soon enough, Anneke. But for now, we sure know who you are. Do you want to go upstairs and look at the rooms? Maybe if your mommy lets you, you can pick which one you want to sleep in."

Another solemn nod and then, to my surprise, she wiggled out of my arms to the floor and took Judy's proffered hand.

I looked around the large empty kitchen. The avocado green flooring I'd seen in pictures of Dan as an eager toddler did what it was bought to do. Last. The bright yellow painted cupboards almost hurt my eyes. I knew Wilma had painted the cupboards and chosen the flooring, and I felt her eyes watching me as I inspected my new kitchen. To insult her handiwork was to insult her.

Though Wilma was always unfailingly polite, I knew she had a hard time with me. When Dan first introduced me to the family, he told the story of our meeting in the bar and laughed. Wilma gave me a polite smile and never really warmed up to me after that. Though she never overtly referred to it, the subtext of her comments was that I had been the brazen hussy whose siren song lured Dan away from church and turned him into a lush. From that auspicious beginning, things went decidedly downhill. I was the daughter of an absent single mother, which had made the wording of our wedding invitations an awkward situation I got to hear about until Dan and I said "I do." In Wilma's mind, to not have a father was misfortune, but to misplace both parents was irresponsible.

In addition to the lack of parents, I had a sister who smoked too much and laughed too loud when she drank too much. Which she did. At our wedding.

I was the woman who kept her beloved Dan in Markham, then dragged him to Fort McMurray and finally Vancouver, all places too far away for casual visits. Easier to blame me than acknowledge that Dan's restless spirit had us packing up and heading out every two years. Wilma even cast me as the impediment to Dan's return to the farm when that sinister role obviously belonged to Dan's stepfather.

To add the growing list, I had put her dear grandchildren in daycare while I sauntered off to make bags of money saving up for an extravagant home that Dan would have to work all hours to keep up and furnish.

Over time, our relationship became a one-way trip from bad to worse as Dan slowly became more my husband and less Wilma's son.

Now we were back in the sheltering, smothering bosom of the family. Though I knew I would have to make a solid stand, I also realized I needed to be sensitive to Wilma's current emotional state.

I glanced at her, trying to catch some hint of the humiliation and sorrow I was sure she felt at the moment. It had been only a few months since Keith left. Wilma had been crushed in a public way and now stood in the house where she'd enjoyed much happier memories. I tried to imagine how difficult it must be for her.

"So how have you been doing?" I lowered my voice in an attempt to sound sympathetic, warm, and friendly.

Wilma gave me a puzzled frown. "I'm fine. Had a bit of a cold the other day, but otherwise, I'm fine."

And the sharing moment collapsed like a cheap tent in a light breeze.

Okay. On to chirpy and mundane.

"I see you left the electric stove behind."

"The last renters didn't have any appliances." Wilma glanced down at Nicholas. "I'll go clean him up."

As she swept out of the kitchen, I sucked in a big breath. Suddenly I had room to breathe and allow myself a little bit of self-pity. Compromise had brought me here and, as with so many compromises, it resulted in two unhappy people.

I glanced around, trying to see positives. I had more space in this kitchen than in our two-bedroom condo and more cupboards. I swept the room with a glance. My gaze snagged on the large, fly-specked window facing south. Through it I saw the unfamiliar expanse of fields, fences, and hills.

Open, empty spaces.

If my life were a movie, this would be the moment when the soundtrack would get all quiet, intimate, and trembly and the focus would go soft. I would gracefully drift to the floor, holding my head in my hands and curling into the fetal position to chew on the cuffs of my sweater and mutter incoherently.

Okay, so it wouldn't be an Oscar-winning moment, but the way I felt, it had the elements of pathos, if not elegance. All the way here, I had tried to be positive and upbeat, putting on my smiley face whenever Dan asked me how I was doing. But right now, faced with the reality of where we would be living for the next year and with whom, I felt a jolt of panic, if not Oscar-worthy emotion.

Upstairs, I heard Anneke bopping along behind Judy. Downstairs, water ran in the bathroom off the kitchen as Wilma repaired the damage done to Nicholas's jacket. Then, above that, the rattly growl of a diesel engine.

The truck pulling the trailer lumbered into the yard and drew up behind my little car. Dan had arrived with the remainders of our other life. Time for smiley face number three.

After a moment, Dan stepped out and stretched, twisting his upper body the way he always did when he wound down after a stressful day. His dark blonde hair looked as if he had run his fingers through it in five different directions. But as he walked away from the truck, stretching out his arms above his head, I could see that the smile creasing his face was one of a man arriving at the Promised Land.

"Dan's here!" Judy called out from upstairs. Her feet beat out a joyous tattoo down the stairs, Anneke close behind her.

"My boy is home." Wilma's soft exclamation from the hallway laid further claim on him. Still holding Nicholas, she strode out of the house down the walk, waving her free arm. Calling out his name.

Dan turned and ran toward his mother, like a soldier returning from battle. He caught her in his arms, Nicholas and all, pulling them toward him in a hug that shouldn't have made me jealous.

From: tfroese@centermail.com
To: lesismore@hccrossing.net
I can't believe U took three hundred and sixty-five Lindor chocolates along to Holmes Crossing. You really are serious about this countdown thing, aren't U? How are U going to keep track if U suddenly have a snack attack or Dan finds them? BTW, love the new e-mail name. How's life in La-la-land? Has Wilma told U she loves U yet? <g> Will be a full-time job keeping her claws out of handsome hubby. I still can't get

over how she ignored me at UR wedding, though I did my best to let her know I was there. Ha. Ha. Put a crust around that soft heart of Urs. Don't let her get2 U. Thankfully U got me giving pithy advice. Pithy I don't live closer. <g> Keep UR house money in term deposit, else U will have nothin' when U head back to Vancouver. I think UR crazy not to work. U'll find a job like that (me snapping finger) and U can use the money. I'm off to San Francisco next week. Try to find a job there. Kiss the kids. I'll send pics when I have some. Heard anything from Mom? Me neither. Sigh.

Terrific Terra Testing The Tides

P.S. Did U ever hear more about that chick Dan worked with, the one you said could speak two languages? Forget her name.

FROM: leismore@hcrossing.net

To: tfroese@centermail.com

I forget her name too. Not. I figured I would let sleeping dogs lie, if you get my drift. Near as I know, she moved back home to PEI. And the three hundred and sixty-two chocolates are in a box under the bed. Oh. Goody. It's almost 6:00. Suppertime and time for another chocolate. Must snack.

Lonely Leslie

FROM: lesismore@hcrossing.net

To: josiepussycat@hurray.com

Hey Josie. I'm here. And, well, I'm here. And, like you said, things are interesting. Please keep me posted on what's been happening at the hospital so I'm not so out of it when I come back.

Les

CHAPTER 2

"First thing tomorrow we should empty the rest of the boxes," Dan whispered, as he slipped into bed late Saturday night.

I pulled my attention away from the water spots I'd been counting on the ceiling of our bedroom.

"I won't need the stuff out of them. Why bother?" I had been all for leaving them back in a mini-storage in Vancouver to create an anchor that would eventually draw us back there, but Dan wanted everything we owned moved back here.

"I want this place to feel like home, and home means having our stuff around us."

"You haven't listened to half those cd's for years, and most of the books have a layer of dust on them."

"You might want to read them. You might even have time to start a hobby."

Me and hobbies were only nodding acquaintances, something I'd read about in the obituaries of older women. I stifled the jitters bubbling in my chest at the thought of being home day after day, trying to fill my time with knitting and making scrapbooks out of the few pictures of the kids still stored on my computer. Somewhere.

All I knew was work. From the time I turned fourteen up until the day I graduated with my nursing degree, I had been working and going to school. All of this was an investment on a future life that I had promised myself would be light years away from my mother's. A life that included a husband, one, maybe two kids, and a beautiful home in the suburbs of a suitably sophisticated city. I could put a check mark beside two of my goals.

The home in the suburbs was put on hold.

"I think the roof leaks." I pointed up at the water spots.

Dan and I had taken one of the upstairs bedrooms, his sisters Gloria and Judy's old room. Anneke and Nicholas each had their own.

"I don't understand why we couldn't take the downstairs room." Dan settled in, ignoring my comment.

"I wanted to be closer to the kids," I whispered. "They're not used to this house yet." Nor was I. It smelled wrong and made me feel disoriented. The last time we'd been here, Dan and I had slept in the spare room, Anneke and Nicholas in this room. Though our furniture graced most of the rooms, this was still Wilma's domain, and if I listened hard enough, I could still hear the echo of her voice the day Dan brought me to meet her for the first time.

I think she wanted to be nicer that day. I sensed it in the puzzlement I caught in her eyes and the hesitant way she took my hand as if she was more used to giving hugs than handshakes. I wouldn't have minded the hug. Then.

Now there had been too many silent skirmishes behind the lines, too many forced courtesies as I slowly drew Dan outside of her sphere of influence. A hug from Wilma would feel even more forced now.

"Gloria thought we could have a family dinner here sometime."

Family? Dinner? All those VandeKeeres in this house? Me? Cooking?

"That sounds like a good idea, but really, Dan, I'm still an apprentice in this whole family supper deal."

"Leslie, you're a great cook." He lifted himself up on his elbow, and in the half light of the bedroom, I could see his eyes shining down on me. He touched my cheek with his finger, a tentative movement that I welcomed, but his comments distracted me from this hesitant move toward unity.

"Are you kidding? If it's tacos or barbecued steak, I'm your girl. But Sunday dinner? I've never met a turkey that I didn't dry out. I hate cooking ham, and I don't know how to make my own croutons." I pulled out another excuse, determined not to get rail-roaded by his crooked smile and soft voice, something I hadn't seen or heard since what's-her-name. Though the shadow of Miss Bilingual still hung like a silent specter over our marriage, she was slowly getting eased away by the obligations and expectations I was sure Dan felt from his family.

"Ah, Leslie." Dan went down softly on the E part of my name. I hate that light intonation even when I know it's coming. It signals his intention to be long-suffering and patient with a woman he promised to stay faithful to until death do us part, but oh, Lord, it shouldn't have to be this hard. "It doesn't have to be Sunday dinner. We can buy pizza and ice cream and have them over during the week. We haven't gotten together in this house since Mom and Keith moved out."

"I don't know what kind of pizza they like."

"Buy a bunch of different ones. Mom would love it."

The burden of moving into the flagship of the VandeKeere line dropped like a yoke on my shoulders. This house had been built by Dan's grandfather, replacing the older house now overgrown with willows and poplars that had replaced the small dugout that great grandfather Willem VandeKeere had moved his young bride into when they first moved to Holmes Crossing from Holland.

This yard was a veritable museum of VandeKeere history, and I had taken reluctant possession of one piece of it. And if Dan's sisters wanted to have a family supper, it was a sure bet that in the long run, I was helpless to stop the plans. But for now, the home was mine, and the control was mine.

"Let me think about it, okay?" I reverted to Ambiguous-Wife as I turned to him, trying to recreate the faint moment of warmth he had kindled in me.

"Sure. Whatever." Dan flopped onto his back, replying with What's-so-Hard-About-This Husband.

I deflected my automatic sigh into a safe place. No need to fan the flames with that outpouring of breath. I had a feeling I would need to save my ammunition for bigger battles.

"Oh, by the way, Mom's coming over tomorrow." Dan adjusted his side of the covers.

"Does Wilma think we need more help?" I had used my limited powers of persuasion to convince her to stay home today. I couldn't maintain a loving façade and deal with another litany of "suggestions" on how to arrange the kitchen or veiled criticisms about the number of appliances I owned. So what's wrong with having a crepe maker and a waffle iron? "Isn't she tired from helping out all day yesterday?"

"She said she'd like it if you'd call her Mom." Dan's comment was delivered in quiet, reasonable tones.

Not happening, though. I already had a mom. Not the best mom, but she was my mom.

"She wants to talk about our finances." Dan dropped that bomb as casually as I would a dirty diaper. "To give us some advice."

I pressed my hand to my thumping heart, trying to keep it in my chest. *Swallow*, I commanded myself. *Breathe. Relax. Again.*

Good girl. Now you can talk. Use short words and...smile...and you're on.

"That's okay, Dan. I'm sure we don't need her help."

"She doesn't mind."

Obviously the smile had worked too well. I needed to lay down hard and firm boundaries. With each dish I put away and each item of clothing I hung up, I felt tiny threads anchoring me to this unfamiliar place that was Dan's home and territory. "We've managed for years without her help. I'm sure we'll be fine now." Nice firm delivery, strong intonation. Much better.

"But the farm belongs to her."

"I don't see the connection."

"She'll be writing the checks."

Don't panic. Do not panic.

"Mom's real good with money. She can help us out. Said she had a budget drawn up for us."

"I don't think... We never really... Budget?" I couldn't grab the right words from the hundreds that swirled around my head. "I thought you would be doing the finances."

He looked up at the ceiling, avoiding me. "Mom asked if you would mind if she kept doing it. I said sure. It will make things easier for us, and it gives her something to do."

Dread spiraled in my stomach and made a home. Wilma. In charge of the farm finances. Our finances. It didn't take a gourmet cook to know this was a recipe for disaster. "But how is she going to figure out..." I faltered, still trying to absorb this latest information. "Why didn't you ask me?"

"You had enough to do getting the house set up. I didn't want to bother you."

"If we're going to be talking finances, are you going to tell her about the assessment?"

When Dan and I had talked about giving a year of our time to help out his mother, we decided it would be in our best interests to have an assessment done of the farm. We assumed that, once we left, the farm would be sold. I knew Dan. Every place we'd lived in, he fixed up. Every place we'd lived, he hadn't been paid for his work. This time I wanted to make sure Dan got recompensed for any improvements he did.

"It seems a bit soon for that." Dan was hedging.

I was about to press my case when I heard Nicholas whimper in his sleep. Kiddy timing. As I slipped out of bed, Dan caught me by the arm, belatedly catching my faint cue. "You don't need to go to him every time he fusses. It's probably nothing. Let him cry."

I glanced back at Dan, the wife part of me struggling with my inherent guilt where Nicholas was concerned. Our boy needed me so seldom. I didn't want to miss any chance to connect.

"It's probably nothing, but he's in a strange bed in a strange place." Like me. I glanced around the room that still had posters from its previous inhabitant, Judy, on the wall. "I'll be right back."

But as I walked down the hall, Nicholas's already loud cries grew in intensity, and by the time I got to his door, his screams filled the room, and he thrashed about, kicking his feet, his adorable face squinched so tight, his eyes had disappeared.

This is going to take a while. I lifted the stiff and unyielding bundle of terry cloth that was my son out of his crib, his screams piercing my ears. Then Anneke appeared in the doorway as I tried to rock Nicholas out of his snit. She sidled up to me, sniffing. "I'm scared," she called out above Nicholas' cries.

And I knew by the time I got back to the bedroom, Dan would be snoring.

From: lesismore@hcrossing.net
To: tfroese@lakeshore.com
My husband is morphing in front of my eyes. From stressed out mechanic who gave me a sullen wave as he trudged out the door to a man who seems to want to make an effort to make this marriage work. From a man who sat at the table and dived into his food to a man who spends a meditative moment before eating. Like he's going to pray. It's Sunday tomorrow. I'm scared that the next move is church.
Laggard Leslie Lamenting her Life

FROM: tfroese@lakeshore.com
To: lesismore@xplornet.com
May B all the chemicals he's using? Anyway, hope not catching.

"The farm has to support two families now." Wilma folded her hands over the checkbook as if defending it from my grasping clutch. Her gaze flicked from me to Dan and back again. The significance of the equal triangle we formed around our circular kitchen table wasn't lost on me. Dan sat equidistant from me and his mother, torn between two women again. I almost felt sorry for him. Emphasis on almost. "We will have to watch every penny," Wilma continued.

Considering that Wilma already had that department well in hand, I didn't think the pennies needed my eagle eye on them as well. I glanced at Dan, sitting across from me at the kitchen table, wondering what he thought of the check that lay on the table in front of him.

Dan had been up before me this morning, so before I could tell him I didn't want his mother coming over, she was striding up the sidewalk, farm books in hand and a take-no-prisoners look in her eye.

"We won't have lots of expenses." Dan stroked his chin with one hand as he picked up the check with the other. "If the farm pays for fuel for the truck, power, and upkeep on the house, we won't need to use this for more than our personal stuff." He smiled up at me. I felt heartened by the glimpse of disappointment I caught in his eyes.

"Of course, if things go well this year, I'm sure I'll be able to give you extra money." Wilma smiled as if she had just granted us stock options in a blue-chip company. "Though I think the amount you are getting is a fair bit."

A fair bit? If she knew how much I could make in a week, she would choke on her decaf.

"Now if you will look at this budget, you'll see that it won't be hard to live on what you are getting." She handed me a paper. Call me stubborn, but I didn't spare it so much as a glance. Dan, however, dutifully picked it up and looked it over, nodding his approval.

"I did put in an entry for contributions to the church..." Wilma let her sentence drift off, her eyes on her son. "That is, if you will be coming to church. Of course, there's no obligation..."

Of course there was. While her words were meant to let us off the hook, the raised eyebrows and the tilt of her head caught Dan neatly in a snare of expectations.

"It would be wonderful if you could come."

"Of course we will." Dan sat back and set the paper down. I caught the question in his eyes as he looked at me, and I subtly shook my head.

"I wouldn't be comfortable," I said. "I'm not familiar with church."

"C'mon, Leslie. You've gone at Christmas and Easter." Dan's awkward laugh made me nervous. "And you, your mother, and sister used to go when you could get..."

"That's enough, Dan," I said sharply, cutting off his sentence.

Wilma's eyes darted from Dan to me and then back again, as if hoping she could ferret out what I had stopped. Not a chance.

"Well, I hope you will reconsider coming to church." Wilma continued, as always brisk and efficient. "And look over that budget and tell me what you think."

I already knew what I thought of it. Not much. But she was the payer, and we were the payees. Powerless and puny.

"There's one more thing. I would really like to have the family together to talk about the farm. We are in a bit of a cash crunch." She paused and I immediately thought of Keith, but she rallied and forged ahead. "So if Gerrit and Dayton could offer us some advice, that would be helpful."

"That's a good idea," Dan said.

"Your Grandma VandeKeere has been asking after you and the kids," Wilma said to Dan. "Once seeding is done, you should go visit her in Edmonton."

"I haven't seen her since Christmas. How is she doing?"

Wilma leaned a bit closer as she brought him up to speed on the care and maintenance of the family tree.

I picked up my coffee mug and washed it out as their conversation covered all the twists and turns of names and connections I doubted I would ever master. I didn't feel left out. Not a bit.

How was I going to make it for another eleven months, two weeks, and five chocolates?

Wilma finished her coffee, wound down the conversation, then went into the living room to see Anneke and Nicholas.

"Sorry about that church comment." Dan set the coffee cups beside the sink.

"It's okay." I shrugged off his apology. But it wasn't. I had been given a budget. Really?

I looked over at him in time to catch him looking at me, something akin to sorrow on his face. Our eyes held for a moment longer than they usually did. He took a breath, like he was about to say something.

"I'm going now," Wilma called out, coming into the kitchen.

That tender moment was gone.

Dan pushed away from the counter. "Thanks for coming Mom." He gave Wilma a kiss.

"Bye, Leslie." She tossed me a quick wave, then tucked her arm into Dan's. "Son, I was wondering if you could have a look at my car. There's a funny knocking sound in the engine."

As they walked out the door, Wilma took him by the arm and pressed her head against his shoulder. Dan bent closer and gave her a hug. They talked a moment as Wilma brushed her fingers over his cheeks.

I really wanted to give her the benefit of the doubt. I really wanted to be a good person and feel sorry for her. But as I watched her clinging to Dan, I felt that although Miss Bilingual had been left behind, she had been replaced by another, more powerful combatant for my husband's heart.

FROM: tfroese@centermail.com
  To: lesismor@hccrossing.net
  So Dan is making noises about going to church? So not fair. Tho I figured that would happen once he got back to Mommy. She's got a hold

of him U gotta watch. And the whole finances and Wilma thing? Lee-lee, be afraid. Be very afraid. I don't think this woman has met a dollar she couldn't put in a bank account. Speaking of, mine should be out of the red soon. Got a job. Not great, but we can't all be brilliant nurses. And hey, I think I have a right to push U back to work. After all, I had a part in UR edjumacation, sugar plum. If anyone can prove the Froeses can be productive members of society, U are the one. Two kids, one husband that UR still married to. :) Give my darling nephew and niece a hug kiss from their

Adventurous Aunt, Alive and Adorable

FROM: lesismore@hcrossing.net

To: tfroese@centermail.com

The noises about church have become actions. He went this morning and took Anneke with him. I just remind myself to grow accustomed to this phase. Once we're back in Vancouver we get normal back.

Laconic Leslie

I STEPPED out of the computer room Sunday morning and glanced around the main floor, mentally going over my to-do list.

Anneke's bedroom cleaned.

Check.

Chocolate washed off Nicholas' face and the couch and sponged off the carpet.

Check.

Remnants of Nicholas's orgy with an unsupervised bag of chocolate chips remained imbedded in the shag carpeting, but enough had been scraped and wheedled out that I considered the job done.

I had already cleaned up the broken plate Nicholas pulled off the counter, read him a story rather than let him watch a televangelist plead for money, cleaned up the baby powder he had gleefully tossed around the bathroom, unloaded the dishwasher, wiped up the syrup he had spread all over his hair and clothes in the four point one seconds I had been staring out the window. I gave him a cookie and foolishly left the bag on the counter while I hurried to the bathroom to stop the toilet from running through and wasting precious water.

Now Nicholas was in bed, and I was exhausted.

From where I stood I could hear a few half-hearted cries, a lackluster attempt at manipulation.

The only other sound I heard in the eerily quiet house was the rattle and hum of the refrigerator. No cars rolling past our home, no cries for "Mom," no obnoxiously loud television personality yelling at me to "come right down and help us move this over-stocked inventory," no Dan asking me where I put the sugar bowl this time.

Dan and Anneke were out of the house for now. At church. And I wasn't.

I picked up the laundry basket, went downstairs, and let my gaze flicker past the windows. All I saw was a vast expanse of fields. No houses and no vehicles broke the expanse of field and sky. Just land and more land, and every acre, as far as I could see, belonged to Dan's family.

I caught hold of the back of a chair with one hand as a wave of dizziness washed over me. It still caught me unawares, this endless space. It was as if my world had been sucked empty, and Nicholas and I were left behind.

I stuffed the clothes in the washing machine, turned it on, and strode back to the kitchen.

A pile of cookbooks on the counter in the kitchen caught me mid-stride. Yesterday Wilma had come by with her flawless smile and these cookbooks. She had helpfully bookmarked the pages that held Dan's favorite recipes. I gave her my best imitation of dutiful daughter-in-law smile, took the cookbooks, and set them aside.

Now I picked up one of them, wondering if I dared venture where I had seldom gone before. I knew I had skills. I could start IVs, autoclave instruments, and spot a drug seeker at twenty yards.

How hard could this be?

I reluctantly opened the book and stopped at the fly leaf with its dedication.

"The ladies of Holmes Crossing Reformed Church would like to thank all of the members for sharing the recipes that make our kitchens worthy of the woman in Proverbs." Below that another inscription headed by the words, Psalm 104: 14.

"He makes grass grow for the cattle and plants for man to cultivate, bringing forth food from the earth. Wine that gladdens the heart of man, oil to make his face shine, and bread that sustains his heart".

These women had put this quote from the Bible in a simple cookbook sold to raise funds for the local church?

Clearly the ladies of Holmes Crossing Reformed Church took their faith seriously.

I opened the cookbook, and of course it fell to one of Wilma's bookmarked pages. "Gloria's Yummy Bars."

Some residual resentment reared its ugly head, and I sailed right on past Gloria's Yummy Bars recipe and its self-aggrandizing title. I paused at some of the names of the recipes. Speculaas. Koek. Krentebrood. Roggebrood. Probably Dutch and probably Things I Would Never Make. I turned the page and stopped at Kathy's Everything Cookies.

As I read through the list of ingredients, then the instructions, I realized I teetered on the threshold of another world with its own language of "creaming" and "separating" and "sifting." Did I really want to go there when perfectly good cookies in perfectly good bags could be bought in perfectly good grocery stores?

Okay, they weren't exactly around the corner, and the store in Holmes Crossing wasn't open on Sunday, but a cookie was a cookie, right? And someone had to keep the economy going? Wasn't that my duty as a North American consumer?

I skimmed through the rest of the recipes in the same way I read science fiction. With skepticism and disbelief that people could even think this stuff up. I had enough to master the next few months. For now, baking had to be put aside. I was in charge of my home, and this home bought cookies.

I closed the cookbook, gathered up the rest of them, and put them in an empty drawer. Out of sight and all that.

From: lesismore@hcrossing.net

To: tfroese@centermail.com

My husband is changing right in front of my eyes. Today Dan got some old-time religion. Of course as far as his family is concerned, he's misplaced it for a while thanks to me who kept him in the realms of pagan night. He asked me if I wanted to come with him to church, but I ix-nayed that idea. Couldn't imagine bringing The Tyrant along to church. Anneke overheard Dan's plans, and she immediately got religion as well. So this morning I had to find the box of clothes with her one and only dress in it. Of course the dress needed ironing. I spent half an hour finding Dan's dress pants he hasn't worn since the Christmas party from my work last year. Anneke's fingernails needed trimming. Then she got gum in her hair, and I had to find a hairstyle that would hide the chunk I cut to get the gum out. I don't know why Sunday is called a day of rest when it takes that much work to get ready for it. I'll take my rest at home, thank you very much. Besides, I have to conserve my energy. Your sister is going to "help with the cows," whatever that entails. Family is coming over to do said deed. Figured I should make a stab at being a farmer's wife for the short time we're here.

Lionhearted Leslie out of her League

From: tfroese@centermail.com

To: lesismore@hcrossing.net

Good call on staying at home. Church is overrated. Full of hypocrites and all that self-righteousness. Bad call on the cows. U dn't know cows. Being in charge might mean being in the way of a charge. Besides, U wl B working sn, won't you? Your not a farmer's wife and never will be.

CHAPTER 3

"What are you doing?" As Dan bent over my shoulder, the scent of hay that he had been feeding the cows mingled with his warm skin and teased my nose. It was a kinder, gentler smell than the gag-me-in-the throat odor of gear oil or gasoline fumes that usually swirled around him after a day of mechanic work.

Doing farm chores had turned Dan into a kinder, gentler man I was still dealing with. Vancouver Dan never would have had time for lingering in the kitchen watching me work. Then again Vancouver Leslie would not have been frowning over the arrangement of cookies on a plate for company.

"I'm trying to make these cookies look tastier than they are."

"I don't know why you bothered." Dan rested his hand on my shoulder. "My mother and sisters said they'd bring dessert."

"Well, I felt duty bound to provide my own temptation." I sighed as I moved away from him. I hoped he took the hint. I didn't have time to nuzzle, and I was still trying to adjust to this new place in our marriage. I couldn't help it. Every time he came close, I pictured him doing the same with Keely. I knew I had to get rid of her, but for now she was sticking around.

In a moment of insanity, I had decided to go along with Dan's idea of a family dinner and invited everyone over for pizza afterward, then made a quick run to the grocery store in Holmes Crossing to buy said pizza and, of course, cookies that I knew would be required.

When Dan had come home from church on Sunday, it was to inform me that his mother, Gloria, Gerrit, and their kids were coming over on Tuesday to help with the cows. This was said with an expectant look that I could translate only as, *Could they stay for supper?* In a moment of insanity I caved in to familial pressure. Then, as if to make my breakdown complete, I invited Judy and her family to join us for pizza afterward, as well. This necessitated making a quick run to the grocery store in Holmes Crossing to buy said pizza and, of course, cookies that I didn't have to bake myself.

Wilma had made her bi-daily visit yesterday with her take-no-prisoners attitude... and a pile of cookbooks. She had helpfully folded over the pages that held Dan's favorite recipes. I put the books in an obscure corner of a cupboard and closed the door of self-preservation on them. I may not be in charge of the farm checkbook, but I was in charge of the home and this home *bought* cookies.

"You don't have time for me?" Dan asked.

The hint of hurt in his voice created a guilt I wasn't ready to take on, though I knew where he was coming from. Time was what we moved to the farm to create for us.

In Vancouver I worked night shifts so that Anneke and Nicholas would spend minimal time in Daycare, and Dan's and my lives slipped past each other. When Dan's business declined, he started working extra hours in a futile attempt to save the business. That gave us time for nothing more than an occasional heart scrawled on a Post-it-Note and slapped on the fridge. Hardly enough to keep the fires of passion burning brightly and barely enough to keep them glowing.

"Later." I thought about hugs we used to share in the kitchen, how the first time Dan kissed me, his fingers played over my face as if reading my features by Braille. The little shiver I always got whenever he smiled at me.

Did he smile at Keely like that?

And an unwelcome image of "her" surged into my tired brain.

Seriously, I needed to let go, hoping the forgetting would come soon.

And I needed to stay on task.

"Are you going to talk about the assessment at the family meeting tonight?" Maybe not the best time to bring it up, but someone had to look to the future away from this place. "We agreed to make sure the year we are here is recognized."

"I don't think tonight is a good time. We've got other important things to discuss with the rest of the family."

"The longer we wait, the longer your family will think we're staying." Dan's stern expression made me feel like an unwelcome negotiator in a hostile takeover. I wanted to be on the same page as Dan, but lately we weren't even in the same story. We had to be practical, I reminded myself. We had to take care of our little family. "Once the year is over, we're moving back. It's not fair to raise your family's expectations and then dash them."

We had gone over all of this before we came here. Talked about it endlessly while we checked out all our options. He couldn't switch allegiances on me now.

His resigned sigh told me he was easing back to my side. "Okay. I'll try to work it into the conversation tonight."

The hard block of tension that had lodged in my chest slowly dissolved. I gave him a look that hopefully transmitted some type of affection, but to cover my bases, I added a cookie.

"Thanks," he muttered, then leaned back against the counter as he ate it, his one hand cupped under the other to catch the crumbs. "I remember eating cookies straight out of the oven in this kitchen."

It was a throwaway memory, but saying it in the kitchen where thousands of homemade cookies had been baked, eating one that wasn't added a bit of a sting. "Good thing you didn't marry me for my baking skills." I gave him a quick smile to show that, on the surface at least, I was okay with the memory. On the surface at least.

"I married you for other reasons." Though his declaration was imprecise, his sincere look created a warmth I hadn't felt in a while, and I reached over to touch his cheek.

The screen door slapped open, and Anneke burst into the house shattering the moment. "Mommy, mommy, I found a worm." She held it up, a long pink string that bunched and pulled and made my stomach curl. That was no string. That was a worm. In my house.

Okay. Calm voice. Soothing voice. "Honey, Mommy doesn't like worms in her kitchen." I spoke quietly hoping she wouldn't drop it.

Anneke held it up in front of her face as if inspecting it further, then with a light shrug, turned around and ran directly into her little brother, who had followed her. Nicholas fell back on his diapered bottom, his expression registering only mild surprise.

But Anneke collapsed in a tangle of long skinny legs and flailing arms and cries of indignation.

"I lost my worm," she wailed, scrabbling around on the kitchen floor.

Two words, "lost" and "worm," galvanized me into action.

I pushed past Dan and snatched Nicholas into my arms before he found Anneke's new pet and inspected it the way he did with all new discoveries. With his fingers, then his mouth.

I quickly scanned the floor. A pink worm should be easy to pick out on the DayGlo linoleum. "Honey, stop crawling. I see it." I juggled Nicholas, reaching for her arm just as she put her hand down in the wrong place.

And Teddy was no more.

Anneke discovered this the same moment I finally snagged her hand. The wail she let loose would send air force pilots scrambling to their planes.

Dan made it to the murder scene in time to catch his sobbing daughter in his arms.

"A little bit of speed would have been nice," I muttered, shifting Nicholas's chubby weight on my hip.

"It's just a worm, Leslie."

"That's now squished all over our kitchen floor and your daughter's hand."

Dan inspected Anneke's hand, then wiped it on his shirt. He cuddled Anneke, whose sobs didn't show any sign of shifting to normal.

"Dan, for goodness sakes wash her hands." I raised my voice to be heard above the growing din. *Great, Leslie. Way to motivate him.* I opened my mouth, apology ready to spill out when I heard the door open behind us, followed by the thump of shoes and two young girls burst into the house.

"Hey, Uncle Dan" "Hey, Dan." They spoke at the same time.

I looked over my shoulder to see the grinning faces of Tabitha, Gloria's daughter, and Allison, Judy's oldest girl. Tabitha was fifteen, Allison thirteen, but to me they were interchangeable. They could be sisters instead of cousins.

"Is your dad at the corrals already?" Dan turned to Tabitha, obviously thankful for the interruption.

"He's backing up the trailer with the horses in it." She answered in a tone that made it clear she was Gloria's daughter. Informative with a soupçon of authority.

"Then I'd better get going." I saw an unfamiliar light of pleasure in his eyes as he scrambled to his feet. Dan had been talking all day about the horses that Gerrit was delivering, and the sparkle in his eyes left me with a flicker of jealousy.

He handed a still sniffing Anneke to Allison, flashed me a quick smile, and left.

Nicholas let out an angry wail, but Allison, still cradling Anneke on her hip tickled him, distracted him from the departure of his beloved father. I often wondered how Dan got such a huge return on such a small investment of time. I spent precious hours playing with our son and reading to him, and still he resisted my charms. A quick tickle and a brush over his chubby cheeks were all Dan had to bestow on him, and Nicholas was devastated whenever he left.

"So how do you like being on the farm?" Tabitha asked, watching Allison playing with Nicholas and Anneke but making no move to join them.

Time to put on my hearty voice. "It's really beautiful here. Such an abundance of scenery."

"We don't have mountains though. Could you see the mountains in Vancouver" Allison scrunched her face as Nicholas's chubby hands reached for her long hair.

"We did, but I could only see them out of the upstairs window of our condo." And only if I leaned my head against the window frame to look past the rows of other condos that blocked my view.

"So why didn't you have your own house?" Tabitha now leaned back against the counter inspecting her nails.

"We were going to buy one..." I stopped the note of self-pity creeping into my voice.

"But you decided to move here instead." Allison gave me a quick grin. She got up from the kitchen floor, swung Nicholas into her arms, and held out her hand to Anneke. "Is it okay if I take the kids outside? I thought they might like seeing the horses."

"They might be scared," Tabitha said. "They're still city kids."

Allison simply shrugged her cousin's comments away with a grin. "Not anymore. They're farm kids now."

"Give me a few minutes, and I'll come with you," I said.

Allison may have allowed Alberta to make its hurried claim on my children, but I knew that the horses and cows that Allison felt so comfortable around would make my children afraid.

"Are you going to help?" Tabitha looked skeptical.

"Isn't that what farmers' wives do?" I would try to make the best of the short time we were here, and if working with large unwieldy creatures was part of it, I could play *Little House on the Prairie.* Helping hadn't even been a consideration until Gloria called. I don't know whether it was the take-charge note in her voice that spurred me on when she said she and Gerrit and the kids were coming or the blanket assumption that I wouldn't be able to help. Pride makes a woman do foolish things.

With a faint shrug in my direction, Tabitha followed her cousin out the door leaving me alone to do what preparations I could before the Vandekeeres invaded.

Twenty minutes later I was out in the yard. I glanced around but could neither hear nor see Tabitha, Allison, or my children. I heard the distant whinny of a horse but couldn't place the direction. Suddenly the rattle of a truck penetrated the stillness, and an empty stock trailer came toward me from behind one of the barns. Gloria was driving, and behind her in the cab of the truck, I saw a jumble of heads.

The truck screeched to a halt, and three boys piled out in a tangle of arms and legs and laughter followed by a barking dog. The boys glanced my way, nodded, and gave me the sheepish smile of a self-conscious teenager. The dog ignored me.

I remembered the boys names. Joseph, Douglas and Nathan. Gloria and Gerrit's boys.

During our time in Vancouver I had accompanied Dan home once for Christmas and once for a family get-together. All I remember of the nieces and nephews was a bunch of kids sitting still long enough for the obligatory prayer before the meal, then filling their plates and running off to various rooms in the house.

Just as Gloria turned the truck off, Allison and Tabitha joined us, coming out from one of the older barns on the yard. Allison was pulling Nicholas in a small, red wagon, and Tabitha held Anneke's hand.

The boys left, the dog following, its tail waving like a plume, it's mouth open, like it was smiling at the prospect of moving cows.

"Good morning, Leslie." Gloria, a slimmer, more nervous version of Wilma, got out of the truck. She was pretty in an uptight way. "So. Here you are." She twitched out a smile. "It's good to have you with us. Mom's so happy about that, too."

I almost mouthed those last words along with her. Each time I met Gloria, she said precisely the same thing. Like she had written down somewhere, "Things to say when I meet Leslie," and each time I got a sense of her watching me, looking for cracks or possibly the same lewd behavior that my sister exhibited at the wedding.

And now the next thing would be... Wait for it...

"So how have you and your lovely children been doing?"

Bingo. Sure, these were often the same blank phrases tossed out when people first meet. A conversational equivalent of letting your car run to warm it up. But with Gloria, the conversation was always the same phrases in the same order and she always started with, "So—" Pause. "Here you are." As if my presence was something she'd have to get used to all over again.

Today she had her long blonde hair tucked under a farmer's cap. She wore coveralls with a pair of gloves hanging out of the back pocket. In spite of the farmer attire, she still managed to look like she was setting some new fashion trend.

I couldn't help but glance down at my clean blue jeans and pale pink jacket.

"Sweet coat, Leslie," Allison said.

I didn't detect any irony in her voice, though I noticed too late that she and Tabitha were wearing faded and worn jackets and jeans.

"What the well-dressed farmer's wife wears," I quipped.

"You won't be doing much." Gloria waved her hand at me, dismissing my capabilities with the flick of her wrist. "So you won't have to worry about getting dirty." Another twitchy smile.

Down, hackles.

"I'm a farmer's wife now," I said with a blustery confidence that was ninety-seven percent fake. I still couldn't tell barley from wheat or hay from straw, but I was undaunted. "I can help."

"Well then," was all she said.

"Are the horses unloaded already?" Tabitha glanced toward the corral.

"Dan and Dad are already headed out to gather up the cows. And Oma is getting the needles and medicine ready." Gloria pulled the gloves out of her pocket. "We'd better get going."

"Wilma's here, too?"

"Of course." Gloria frowned. "The cows belong to her."

I nodded. My big attempt at integration struck aside by the reality of ownership. Wilma's cows. Dan and I were simply hired help.

"We'd better get going." Gloria's command became everyone's wish, so we started off. Nicholas babbled as Allison pulled him along in the wagon. Anneke sang. And I had to look back to make sure these happy children were my offspring. My long nursing shifts had left me with the tired and cranky version of my children after they had spent ten hours in daycare. My mission had always been to pick them up, feed them, and clean them up before Dan came home, then get ready for another twelve-hour shift at the hospital.

Beside us, Gloria and Tabitha chatted about the weather, school, the cows, the farm. At one point Tabitha laughed and dropped her head onto her mother's shoulder.

The little gesture made me feel a tad despondent. Gloria just seemed too good to be true. Like her mom. Inadequate me had been secretly looking for chinks in Gloria's armor that would make me feel less deficient, but so far she seemed well and truly in charge of her family and her world.

"So, what do we do with the cows?" I asked Allison, slipping my hands into the pockets of my "cute" jacket.

"We process them. Give the calves shots for blackleg before we put them out on summer pasture in a few weeks. You never did this before?" Allison's voice suggested that processing cows was something normal people knew all about.

"Honey, the first time I found out that the milk I bought in those nice cardboard containers actually came from a cow, I was physically ill."

"You've gotta come and see my dad's milking parlor," Tabitha said with a touch of pride as she glanced over at us. "It's so clean, you can eat off the floor."

"That might not mean much. I can sometimes eat off my kitchen floor, but that's only because I didn't manage to pick up all the crusts that Nicholas threw off his high chair in the morning."

Tabitha and Allison both laughed at that. Auntie Leslie. What a cutup.

"I don't believe you're that messy," Allison put in, the wagon bumping along behind her. "Auntie Judy always said your place in Vancouver was immaculate."

The secondhand praise from my favorite sister-in-law warmed my heart.

"You lived in a condo, didn't you?" Gloria asked.

Judy and Dayton had managed a trip to Vancouver to visit us a couple of times, but Gerrit and Gloria could never get away from their dairy farm long enough to make the trip. So they never saw our place in Vancouver. Nor the other places.

"Yes. We were hoping to get a house, but when Dan went broke, that was the end of that dream." I kept my voice detached, breezy, skimming over the soggy ground of disappointment. "I know it bothered Dan-"

"It wasn't his fault." Gloria rushed to her brother's defense, no surprise. What did surprise me was the anger in her voice. And the flash of accusation in her eyes. Did she think the fault was mine?

I looked ahead, trying not to take this personally. She was simply upset for her brother. That was all.

"Hey, Aunt Leslie, did you ever go see Granville Island?" Tabitha asked. "I heard it's really funky."

Bless you, child, for validating my existence.

So I told her about the tour I had taken one afternoon when a friend from work and I had finally managed to make a coffee date sans children.

While we talked, we made our way around the shed where the machinery was stored. As we came through a break in a line of trees that surrounded the farm yard, it was as if the land opened up in front of us. All I saw was a vast expanse of field that stretched and rolled away from me. It still caught me unawares, this endless space. It was as if the world had been sucked empty.

"You okay, Auntie Leslie?" Allison asked.

I flashed her a nervous smile. I had to be okay. I had no choice. I glanced over at Anneke, who didn't seem to be feeling the same vertigo I was.

"So where are the cows?" I pulled a long, slow breath into my oxygen depleted lungs.

Tabitha pointed past a barbed wire fence that bordered the field.

Against a tree line that bordered the field beyond the fence, I saw the herd of cows moving toward us. A cowboy with shaggy blonde hair anchored by a baseball cap was waving a rope, whistling through his teeth at the cows slowly moving ahead of him.

What made all of this unusual was that he was doing this from the back of a dark brown horse, and the cowboy was my husband.

Gloria and Tabitha forged on ahead while I stopped in my tracks to watch. I knew Dan had a horse. Its name was Taffy, and it was part quarter horse, part Morgan. That was information I had absorbed casually without understanding the implications for me and my life until now.

"Is that Daddy. On the horse?" Anneke asked.

"Yes. It is," I said still trying to morph Mechanic Dan with the Marlborough Man in front of us.

My husband was an honest-to-goodness cowboy.

One of Gerrit's boys rode up on the horse they had taken along, and soon he and Dan were moving the herd inexorably toward us. The cows and Dan silhouetted against the blue sky was truly a calendar worthy picture. I was sorry I hadn't taken my camera. It would have made a lovely memory.

"That's good, right?" My eyes caught Gerrit and the boys moving the herd in our direction. My heart sped up as I glanced from the cows to the kids. "The cows coming at us like that."

"Yah. Though one of them could take off for no reason." Allison gave a casual shrug. "Cows aren't too smart."

Her words were almost prophetic. As we watched, a cow swung its head to one side, took a few steps, then veered off, running out toward the open field, its calf right on its heels. One of the boys ran toward it to cut it off as another cow started following. Then Dan turned his horse around and was galloping after the cows, the dog racing alongside of him. The cows turned, but the rest of the herd that had been heading toward us stepped up the pace, and soon they all were running, a lumbering, bellowing group of bovines, calves skittering away from the pack, but then returning. All that lay between this thundering herd and us were four suddenly feeble-looking strands of barbed wire strung between fence posts that now seemed way too far apart.

"That's not so good." Allison spoke with an air of nonchalance that I envied deeply.

"Okay, I don't like this." I didn't even attempt to keep the shakiness out of my voice. I felt fear rising up at their relentless progress. But Gloria and Tabitha, who were ahead of us, kept going, following the fence. And Tabitha, pulling my fragile youngsters in the wagon, followed them.

"Gates. Open the gates." It was Dan. Yelling. Loudly.

I'm not your typical submissive wife, but when Dan yelled, it invariably sent me into action. Trouble was, I had no idea what action to go into.

Gloria and Tabitha did and started running. They clambered up and over the wooden fences and disappeared, only to reappear on the other side between the corrals and the cows. Above the bellowing of the cows, I heard the screech of metal. Gloria was pushing open half of a large gate, Tabitha the other.

The cows saw them, and their forward momentum slowed, but only a moment. Then they veered off in a cloud of hooves and bellowing heads and dust, away from the men and dog behind them and away from the corrals.

Dan yelled. Gerrit waved his arms. The boys tried to cut them off as the dog raced alongside the cows. But the animals thundered on oblivious to their cries.

I guessed this wasn't the desired effect.

"Uncle Gerrit's gonna be ticked," Allison said in a matter of fact voice. "Better head over there and see what we can do."

I looked back at Nicholas and Anneke, who had been watching the entire production with wide eyes. "I don't think the kids should get close to this."

"They'll be okay. They'll be on the other side of the corrals." Allison shrugged.

I didn't share her optimism. Those cows were big and heavy and loud. The corral fencing didn't look strong enough to hold them back. I had two children here. Which one would I be able to save if the cows burst through the boards?

"Hey, Aunt Leslie, the kids will be fine." Allison apparently sensed my unease. "Uncle Dan would never let anything bad happen to them." She gave me a crooked grin that was so much like Dan's, I felt suddenly like I could trust her.

"Okay. You're the farm girl."

Allison punched me lightly on the arm, the ultimate teenage compliment.

Dan was leaning down from his horse, which was snorting and stamping one hoof as Dan conferred with Gerrit, Wilma, and Gloria, who had joined them outside the gates. The dog lay at Gerrit's feet, his head on his paws, looking bored. By the time we got there, they had come up with another plan.

Gerrit and Gloria's youngest boy—Joseph, I think was his name—was assigned to gate duty. He was only eight years old and small, even for his age. He would get trampled.

I don't know what got into me. Delusions of grandeur? A desire to show Gloria and Wilma that I could do this, too?

"I can do the gates," I said with false bravado, before my brain could catch up with my mouth. I gave Dan a quick smile. "How hard could it be?"

Dan straightened up in the saddle, and his expression made my moment of stupid self-sacrifice worthwhile. His features softened, and he winked at me. "Are you sure?"

"Yah." I glanced back at Allison, who gave me a thumb's up. "I'm sure."

He told me what I needed to do. As soon as the cows were inside the gates, I was to swing them both shut. There were two gates, and they needed to be chained up in the middle where they met. Simple. And Dan assured me that the cows would respect a shut gate. I had to trust him on that. As a backup, he gave me a long flexible stick covered with woven nylon with four small knotted strands waving from the end, a whip that he assured me the cows would respect as much as the gate. A feeble defense, to my way of thinking, but he seemed to think it would work. So I nodded, still wondering what I had gotten myself into.

Dan gave me another smile, then clucked to his horse, turned it around, and cantered off toward the herd of cows, the dog racing alongside him.

My heart kicked in my chest. That was my husband looking so masculine and western. So at ease on the back of the horse, one hand holding the reins, the other resting casually on his thigh. So in charge of his world. So different from the worn and tired man I had seen the past few months. This man I could get used to, and an old affection rose up.

I hugged the emotion close. Affection, let alone love, hadn't factored into our interactions the past few months. Fear, frustration. And, oh yes, betrayal.

Definitely not one of the five so-called love languages that the book Gloria had sent us once talked about.

So, who knew? I thought as I watched my man slash cowboy being all manly and magazine ad-worth. Who knew what could happen.

Twenty minutes later the cows were moving our way again. As they picked up speed, heading toward the gate, my previous bravado and confidence were replaced by a slow fear that started in my stomach, then spread its icy fingers out to my arms, my legs, my head. I clenched the gate in a death grip, the chill of the metal adding to an ominous feeling that something terrible was about to happen.

C'mon, Leslie, an eight year old kid was going to do this.

And I had my whip, I reminded myself, clinging to it with the other hand. Don't forget the whip.

The cows kept coming, the ground shaking. I was facing death. Behind them, Dan was a blur through the dust.

An unwelcome thought pierced my bluster.

We hadn't updated our wills.

Our children would be parceled out among family members. Separated. Would my mother push for guardianship? Would she and Wilma fight over the kids? I could already see them facing each other down, our poor children crying, calling out for their mommy and daddy.

I almost got a lump in my throat. But then the pounding of the cows' hooves grew. I stood perfectly still, trying to make myself insignificant, unthreatening.

They got bigger and bigger, noisier and heavier the closer they came, and the only thing that kept me at my post was a larger fear of ridicule and the fact that I was wearing an unsuitable pink jacket. I wanted to prove to Dan, to Gloria and especially to Wilma that I could do this in spite of my lack of experience and farm fashion sense.

I thought the cows would come in a huge rush, but as soon as they saw the corrals, the ones in front slowed down. But the momentum of the herd behind them kept them moving, and they pushed past me, a jumble of brown and black bodies, snorting and bellowing their displeasure as they swung large shaggy heads and rolled their eyes in my direction. Heat and steam engulfed me in a bovine sauna. I fumbled with my whip, ready to close the gate that they would respect.

Yeah. Sure.

"Wait, wait," Dan called out, as the herd going past me thinned out. But the cows in the front had seen the end of the line and spun around, using their large heads to push the cows behind them out of the way, bellowing and snorting and straining against the boards of the corral. They creaked, and I hoped they would hold the churning herd. I thought of my precious children but couldn't see them in the mass of bodies.

Gerrit whistled, and his dog started barking, nipping at the stragglers' heels. A few kicked, but the dog danced out of harm's way, and the herd slowly pushed its way into the corral. The last dawdler was moving past me when I heard Gerrit yell, "Shut the gate, shut the gate."

That was my cue. I pushed one half of the gate closed, wincing at the screeching sound that would surely clue the cows in as to what was coming down.

I ran across the opening to get the other half just as Dan yelled, "Watch that cow!"

I looked up in time to see a large and angry looking animal turning around. It was huge, with buggy eyes that looked bloodshot. It was ten times my size and coming straight for me.

"Stop it from getting through," Dan yelled.

He was being crazy, yes? He was making a joke, right?

I stood in the breach, holding the narrow whip he promised they would respect. I waved it threateningly, but the cow was coming and building up speed.

A hero I was not.

I jumped.

The cow thundered through, then stopped.

From my vantage point behind the gate I saw the dog scoot out around the cow, face it down. To my shock and surprise, the cow spun around, kicked out behind her, but ran back inside the corral.

Here was my chance to vindicate myself. Still clinging to the gate, I ran, the opening growing smaller, smaller. The cow turned, faced me again, and started coming as I caught the chain from the other gate. With trembling hands I flung it around, hooking it like Dan had showed me, realizing that my pink coat and I were drawing the cows' attention, hoping, praying, that the cow wouldn't charge.

But it only blinked, shook its head once, as if warning me, then turned and trotted back to join the herd, its moment of rebellion quashed.

My heart thundered in my chest, and my hands were like pieces of limp spaghetti. I had overcome. My children weren't motherless. Dan wouldn't have to find someone over the Internet to marry him. I took a long, slow breath as the adrenaline eased.

Dan vaulted off his horse and came running over. "Are you okay?" All solicitous, he put a dusty hand on my shoulder, and I didn't even mind.

"I'm fine." I trembled with relief.

"You did good." He gave me a quick hug. "You did fine."

"Way to face that cow down, Aunt Leslie," Allison shouted from the other side of the corrals. She was holding Nicholas. Anneke stood on the fence beside Tabitha, her tiny feet clinging to an opening, her arms hooked over the rough lumber. She was laughing at the cows milling about in the corral below her, showing absolutely no fear. Nicholas was waving one arm, grinning a wet, drooly grin.

Nathan, the middle boy, strode over and high-fived me. "Good job, Auntie."

Dan winked at me, then vaulted over the corrals to get ready for the next stage.

I clung to the wooden fence, glancing at the cows. Some were standing quietly, others were wandering around bellowing. But on my side of the fence, I felt safe. I felt strong. I was woman, hear me roar.

And I was definitely going to walk over and join Wilma, Gloria and Dan.

As soon as my knees stopped trembling.

CHAPTER 4

"*L*eslie, do you have pastry forks?" Gloria cornered me as soon as I stepped back into the kitchen, face sore from scrubbing and my wet hair pulled into something resembling a rat's tail rather than a ponytail.

When we got back from working the cows, I had ducked out to wash dirt out of my hair and try to create a kinder, gentler Leslie. No mean feat, considering the dust from the cattle caked every inch of my body, inside and out. My "cute" pink jacket was now a sickly gray, and my jeans sported a rip in the knee I probably got from clambering up and down the wooden fence. My head rang from the constant bellowing, so I could hardly see straight. Hardly the idyllic afternoon experience I had pictured in my head when Dan first spoke of this adventure.

Gloria had brought extra clothes along and made the transformation from farmer's wife to hostess in less time than it takes to say "lightning change." Her tidy hair and impeccable lipstick put me to shame. *I should take notes.* Wilma had gone home to change, leaving her alter ego in charge of domestic duties.

"We'll need the forks for the cheesecake," Gloria continued.

Ah yes. The cheesecake. Gloria had brought it. Dan's favorite, she had explained as she put it on the kitchen counter.

I took one look at my artfully arranged trans-fat-laden store-bought cookies and discreetly hid them under a cooking-pot lid.

"I thought I saw them when I unpacked." My mind scrambled as I pulled open the utensil drawer. The faint odor of burning cheese rose from an oven overloaded with pizza, but I couldn't shake this mission.

"I looked in there already," Gloria said. "It would be nice to have them."

That comment, plus the fact that I got the pastry forks from Gloria as a fifth-anniversary present, was a surefire recipe for pressure. I dove into the pantry. No luck. I tried the disastrously disorganized odds-and-ends cupboard. Nope.

Coming out empty-handed and desperate, I almost collided with Judy, who had arrived carrying a large crystal bowl full of layers of cake, whipping cream, and chocolate shavings. If I didn't know she loved to bake or that the nearest bakery was a half hour's drive away, I would have guessed she bought it and was trying to pass it off as her own.

"Hey, Sis." She handed the bowl to Gloria with a casual gesture. "Dump this wherever."

Judy turned back to me, and her smile shifted. Grew warm and welcoming. "So, farmer's wife, now you can add processing calves to your résumé."

"The employers will just snap me up."

"So, what should we do about the pastry forks?"

I stifled a sigh. Persistence, thy name is Gloria.

The door opened again, and the kids burst in, enveloping me in another round of hugs and kisses and well-wishes and noise.

And all the while my pizza was overflowing and burning to the bottom of the oven, and Gloria's fingers were tapping out her desire for my elusive pastry forks.

This was going to be so-o-o much fun.

* * *

"STOP DISSECTING THE DESSERT." Judy pulled the large crystal bowl away from Dan, who was mining Judy's trifle for leftover chocolate. We were all gathered in the kitchen digesting the remnants of the various delicious desserts. It was a tight squeeze, but the family insisted that it was cozy.

"I'm making sure I get all the chocolate." Dan pulled the bowl back toward him.

"You poke to your heart's content." Wilma sent a benevolent smile in Dan's direction. "You're probably going to throw it away when you get home anyway, aren't you, Judy?" Wilma lifted an eyebrow that turned the question into a suggestion.

"Gee, Mom, not so sub with the subtext." Judy laughed as she patted her ample hips.

I was surprised she could be so blasé. Even as my anger rose on her behalf, Judy seemed completely unfazed.

"Dan always did love chocolate." Gloria gave him an indulgent smile.

"But he didn't always respect it. Remember when Dan and Cousin Nicholas had that food fight here on his birthday?" Judy laughed and leaned over the table toward Gloria. "That chocolate cake that you made?"

"It would have turned out if you hadn't distracted me."

Judy dropped her head back and let out a hearty laugh. "Still blaming it on me. I bet you still think I was the one who ate your Halloween candy when really it was Uncle Orest, who always pilfering it when he came over."

"I did catch you with a Hershey bar."

"That was my Hershey bar." Dan came up for air to join the walk down memory lane.

Everyone laughed as the conversation splintered, then separated and flowed past again, memories intertwining with conversations about work, kids, and people I had heard only vague mentions of from previous visits. I sat back and let it flit past me. I didn't know the people they talked about, and by the time I caught the connection, they were off on another topic. Hard not to feel like a stranger in my own house.

Tabitha and Allison huddled on the floor at one end of the table, their conversation liberally sprinkled with prepositions and exclamations. Near as I could tell, for the past half hour, they had been analyzing the latest romance of a mutual friend and hadn't, to my knowledge, come to any conclusion as to whether they approved or disapproved of the liaison.

Allison bounced Nicholas on her lap, playing peekaboo with him.

The little piker had been a tangle of misery all evening, crying and rubbing his red cheeks against my face when I tried to comfort him, twisting his blankie around his hands when I tried to entertain him. And now he giggled at everything Allison and Tabitha threw at him, charming them with his tenor belly-laugh and clapping his chubby hands.

Lovable little turncoat.

And Dan, well, he was looking around at his family, that half-smile of his that never failed to give my heart a little kick hovering over his well-shaped lips. He looked so content and so at peace that for a quick, sharp moment, I was envious of him.

"So, Leslie, when are you going to put the garden in?" Wilma asked.

What? Where did that come from?

"I ...I didn't plan on it." I flailed into this new topic like Nicholas waking up from a nap.

"You'll like gardening," Judy said. "Besides, fresh vegetables are so much better than those strip-mined, poor excuses for food that the local Co-op tries to pass off." Her vehement tone surprised me.

"Did that nasty Co-op turn down your application to sell your vegetables to them again?" Gerrit made a face. I was guessing this was an ongoing family joke, and I was glad for the deflection away from me and anything botanical.

"Without even giving us any kind of explanation." Judy poofed out her lip and blew her bangs out of her face.

"I think they should be happy to get fresher vegetables." Wilma was obviously put out with a store that wouldn't take produce from her own child. "I'll have to talk to Dennis Verweer."

"No, Mom." Judy rolled her eyes. "I can take care of this myself."

"Dennis is an old friend of the family."

"Mom, if I find out that you even mention the word produce and my name in the same sentence in front of Dennis, I won't come for Sunday dinner for two months."

Wilma's and Judy's gazes held as I sucked in a breath, amazed at the stand-off happening before my very eyes.

"But, darling, surely...."

"Three months." Judy held up three fingers. "Three, do I hear four? Four?" She sounded like an auctioneer.

Wilma pressed her lips together, glancing at Dan as if hoping to enlist his support, but Dan was still buried in the trifle.

Full of admiration for Judy's bold move, I kept watching, mentally taking notes. Guess I knew where to go for "Coping with Wilma and Gloria" advice.

"Hey, Judy." Gloria clicked her tongue. "Mom's just trying to help."

"And we have Four. Four, bid now, four, I need five, five." Judy grinned.

"It was merely a suggestion." Wilma's voice held a grudging note. Her glance skittered away from her daughter and grazed over me, caught and held. Her eyes narrowed as if warning me not to try this at home. I almost held up my hands in a gesture of surrender. Judy was clearly in a league of her own.

Dan looked up from the trifle bowl and wiped his mouth. "Speaking of gardening, once the crop is in, we could work on ours, Leslie." He shot me a helpful grin, as if I had been restlessly hovering on the edge of the garden, rake in hand, an avid desire to stake beans and thin carrots burning in my heart. He must have caught my bemused look, because he turned to our daughter. "Wouldn't you like to put a garden in, Anneke?" She had gravitated from the kid's table and pulled herself onto his lap.

"That would be fun," she chirped. She laid her head on Dan's chest and wrinkled her nose at me. From any other child, this could be misconstrued as a taunt. From my Anneke, a sign of deep affection. I took what I could get from her.

I reached over and stroked a delicate strand of hair away from her face, slipping it behind her ear in a moment of motherly connection. Dan caught my glance and the smile deepened. I couldn't look away as older emotions trembled upward.

"So, do you want us to come over and help you with the garden?" Wilma's helpful question pushed like a conversational wedge through this quiet moment between my husband and me. Anneke pulled away, causing Dan to lower his hand from my neck, and our little warm family moment cooled.

"We could get some seeds at the Co-op. It wouldn't take that long." She had obviously given up on her face-off with Judy and settled for easier prey. I was still working my way through the maze of trying to find my place in this family and didn't want to alienate Wilma or my sisters-in-law. But I resented feeling like I was failing a test I hadn't studied for.

"It's a bit early for that, don't you think?" Judy said airily.

"I'm putting in my garden next week." Wilma pushed, pressed.

"What's your hurry, Mom?" Judy pushed back. "Lay off the poor city girl. She doesn't know from gardening."

"I've planted a few things." I felt torn between accepting Judy's offhand definition of me and Wilma's push to assimilate me completely into rural life.

"And they all died." Dan laughed lightly.

"Not right away."

"In fact." He turned to Judy. "Leslie brought a plant into the house once that wilted as soon as it saw the other plants. It obviously saw its future and gave up before Leslie could torture it."

Wilma and Gloria didn't need to laugh nearly as loudly as they did.

"I doubt it was that bad." Judy shook her head at her brother's humor.

That's it. In my new will, Judy is getting my diamond earrings.

"I'm good with the greenhouse, but death on house plants." Judy shrugged. "I think they get jealous and die out of spite because I spend so much time away from them." She gave me a wink.

And my opal necklace.

"I think that's why my houseplants died. They got jealous and died of spite because I spent more time with my patients than with them."

"Thankfully you won't have to worry about that now." This from Gloria. "I'm sure you're looking forward to taking time away from your job."

"I like being a nurse." I tried to keep my tone mild. "I'll miss working."

"Yes, but now that you're on the farm, wouldn't you rather stay home and putter around the house?"

"I never perfected the fine art of puttering." My feeble attempt at a joke.

"Judy could give you a few tips." Dayton pulled himself out of the conversation he was having with Gerrit. "Didn't you give a course on puttering at the ag fair last year?"

"That was pottery." Judy rolled her eyes and turned to me. "You'll have plenty of time to visit us if you're home all the time. I could teach you to sew. We could have a lot of fun."

"I don't know about fun. All that cutting and pinning. I doubt I can be trusted with so many potentially lethal instruments. One of the reasons I never went in for surgical nurse." I smiled at my little occupational humor, but it fell flat. Guess I wasn't taking this gig on the road.

"Leslie was the kind of child who ran with scissors." Dan gave me a gentle poke.

"Sewing is a good way to save some money on clothes," Wilma said. "You might want to think about it."

No pressure from the family here. Sewing. Gardening. Who did they think I was? Ma Walton?

"And if you're not going to be working, that is something to consider," Gloria added. "Farming is a wonderful life, but there isn't always a lot of money left over after all the bills are paid."

"Great, Gloria," Dan said with forced jocularity, "You're going to make her think we're two cheques away from being broke."

"Been there," I muttered. And from the looks of the cheques we were getting from Wilma each month, we were still only a few dollars from "there."

Dan shot me a hurt look, and I regretted my quick tongue. No need to make him feel worse. I lifted my arm to connect with him.

"Anneke, can you come to Oma?" Wilma's quiet request pulled Anneke off Dan's lap and pushed my arm aside, and the chance was gone. "Could you get me the Bible?

Bible? Low-level panic struck again. I knew we had it around somewhere. I knew we had our own around somewhere. Someone from Dan's church had come to our wedding and given us one. I had used it once to dry some flowers. I remember being afraid Dan would find them and get upset, but the flowers came and went without Dan knowing. He never cracked the Bible open himself.

Anneke danced toward her grandmother, then stopped, looking puzzled. "What's a Bible, Oma?"

Wilma's expression didn't shift, but I could see a tightening around her lips.

"It's this book over here." Wilma pushed her chair back and

picked up a large black book from the countertop. I relaxed. I guess Wilma figured that in this house you had to BYOB, Bring Your Own Bible. "Why don't you hand it to your father, and he can read something to us."

"That's okay." Dan held up a hand in protest. "Someone else can read."

But it was too late. Anneke, bursting with pride at her own importance, was already hustling over to our end of the table with her sacred burden and duty.

Dan bit his lip as he took the heavy book from her before pulling her onto his lap. "Anything in particular?" He flipped through the pages, their rustling the only sound in the reverent quiet that had descended the moment he had laid the Bible on the table.

Even the teenagers who had, until now, seemed oblivious to what was going on with the adults, had become quiet. I glanced around the table as people sat back, folded arms across chests, or leaned forward, waiting. Everyone seemed to know the unwritten rules...except me.

"Read what you like, Dan," Wilma said quietly.

Dan bit his lip, frowning as he paged through the Bible. Then a gentle smile eased over his lips as he stopped. "I've always liked this piece." His hand smoothed over the page like a caress.

"This is from 1 Corinthians 13. I know it's read a lot, but I want to read it again." He cleared his throat, took a slow breath, and started reading.

"Though I speak with tongues of men and of angels, but have not love, I am a resounding gong or a clanging cymbal...Love bears all things, hopes all things endures all things. Love never ends."

I listened to the cadence of the words and caught a tone in Dan's voice I had never heard before. It was gentle, soft, and carried warmth and comfort.

Everyone else seemed to pick up on it as well. I saw lines ease away from Wilma's forehead, saw a genuine smile warm Gloria's face. Judy stared off into the middle distance, as if remembering other Bible readings around this table, in this room.

Even Anneke, my original wiggly worm, now leaned against her father, her head on his shoulder the quiet sound of his voice soothing her restlessness.

I turned my attention back to Dan and what he was reading. "...Now abide three things. But the greatest of these is love."

The warmth in Dan's voice pushed the last words deep into my being. And not only the words, but the tone and timbre of his voice, as if he had become another person right in front of my eyes.

"Thanks, Dan." Wilma's quiet voice like a benediction. "That was lovely. Could you close in prayer?

I felt instantly nervous for my husband. Reading the Bible was one thing, but praying off the cuff? The only thing resembling a prayer I'd ever heard from Dan was a muttered "Good Lord" when he was especially frustrated with Anneke or Nicholas.

But Dan nodded slowly, glancing around the table at everyone but me, then lowering his head. And as he prayed, I got another surprise. His voice filled with an emotion I'd never heard before. I glanced carefully around the room. Everyone, even the teenagers, had their heads bowed and their eyes closed.

Once again I felt peripheral to a family I couldn't understand.

A brief pause followed the end of Dan's prayer, and then the family erupted into a cacophony of noise and busyness.

I'd started clearing away the plates when Judy put her hand on mine. "Don't. The kids can clean up. We'll move to the living room."

Ah yes. The next stage of the evening. The family meeting.

* * *

THE SEVEN ADULTS seated themselves in chairs, on floor pillows, laughing and chatting as they settled in. I perched on the edge of a kitchen chair that had been hauled in, feeling like the clichéd homely girl at the prom who people smiled patronizingly at but never talked to.

The noise from the kitchen counterpointed the buzzing talk in the living room. Judy and Gloria's kids alternately cleaned up and entertained mine.

I shot a yearning glance over my shoulder at the chaos of the kitchen and the kids. Call me immature, but that party seemed like more fun.

"So, Mom, how are you doing? Really?" Judy asked point blank during a lull in the conversation. "Keith's been gone two months now. Have you heard from him?"

Wilma shook her head as she toyed with her wedding ring and released a long, slow sigh. "Not a thing. It's like our marriage never existed." Wilma's voice wavered. The hint of vulnerability softened the starch in my spine I habitually felt around her. I grasped that moment of pity I couldn't find when she was her usual pillar of strength. She pressed trembling fingers against her cheeks. "I wish I knew what God was trying to teach me through this."

A heavy silence followed that remark, and I resisted my usual urge to fill it. I truly had no idea of how to give her any kind of comfort. Give me a sucking chest wound or a broken arm, and I was Mrs. Capable and Efficient.

Broken hearts and questions about God were best left to those with more experience and wisdom.

Gloria patted her mother's shoulder. "God will make his purpose clear, Mother. We have to be patient."

"What are you and Dan going to do about the farm in the meantime?" Ever-practical Judy rested her elbows on her knees man-style. "Let's be honest, Mom. Keith was a worse farmer than he was a stepfather."

"Judy, you shouldn't say that." Gloria scowled at her sister. "Keith did the best he could with what he had."

"Glor, seriously. Is it time for your medication or mine?" Judy said in exasperation. "Keith was lazy. Straight up."

"Judy, that isn't humorous," Wilma chided, but her tone held an air of resignation. As if she saw a truth in what Judy was saying.

"I'm dead serious," Judy continued. "Forgive and forget is important, but let's be realistic, Mom. He wasn't treating you well the past few years. And we all know Dan left the farm because of Keith. This isn't classified. I'm sure Leslie knows he was a lousy stepdad." She glanced at me, singling me out, and in a moment of what could only be described as non-inspiration, I gave a lame shrug.

"Now, now, Judy. That'll do, girl. That'll do." Dayton put his hand on Judy's shoulder in a "down girl" gesture that netted an angry glare. But when she saw Dayton's smile, she laughed herself and sat back. Dayton turned to Dan. "Now that we've touched on the past we're supposed to forget, I'm sure you and Mom have gone over the bank stuff. Why don't you tell us how things look?"

Dan's shoulder lifted as he glanced at Wilma. "Mom has a better handle on the money part than I do right now. I've been concentrating on getting the cows fed and going over the equipment in time for spring seeding."

I felt embarrassed for my husband. Wilma should have brought him up to speed on the farm's finances, but it was as if Wilma had regained control and wasn't going to relinquish it too quickly. Which made me even more convinced that the farm needed to be assessed before Dan did one more minute of work on it.

"I know each of you has your own farm and your own problems to deal with," Wilma said, "but I hoped you could give Dan some advice. He's been away from the farm for a while, and I'm sure he could use the help."

I tried to catch Dan's eye, but the shag carpeting held his intense concentration.

Wilma informed everyone of the farm's financial affairs. Though it seemed the farm was doing well, it hadn't prospered under Keith's tenure. Equipment hadn't been maintained, and land had been mismanaged. Income was steady, but it was down. The farm would need an input of cash before Dan put a crop in. Gerrit recommended a short-term loan. The wheat futures were good, as were cattle prices. Suggestions were thrown out on whether to plant barley or wheat. Whether to hay the one quarter or silage it. Gerrit and Dayton launched into a lively discussion about crop yield and the high cost of fertilizer, spray, and fuel.

Everyone had something to add, some piece of advice to give. The women as well as the men.

Everyone except Miss I Grew Up in an Apartment. Call me crazy, but I couldn't catch the wave of enthusiasm these people were projecting over inanimate objects. Land. Seeds. Equipment.

"Interest rates are low." Gerrit ran his fingernail along the edge of the financial report. "You can borrow against the farm. I'm pretty sure there's enough room."

"I hate to borrow more if we don't have to." Dan folded his arms across his chest and leaned back against the couch, chewing on his lower lip the way he always did when he was thinking about weighty matters. "I just got out of a bad debt situation. Not too keen on reliving that. Especially because we've got two families who have to be supported from the farm."

I had seen that gesture too much in the past half year. Dan chewing his lower lip denoted money problems and stress. During the whole Dansworth Contracting debacle, he chewed his lip so much I was surprised he had anything left to kiss me with. Not that we did much of that because he was never around, but I was holding out hope for future smooching when things slowed down.

My heart downshifted, as it always did when I thought of Lonnie Dansworth. I still dreamed that after the court case we could get some money back from him. Because when that happened we could move back home again.

"I don't want to borrow money either." Wilma twisted her hanky in her hands. "Your father worked too hard to get this farm where it is now."

"But the farm has a value, Mom," Dayton said.

I could feel my heart pushing hard and fast against my chest. Dan wasn't saying anything. His mother assumed we were staying here. This had to be stopped.

"Has there been an assessment done on the farm lately?" I blurted out.

"There's never been a need." Gloria frowned.

"I'd like to see one done before Dan does any more work here." *There.* It was said and out in the open.

"Why do you want that?" Judy snapped a cracker in half.

I took a deep breath, ignored my husband's warning glance, and plunged in. "I think it's important we ascertain the value of the farm at the present moment." *Listen to you, Leslie. You actually used the word* ascertain. "Because Dan will be working on the farm and, hopefully, increasing the net worth, I would like to make sure that he is recompensed for our work."

And now recompensed. *Aren't you the business whiz?*

"Well, you'll be drawing a wage from the farm." Judy sounded puzzled about where I was going with this. "And you'll be building up equity long term."

"Leslie means..." Dan started.

I cut him off at the impasse. Too late. I had the conversation reins. "What I mean is *when* Dan and I leave—" I made sure to put exactly the right amount of emphasis on the *when.* "—I want to make sure that Dan is paid for the work he does on this farm. I don't know how much growth will happen in the year we are here, but Dan is a hard worker, and I want to make sure that this is recognized."

If it weren't for the shag carpeting in the living room, you could have heard a pin drop. As it was, I heard a whistling intake of breath, then a "well." Without moving my eyes from my fingers, twisted nervously around each other, I knew these ominous sounds had come from Wilma.

I felt myself mentally back pedaling. But I pressed my lips together, as if holding back any verbal retreat I might be tempted to indulge in. I risked a glance at Dan, who was now tapping his fingers against his arm and staring at me.

I've seen a lot of looks in our married life, but this was a new one. And I didn't like it.

"I agree that we should have an assessment done," Dan said, and I slowly felt the tension in my shoulders relax. *Finally.*

"Why?" Gloria asked. "It's going to cost the farm money and for what purpose?"

"The purpose is to make sure that, if the value of the farm goes up because of the work Dan put in it, that this is acknowledged when it's time for us to leave," I said.

Judy's puzzled look glanced off me before settling on Dan. "You just got here. Why is Leslie talking about leaving?"

Dan had obviously not prepared them for this. Had he been hoping that, once we were here, I would change my mind?

I looked around the room. The sisters wouldn't meet my eye. Worse, they were looking at each other, and I didn't even have to be a VandeKeere to know what they were thinking.

Our poor brother.

I closed my eyes, sucked in some air, and counted to seven. I couldn't wait till ten but knew I needed more than five.

"Our move here was never going to be permanent." I focused on Judy, the one sister I felt the most connection with. Her returning glance was the merest whisper of her eyes over my face, but in that brief look I caught a look of disappointment that hurt. I resisted the urge to explain. Dan was supposed to have done all the groundwork, but it was obvious the sisters knew nothing. His mother, even less.

Retreating and regrouping in the face of overwhelming odds would not have been cowardly. But fear and pride can make people do undiplomatic things.

"We're only going to be here a year, and then we're moving back to Vancouver. That was supposed to have been made very clear." *By your precious Dan.*

Dan sat back, his arms folded across his chest as he leaned back. Away from me.

Any improvement we'd made toward patching our marriage was slowly unravelling in front of my eyes as I saw his frown and downcast eyes.

"Is she right?" Gloria looked at Dan.

"We had discussed it." He lifted his hand in a vague gesture that was wide open to interpretation.

Discussed it? We'd drawn up a plan with a timeline. Stay in Holmes Crossing long enough to catch our breath, get the farm in decent shape to sell. Get Wilma set up, give ourselves a chance to regroup mentally, physically and marriage-wise, and make some decisions about what we would do when we moved back to Vancouver. I had initially lobbied for six months, but Dan had contended that wasn't long enough. A year was better. I knew he was right, but I had hoped we would split the difference.

But all the while we were negotiating the time, Keely, the bilingual secretary, hovered between us, giving me one more realistic and un-ignorable reason to go along with Dan's plan.

"This is news to us. However, if that is your plan." Gloria spoke quietly. "Then we shall have to work with it."

Dan shot me a quick look, and I knew we were going to have a "talk" after everyone left.

"For now we still need to decide what to crop." Dayton tapped his large fingers on his arm. "The tractor needs a new engine. Uncle Orest can help, but you'll still need to pay for parts, and for that we'll need a cash input."

More ideas were thrown around, but it was clear from the lack of eye contact that I was no longer part of the conversation. At some unseen signal, Judy got up and brought coffee around, and Gloria brought out cream and sugar. The sisters worked in an easy, efficient rhythm.

Me? I sat there, inadequate hostess, and ungrateful daughter-in-law.

I got up from my chair. "I'll go and check on the kids."

Eyes swiveled my way, telegraphing unspoken relief.

They wanted me gone. Well, gone I could manage. So I headed out of the room, leaving them to make their decisions.

But as I had my foot on the first stair, I heard Dan clear his throat above the murmur of conversation. Nothing earth shattering about that, but it was the *way* he did it that sent a chill of premonition feathering down my back.

I went back and stopped outside the doorway, feeling like a spy.

"If I can get Leslie to agree, I could use the money we set aside for the house to get the cash flow going again." My heart flopped. Surely he wouldn't? I pressed my hands against the wall to keep myself from charging back into the room. I was supposed to be upstairs after all.

"That would be best," Gerrit said. "You could look at it as an investment."

"Will she agree though?" That was Judy, speaking softly. "Especially if she says she wants to leave in a year."

"Surely she's not serious about that." Wilma snorted, making no effort to lower her voice. "What's in Vancouver, after all?"

My life. I bit lip as I leaned against the wall.

"Doesn't she know how happy you are to be back?" Judy said. "It's just money. You would get it back."

"Hey, if she needs to keep a nest egg, so what?" Rod's comment should have given me comfort, but his tone was dismissive. "Let her have it. We'll figure out another way to get some cash flow going."

I closed my eyes and breathed slowly, deeply as they talked. "Her," "she." The impersonal pronouns pushed me out of the circle. It was junior high school all over again. Except I didn't know why it bothered me that I was being discussed. I was married to a VandeKeere, but I had never harbored any fantasy of completely being part of the family, nor had I ever sought it. I liked my outsider status. I wanted to keep Dan, Anneke, Nicholas and myself *our* little family.

The VandeKeeres were more than Wilma, Gloria and Judy. There were uncles and aunts and cousins and grandparents and nephews and nieces, an entire network of names and faces that I had never been able to keep straight. A history of stories that were interwoven and so ingrained into the lexicon of the family that a single word could elicit laughter and draw out an entire network of shared memories.

And no matter how long I was married to Dan, I would always feel as if I were an alien, a holder of a green card who'd been granted temporary access to this place. As a young girl, I had spent enough time in that territory. Now I had my own little fiefdom, and I was going to fight for it.

I quietly made my way back up the stairs and slipped into Nicholas' room, Dan's old one. He lay curled up on his stomach, his behind in the air, his arms tucked under him like a cat. As I tried to rearrange him into a more comfortable position, he flung his arms out and stiffened. I recognized the first step of wakefulness and pulled my hands back. After a moment, I pulled his quilt back over him even though I knew in ten minutes it would be off again.

Thankfully summer was coming, and I wouldn't have to worry about how to keep him warm in this old, drafty house.

Winter would be another story.

Don't go there yet. One day, one chocolate at a time, was the only way I was going to get through this year. The jar sitting beside my bed down the hall whispered a siren song. *Come eat us. Drown your sorrows in dark chocolate with creamy centers.* If scarfing down the entire contents of the jar would reduce my time here, I'd be unwrapping and chomping quicker than you could say liposuction. But it *wouldn't* shorten our time here, and it *would* make me sick. I glanced out the window but only caught the reflection of the sliver of light coming through the partially open door. I moved to the window and looked out at, well, nothing.

All I saw was my ghostly reflection superimposed on a darkness that was heavy and thick, broken only by pinpricks of light from the stars millions of miles away.

Cue the violins. I turned away and headed downstairs, bypassing the living room where the responsible adults were still talking. I joined the kids playing board games in the kitchen. It was cozy, welcoming and non-judgmental.

My kind of place.

FROM: lesismore@hcrossing.net
To: dfroese@lakeshore.com
I never knew a stunned silence could have such a quiet force. Not only did I demand an assessment on the place, I had the temerity to suggest selling some land to help get the cash flow going. I may as well have suggested selling a few of the kids, who, by the way, seem to like me. I ducked out of the rest of the family meeting and regaled them with stories from the E.R trenches, and they seemed suitably impressed. It was a mistake though. I discovered how much I miss my job. Miss being in the center of things going on. Miss the stress and the push and the energy. But what I miss the most is being in charge. Patients seldom challenge my authority or talk about me like I'm not there. As far as my

patients are concerned, at that moment I am the end all and be all of their lives. Did I tell you how much I miss my patients?

Litigious Leslie Longing for old Life

FROM: *tfroese@centermail.com*
To: *lesismore@hcrossing.net*

I wouldn't sweat the VandeKeere hegemony. Honey U need to get own job. Own paycheck. Remember that dollhouse we got when the Hardistys down the hall moved out? U were always playing with it, pretending family and house. Don't lose the dream. If U Rn't careful that farm will suck U in, maybe even suck U dry of money. And what if you don't end up with anything in the end? U were born to be a nurse. Okay, U R a great mother too. And a good wife. But when I see U with patients, I just know this is what U R called to be. Think about it. BTW, gotta new man in my life. And no, I'm not going to pull a mom. He's a nice guy, and I'm being careful.

Sultry Sister Sashaying in San Fran

FROM: *lesismore@hcrossing.net*
To: *tfroese@centermail.com*

Make sure you're careful. Remember, it's marry first, THEN have kids. I would love to go back to work, but my stock in the family isn't real high right now, and Dan is happier that I'm home with the kids. I have to confess I am too, but I do have a lot of time on my hands. I love my kids, but I really miss my job. The eternal struggle between kids and purpose beyond these four walls that are starting to close in on me at times. But, don't worry. I'm okay. Or so Dan keeps telling me. He's managing to keep busy. I'm still working out the whole "shouldn't he feel guiltier" scenario. He apologized and it helped, but since moving here, he's been happier, more settled, and I'm the one feeling disgruntled.

Lugubrious Leslie

CHAPTER 5

"*I* think next time you plan to throw stuff like that out in front of my family, we should discuss it first." Dan pulled Anneke's toast out of the toaster, then buttered and spread her favorite peanut butter on it.

"We did. Endlessly. One year. That's what you promised me." I turned back to our son, whose weaving head struggled to follow the path of the spoon I waved around. Hard to hold summit meetings and feed a squirmy toddler at the same time.

Nicholas got his plump lips around the spoon and tried to grab it. "And we also agreed to ask for an assessment on the farm." After he pulled the spoon from his mouth, I snatched it from his porridge-encrusted hands.

"You didn't need to bring the assessment up at the family meeting." Dan hacked Anneke's toast into nine small pieces and handed the plate to Anneke, who grimaced at the mangled bread.

Dan glared at me as if the whole subject of the assessment had come from nowhere. Then wiped his knife on the edge of the tablecloth.

I chose to ignore his gross display of temper. I had bigger

issues at stake than bread crumbs and peanut butter on my tablecloth.

"The farm isn't doing as good as we thought. And your mother wants to maintain control." I enunciated each word as if I were talking to Nicholas instead of my husband. "If we're staying, we need to do an assessment and draw up an agreement with her so we're covered for the time you put in."

Dan tapped the knife on the table as if preparing for battle. I wished the battle wasn't with me. I thought I'd get some momentum from the warm and tender moment we'd shared the other night, but my insistence had precipitated a cooling trend.

"What is your problem with my mother? She's not trying to cheat us."

"I didn't say that. You need to get compensated for the work you do while you're here."

Nicholas jerked his head to the side, his little sausage hands flailing at the spoon as he spat out his mouthful of porridge. Telling me in his usual diplomatic way that he'd had enough of breakfast.

"It looks like we don't trust her." Dan dropped the knife with a thunk.

"It's not a matter of trust or greed." I wiped Nicholas's mouth, then his hands, then everything within reaching and spitting distance. I knew I was being practical. My voice was quiet, my body language non-threatening. I was a living, breathing ad for Reasonable and Practical Female. So why was Dan drumming his fingers on the table, telegraphing in a stuttering Morse Code his disapproval of what I had said?

"Daddy, you cut my toast too small." Anneke shoved her plate back toward him. "Make it bigger."

"Daddy can't make it bigger." He rearranged the pieces into a bread shape and pushed the plate back at her. "It makes it look like money is more important than helping my mother out."

"Money is important." I lifted the high chair tray and

unbuckled Nicholas from the harness anchoring him to the seat. "It's the lack of it that got us here in the first place."

"When are you going to get past it? The garage is gone. It's over. We're not going back." Dan stared me down, but I couldn't back down.

"Maybe not to the garage, but we are going back to Vancouver." I clung to Nicholas like a lifeline. "We decided that."

"Maybe."

Funny how that simple word could send my heart rate into coronary territory. "You don't mean 'maybe' do you? You mean when."

"We were barely hanging on there, Leslie. Money was tight and neither of us were happy at work."

I wasn't liking this. Moving to the farm was supposed to give us a reprieve from talking about money. From stressing about how we were going to spend it and where. I'd watched reruns of *Little House on the Prairie*. I knew how this worked. I made the sacrifice of not going back to work when we moved here so we could spend our mornings talking farmer talk. Cows and crops and being all close to the land. Facing the elements together as a family and coming out stronger. United. With one purpose. Stronger in our relationship and ready to take on our future.

In Vancouver.

Instead we were covering the same ground we had for the past two years. Our location had changed, but the view stayed the same.

I lowered my voice, willed my heart to slow, and pressed on. "When we were dating, you told me you could hardly wait to leave this place." I smiled at him, hoping it softened my words. I really didn't want this confrontation. I was hoping we could make the move toward husband and wife, not revert to being calculating business partners. "In all the times we've moved, you never talked about coming back here."

Dan ran his hands through his hair. He needed it cut, but

there hadn't been time. Truth was, I kind of liked the shaggier Dan. Made him look more like an Eddie Bauer model. When he was a mechanic, he kept his hair short. He said it was easier to wash.

I'm sure his bilingual secretary would feel the same about his new look. Which made me hold back and temper my words instead of pushing hard and fast. A fragile relationship needed gentle movements. I learned this from working with the cows the other day. Low and Slow was the name of the game with skittish prey. Don't bring up subjects he'd assumed had been dealt with. Don't ask too many questions. Just get through this.

Realize that someday we would look back at this time in our life, laugh nervously, and then change the subject.

"That was a while ago, Leslie. And I had other reasons for wanting to leave this place."

"Like your stepfather?"

"We had the worst kinds of fights right here in this very room."

Sort of like we're having now. Although on an emotional level, we were only flirting with the "shock and awe" stage.

"Plans change. Life changes." He breathed out a light sigh. "And if we're both honest, moving here works out for the best for all of us."

"I never had a problem with the moving-out-here part." *Big fat liar.* "I'm having a problem with the staying-here part."

I stifled a flutter of panic at the idea of being home all day, every day. Ever since I started working, I may not always have had time, but I always earned my own way. I had agreed to stay at home while we were here. We would squeak by on Wilma's "fair wage," but if my car broke down or we needed to make a major purchase, we would have to dip into the "Dream Home Fund."

I couldn't let that happen. The DHF had to be protected at all costs. I wasn't going to see all the sacrifice of time I could have spent with my family sifting into the black hole of the farm. The lure of our own home on our own piece of property, a safe place where my kids play outside and with room for toys and running and laughing, a home I could put my own stamp on. This Thomas Kincaid vision kept me going to work, saving money, being cautious and careful. I couldn't see all that sacrificed to help out his mother.

"I know that's a problem for you—" He leaned back in his chair, frowning, looking all contemplative and serious. "But with each day I stay here, I feel like I'm seeing things differently. I think it's a clear answer from God for us."

"Answer to what?" I don't remember asking God any questions.

Dan's gaze flickered from me to the window beside the table. "In church on Sunday, the minister talked about how God sometimes closes doors and opens others."

"Losing you, Dan." I didn't attend church with him, so I couldn't partake in the pastor's insights.

"I think we had doors closed for us in Vancouver." He gave me a troubled look. "Maybe they were opened here. Maybe God wants us to be here."

Okay. He was freaking me out now. "Sorry, Dan. I can't see that someone who flung stars into space and came up with something as complex as the human body would care whether we live in Vancouver or Holmes Crossing."

"I don't like my crusts." Anneke gave her plate a quick shove, sending it spinning across the table and onto the floor. Dan ignored her, and I didn't dare take my eyes off of my husband. The discussion was moving in a direction I hadn't practiced for. I was fairly sure he'd received coaching from his family. As for me...a sister whooping it up in San Francisco was hardly a fair competition to Wilma, Gloria, Judy and assorted cousins, uncles and aunts. Terra popped in and out of my life via e-mail and the occasional phone call. His family, however, were always here, always present. Always supportive.

"It's called taking care of us. Taking care of our marriage." I hoped he didn't hear the rising panic in my voice. "Something we haven't done as diligently in the past as we should have."

Dan stared me as silence rose between us, heavy, present, threatening. And swirling around us as we faced off was the sibilant hiss of one name. Missssss Bilingual. "I told you before we moved here, that's over." He zipped up his vest, stepped over the pieces of Anneke's toast, and strode toward the porch.

Coward. I watched as he jerked his bootlaces tight. I wanted to go out after him and finish this, but for now I was chained to the kitchen by two soft but tyrannical obligations and nine pieces of toast scattered all over my kitchen floor.

"I'm leaving in an hour." Dan slipped on his coat. "I'll stop by the house to see if you need anything before I go to the auction."

Dan was going to a farm auction down the road to do some "shopping." I needed a clothes dryer, and Dan needed a few things for the farm. The dryer that had come brand new with the condo had died about eleven minutes after the warranty expired and days before we had to move.

I had assumed we would simply head into town and pick up another one once we got here. But I hadn't counted on the Dutch tendencies lying dormant in my husband and only now, in the bosom of his family, starting to reveal themselves. Last night Gerrit had told Dan that the neighbor down the road was selling out and having a farm and yard sale, so now Dan was going. I kept my mouth shut about where my future dryer was coming from. Choosing my battles was my new mantra.

I cleaned up Anneke's bread and dropped another piece in the toaster while Nicholas rooted around on the floor for crumbs I had missed. I'd had breakfast with my entire family for eight days in a row, a new record. I looked around my finally-organized kitchen. I should be full of warm, soft, motherly emotions, shouldn't I?

Instead I felt like I was running out of breath.

Toward the end of our time in Vancouver, when I worked my crazy twelve-hour shifts and covering any extra ones I could pick up, I would come home in the late morning to the smell of bacon and eggs still lingering in the air. I would feel a twist of sorrow that Dan had been the one to give the kids their breakfast, bonding with them at their best time of the day, singing cute songs and laughing, while I, the ghostly mom, struggled to keep the family and Dan's mechanic business afloat after the Lonnie Dansworth debacle.

Sometimes things that are out of reach become appealing simply because they're unavailable. In my soft and tender dreams, my children were rosy-cheeked, happy, smiling, and neatly dressed sitting at the table, looking at me with happy smiles.

Instead my grimy little boy had pabulum in his hair and emitted a distinct diaper odor as he looked around for new areas of this house to explore. My daughter was slowly working her way up the emotional scale from scattered periods of grief to tsunami of hysteria because her toast wasn't coming fast enough and her tummy felt sore, sore, sore. Pre-farm I'd only had to deal with a slice of these family crises, never the whole loaf. It was exhausting and demanded a relentless creativity I'd never had to utilize before.

I got Anneke's toast buttered and peanut-buttered and cut to her culinary satisfaction, then grabbed Nicholas as he pat-patted his way toward my one and only live plant.

"You are a little worm, aren't you?" I hooked him around his chubby stomach in frustration and spun him around to face me.

"Awwaw du wa," were his eloquent words as wide blue eyes sparkled up at me, kindling a warmth as unexpected as it was welcome. And in spite of the crust edging his mouth and the dirt in his hair and the ever-growing odor from his backside, I felt a surprising rush of affection. I pulled his rounded body close to me and kissed a sticky face only a mother could love, knowing I had time to clean him up later. At home, I would have seen him as another job to squeeze in while I had one eye on the clock. Now, I could see the potential sweetheart that was my adorable Nicholas under the grime and beyond the smell.

Good thing, because right now with Dan? Not so much with feeling the love.

"My worm is dead." Anneke swung her feet while she ate the toast I had given her.

"Yes, he is." I simply gave her a smile, not really wanting to resurrect the memory of Teddy. I clutched Nicholas closer and grabbed the wipes and a clean diaper from the basket I kept handy so I wouldn't have to run upstairs every time I needed to change him.

"Can I get another one?"

"Maybe later," I said vaguely as I cleaned and wiped my son, all the while breathing through my mouth. I reminded myself of the promise to myself. I was going to make the best of it. Be proactive. If you can't change it, adjust to it. *Carpe diem*. Seize the day.

I glanced at the clock and a surge of dread swept through me. I had acres of time to carpe this particular diem. Since Anneke was born, I had been chasing time, trying to catch up to it, to grab hold of it, and make it work for me. After we moved here, it hadn't taken as much time as I thought to get the house set up. My kitchen looked orderly. The house smelled like artificial lemons. The upstairs rooms were sorted and organized.

Now I had time on my hands, and I didn't know what to do with it.

A passing glance at the windows gave me an idea. I could take the kids for a walk.

"Shall we get dressed?" I injected a note of fake heartiness into my voice. My morning conflict with Dan still churned in my mind. As I brought the kids to the porch, I rehearsed alternate endings to the fight and gave myself much wittier dialogue. My intelligence level always rose after our arguments. I would be ready for Dan if the topic came up again tonight. Hopefully it would. Bringing an argument to completion in under twenty-four hours would be a novel concept for Dan and me.

I laid Nicholas down on the porch floor to weave him into his jacket and pants. Anneke was at the "I can do it myself" stage of dressing, which would give me enough time to get Nicholas ready, get dressed myself, file my nails, and maybe read a couple of Shakespeare sonnets.

But today I didn't need to stuff her protesting arms into a jacket, her twisting feet into boots, one eye on the relentless clock. No schedule hung over my head like Damocles' sword as it had at home. We didn't need to rush off to daycare so I could rush off to work where I rushed to catch up to a constant influx of patients, then rushed home through snails-paced rush hour traffic, my thoughts on my waiting children.

I could let Anneke dance around the porch with her mittens on her feet, entertaining her little brother, who was content to sit like a bundled-up Buddha, babbling his incomprehensible jargon while I slowly put on a coat and gloves. I listened to a recitation of a "pome" Anneke had made up about a frog and a ball and laughed with her at the ending. When she graciously allowed me to zip up her coat, I made buzzing noises as I pulled the tab upwards and finished it off with a kiss on her pudgy nose.

"I love you, Mommy." She grabbed me tightly around the neck.

Her four words shot straight to my heart and wound around it, holding it as tightly as her arms held my neck. *She's mine.* I jealously squeezed her hard. She belongs to me fully and completely and wholly. Dan's heart and affections had wandered for a time, Nicholas treated my love for him as something to tolerate, but Anneke was purely and wholly my child.

The warmth her declaration kindled in me lasted as long as it took us to step from the porch to the outside. A faint breeze sifted through the buildings, snaking up through my jacket when I bent over to put Anneke and Nicholas in their plastic wagon.

The resulting chill was a leftover of a nasty winter more than content to stay around like an unwelcome guest who had one more joke in his repertoire.

Beyond the house lay a large open patch of ground bordered by bare red canes of raspberry bushes on one side and a row of apple trees on the far south end. The garden itself was a clean, neat expanse of black dirt, waiting for the planting of the garden Dan and his family thought I was eager to sow. As if. The closest I got to living things growing up was my mother's single ivy plant, which my sister and I watered with leftover tea and, when we had money to spare, soft drinks. And now the indestructible fichus Terra had given me as a joke.

"Let's go, Mommy." The handle of the wagon shook in my hands. The natives were getting restless. Anneke smiled as she rocked the wagon. Nicholas's heavy coat bunched up at his neck, made his head effectively immobile, but his eyes flitted back and forth, taking everything in. As I watched my two children act utterly content in the cold, I realized how long it had been since I had taken the kids out for something as ordinary as a walk.

Smiling, I turned around and started down the long driveway toward the road. Anneke burbled snatches of an unfamiliar song, something macabre about God watching a sparrow falling. Then she belted out the chorus. "He loves me too, he loves me too, I know he loves me too." Every now and again Nicholas burbled some unintelligible comment that I chose to translate as "I'm happy."

I sucked in a deep gulp of biting air and turned my eyes toward the road. In spite of a flush of wellbeing, something nagged at me, scrabbling at the edges of my consciousness. Something eerie and unfamiliar. I paused. Listened. That's when I heard it.

Nothing.

No cars. No horns honking. No airplanes. No people calling out to one another. No music. No neighbors.

I stopped, listening to the great big nothing. Anneke and Nicholas must have sensed my uneasiness, because they grew silent as well.

Emptiness pushed on my ears, pressing deep into my head. I felt the sweep of the wind urging me along over the fields toward the river that snaked through the valley we perched above.

My heart pounded, pushing against my chest. I could hear it as my raspy breath drew in and out, in and out. I thought again of that moment just before I had helped with the cows. The same feeling, but then I wasn't alone. Now it was just me and my two vulnerable, tiny children lost in this huge emptiness.

Don't panic. It's okay.

I breathed slowly like I often told parents of patients to do.

Easier to be the coach than the coachee. I got control of my breathing as my heartbeat slowed.

Then, behind me, I heard the slam of a door. A truck starting up. Dan was leaving. And I would be left behind, all alone in this vast, quiet nothingness.

I spun around and strode quickly to the shop, the wagon bump-bumping over the washboard ruts in the driveway as I honed in on the truck. Nicholas squealed with pleasure, and Anneke laughed as I quickened my pace.

Dan was driving toward the house when he saw us.

"Hey, there. I was coming to say good-bye."

"I thought we could go with you." I had the panic under control now so didn't miss the faint downturn of his mouth. Though I couldn't speak mechanic, I had "Dan" pretty well mastered.

He didn't want us to come.

But Anneke heard "go with you" and, with a high pitched squeal, repeated the words, effectively bolstering my faint suggestion.

"Are you sure? It's not going to be that interesting." If it weren't for the fact that Miss Bilingual had moved to PEI and he had promised me it was over, I would think he was heading out to meet her. He looked that guilty.

"I don't have a lot to do."

Dan adjusted the fit of his ever-present billed cap and sighed. "Okay. I'll get the car seats."

Moments later we had the kids strapped in and the wagon in the box of the truck. As I climbed into the cab, Dan adjusted the radio, cutting off some country singer mid-sob. Dan never listened to country music at home. But then neither did he let his hair get this long or go out in public without shaving.

I climbed in the truck, feeling like I had accepted a ride with a stranger.

"Are you sure you want to come?" He gave me one more chance before he turned the key in the ignition. "The kids will probably get bored and cranky. These sales go on a long time. Mom said she might stop in anyhow."

"I like the idea of spending the afternoon together." I wasn't going to let him talk me out of it. Besides, in my current frame of mind, I didn't know if I could deal with the possibility of a visit from Wilma.

"Okay," he said in the "I think you're crazy" tone that usually set my teeth on edge. But these days, I was trying to construct a new and improved Leslie VandeKeere, and I let it slip under the radar.

We drove in silence as I looked out at the endless landscape of brown ditches, brown fields, and bare trees, stark and clear against the leaden sky.

This is no different from Vancouver this time of the year. Just fewer houses and less traffic. Appreciate it for what it is.

I was getting good at this self-talk.

Dan cleared his throat, laying his hand on my arm. "I'm sorry about this morning. I shouldn't have walked out on you like that."

Usually this was my cue to meet him halfway, acknowledge my part in the argument, then shore up my defenses. But usually

I had most of the day or night shift at work to go over the argument and find weaknesses in his statements, and usually I had the help of sympathetic co-workers who faithfully took my side.

But today he had caught me defenseless and rebuttal-less.

"I still think we should do the assessment." Lame reply, but the best I could do on the fly.

Dan looked away. "If I agree, will you be willing to put our money into the farm?"

Marriage was about give and take, but on this I couldn't give. The money from the house was the down payment on the life I needed to return to. On a future that had security and steady, regular income. I didn't dare risk losing any ground on that. Not the way he'd talked this morning.

"I'm sorry, but I can't."

He held my gaze and I pushed. Had to. "We'll get money from that court case against Lonnie Dansworth, then we'll be okay."

"And if we don't?"

"Then we can use the house money to start up another business and, in time, we'll get it back."

"Why can you talk about putting the money into a business I don't like doing instead of putting it in to something I do like?" He looked ahead again, his jaw clenched.

And we're off... "Because we agreed we were going back." I could do stubborn too. What I lacked in creativity, I made up for in persistence. Dan, however, was exceeding his usual quota. Of course, he had the rallying support of his family behind him. I was on my own. "We agreed, Dan."

Dan reached over and turned on the radio, filling the cab with wailing guitars and nasal twangs. The conversation was over. And now I had put myself in the unenviable position of being stuck in close proximity to him for the rest of the day.

This was a mistake.

CHAPTER 6

A long, snakelike line of pickup trucks--twin metal caterpillars--lined each side of the narrow road leading to the farm sale. As we walked toward the farm's driveway, I wondered where all these people had materialized from. In the twenty-five minutes it had taken us to get here, I had counted maybe twelve yard sites. There were at least eighty vehicles parked along the road.

In the distance, as if in counterpoint to the silence that had risen between Dan and me, a nasal babbling rose and fell, then paused and continued again. After a few minutes I realized the sound came from the auctioneer, his voice carried to us by a faint breeze.

"So, why are there so many people here?" I glanced sidelong at Dan. "Is this a special sale?"

From the glint in his eyes when he looked my way, he appeared to recognize my conversational peace offering for what it was. Avoidance. But his light shrug told me he was game to at least make an attempt. "Not really. I remember going with my dad to farm sales every spring. Most of the people are 'lookie loos.' It's something to do and a chance to visit."

I pulled my coat a little closer around me and thought of a hundred other ways to visit that didn't require standing around in cold weather.

"So why do people have farm sales?"

"This one is an estate sale. Dwayne Harris died about three months ago, and the wife is moving to town 'cause the kids don't want to take over the farm. Been happening a lot lately." Melancholy edged his voice.

I was about to ask him if Wilma would have an auction sale when we left, but his tone told me he didn't need my happy questions.

We turned into a long, narrow driveway enclosed by trees. The amplified voice of the auctioneer lured us on while chiding the bidders to recognize the deals they were getting.

Bargains, folks. Absolute bargains.

The driveway wound for a few hundred feet before opening up onto a wide yard. A large red barn, the kind that come with farm play sets for kids, held court on one side, its doors and windows creating a face that looked with bored tolerance at the large group of people milling about on the yard below it. Beside the barn, a large shed, open in the front, held an assortment of machinery.

The house sat across the yard from the barns, an older two-story affair with a large wrap-around porch. Brown paint peeled off the siding, and a few old pots trailing dead branches and leaves still hung from the beams of the porch. The house looked weary, as if it was ready to move to town as well.

Furniture stood in neat, orderly rows on the grass. A couple of couches, one with a matching chair and loveseat, some beds, a dining room table and chairs.

People looked into boxes, sat on chairs, tried out appliances, inspected items normally secreted in the cupboards of the house behind us but now laid out for anyone who had the least bit of curiosity to look over and comment on.

"Hey, Dan, there you are." A tall, older man wearing a red plaid shirt over a T-shirt strode toward us, waving. Two younger men trailed him. One of them wore a jean jacket, the other a loose hoodie and the oversized pants favored by young city boys trying to look tougher than they really were. I would know. I'd stitched up enough of them in the Emergency Department back in Vancouver.

Both of these clean-cut, strapping young men, who didn't look like they would know beer from iced tea, had the same sandy blonde hair as Dan. When one smiled, I saw Dan as a teenager. They had to be relatives.

"Why haven't you been by?" The man clapped a large hand on Dan's shoulder. "Auntie Gerda made your favorite pie when she heard you were back, and she's been waiting for you to come and eat it." His dark eyes slid over me to the kids, then back to Dan. "And you got your family along?"

"Leslie, this is Uncle Orest and my cousins Nicholas and Jason. This is Leslie and Nicholas and Anneke."

Orest gave me a huge grin and caught my hand in both of his, burying it in a pack of calluses and thick knuckles. "Good to see you, girlie. Heard lots about you."

Which, of course, begged the question, what? But I wasn't going to head down that path and simply smiled, trying not to look too threatening.

Nicholas and Jason acknowledged me with the imperceptible nod of teenagehood, then turned back to Dan.

"So, you here to check out some deals? I saw a Massey here, like the one Keith used. 'Course, Keith didn't use it much after he blew the head gasket on it." Orest shook his own head as if he couldn't understand Keith or his actions. "That man didn't know how to maintain equipment. But this one looks pretty good. A bit old, but you can get it going I'm sure."

Dan's eyes lit up until he looked my way. "I'm going to check out a few things. Do you want to come or stay here? I can take the kids."

I shrugged. I sensed a mini-family reunion, and I would cramp his style. "Go ahead. I'll keep the kids."

He gave me the kind of smile that reminded me of why I fell in love with him in the first place, and I knew I had done exactly the right thing. For a change.

"I'll keep an eye out for the dryer." Dan touched my arm lightly, cementing our brief flash of togetherness. Then he and Uncle Orest and his cousins left, deep in discussion about head gaskets, cylinders, and pistons. I knew the terms but hadn't developed the deep affection for them that Dan had or, it seemed, his uncle and now animated cousins did. What was it with men and internal-combustion engines that put a light in their eyes that even lingerie had a hard time competing with?

In spite of my assurances that I'd be okay, fear nipped at my heart as Dan walked away. I felt trapped in a bubble of strangeness that pushed people away, separated me from the crowd. I tried to smile and make eye contact, but no one seemed to notice or care.

"Mommy, I want out," Anneke called out from her perch.

"No, honey. Stay in the wagon." I couldn't let her go in this strange place. One glance away from her, and she would be gone, lost. And I would be running around, calling out her name, an irresponsible mother full of panic.

No thanks.

"Let me out, let me out, let me out, let me out!" Anneke's voice rose a few decibels with each repetition.

Of course she chose this moment and this place to push.

"No, honey. You stay in the wagon with Nicholas." I kept my voice low and quiet as I concentrated on projecting "be rational" vibes, the only tool available to mothers when their children are spiraling out of control in a public place. I don't know why I tried it here. It didn't work in toy stores, grocery stores, or parks.

And of course she started to climb out just as I turned around to warn her. I went to grab her arm, and she danced out of reach. Suddenly I was giving the auctioneer competition as curious eyes turned toward me and my daughter.

"Hey, little girl. I don't think you should wander off." A tall man with dark hair, brown eyes, and a quirky smile blocked her line of flight by crouching down in front of her. Curious, she stopped, sizing him up.

"My mom says I'm not 'posed to talk to strangers," she said primly, as if her mother's feeble pronouncements were the laws that dictated every action of her day, instead of the other way around.

"That's a good thing your mother told you." He glanced up at me. His dark hair had a wave that would make a woman as jealous as his thick eyelashes did, and when he smiled a slow, lazy smile, I caught the faintest flash of a dimple. He wore blue jeans, a leather jacket, and cowboy boots. Something about the combination, the quality, the way he wore the clothes set him apart from all the other men present. Even my Dan. He could have been anywhere between thirty and forty-five and had that self-assured air that both appealed and sent warning signals up my spine.

Axe murderer, I thought instantly as City Leslie kicked in.

"She sounds smart." He pushed himself up, his gaze still holding mine, his dimple deepening. "You've done a good job with her."

Now he was flirting with me? I glanced down at my farm-wife clothes. No makeup, hair worn in the artfully tousled "mommy ponytail" that looked great on Angelina Jolie and sloppy on me. Yet when I looked back at him, I caught the faintest hint of interest. Had to be crazy.

I caught Anneke by the hand to pull her away just as the man held out his own hand.

"I'm sorry, Leslie. I should introduce myself. I'm John Brouwer."

He knew my name. He wasn't flirting with me at all. Fear grabbed my heart with icy fingers.

Stalker then. Well-dressed, well-informed stalker. Did he know where we lived?

"I was talking to your sister-in-law, Judy, and she told me that you used to work at the ER in Vancouver."

I blinked and stopped edging away from him as reason pulled me off my usual rabbit trail of delusion. "Pardon me?"

"I'm a doctor in the local hospital, so when I heard you were an Emergency Room nurse, I paid attention."

My heart slowed down, and I mentally gave myself a slap on the head. Some animals have a fight or flight defense mechanism when they are frightened. Me? I freeze and let my mind dive into the worst possible scenario and *then* I run with it.

I finally took his outstretched hand, regretting the shoulder cramps he must've suffered while I mentally labeled him everything from Lothario to deranged killer. "Sorry. My name is Leslie VandeKeere, but it seems you already know that. And yes, I did work as an ER nurse."

"You must have seen your share of trauma." Now that his status had been downgraded from psycho to physician, I realized how attractive he was.

"The usual." I waved my hand airily. "Gunshot wounds, stabbings, sometimes a broken arm to keep us on our game."

He nodded and glanced at the kids. "How old is your little one?"

"Nicholas is a year and a half. But I went to work pretty much right after he was born."

"Dedicated, then."

"Broke, then."

"And now?"

"Well, I'm trying fulltime motherhood on for size." I swung Anneke's hand to remind myself that I was still supposed to be interacting with my children, that they weren't mere accessories.

"And how does it fit?"

"Still working out the wrinkles." *Okay, enough with the metaphors.* "Why do you want to know?"

"Again, I apologize. Not too deft with this head-hunting business." He turned serious. "When I heard you were an ER nurse, I thought I'd ask. I'm not a stalker, and I'm not trying to come on to you, in case that's what you were thinking."

I dismissed the comment with another airy wave of my hand, as if that wasn't even worth consideration.

"But I hope I can talk you into coming to work for us."

Desperate much?

"I've decided to take a hiatus from nursing." I tried to inject a note of heartiness into my voice. "The kids are only young once." And wasn't that profound? The "only young once" mantra didn't come into play when I rushed off to work stuffing myself into my maternity scrubs because my pre-Nicholas ones didn't fit.

"If you ever change your mind--" He lifted his hands in a "what can I do?" gesture. "--I'm sure you know where the hospital is."

Forty-Eighth Street, along the main highway going through town as you come to the bottom of the hill heading into Holmes Crossing.

"Thanks, but I think I'll wait for now." I gave him my best motherly smile, then turned and walked briskly away from temptation. Anneke skipped along beside me, happy to be on the move, and Nicholas was smiling, his cheeks rosy, and his eyes bright as his wagon bumped along the frozen ruts in the yard. He looked so adorable, I couldn't help but smile too. How could I even consider going back to work when I had these two precious children to take care of? Surely that should be enough. I was a farmer's wife. I was going to expend my energy on my family.

How? You can't bake or garden, and that cow thing. Did you really think you made a difference?

Of course I did. Dan was proud of me. That had to be worth some sacrifice.

If that cow had come out, you would have turned tail and run. You're going to be here a whole year. You're going to need some kind of distraction. And money would help.

I shoved the thoughts into a box, slammed the lid, and quickly went searching for my husband. I was here to maintain our marriage and build it on mutual trust and respect. At least that's what the book, *How a Marriage can Succeed or Fail*, said. And because I was campaigning for the Succeed part, I figured I'd better stick with my plan even if Dan didn't.

I followed the auctioneer's voice and found Dan. He stood with his hands in his coat pockets, his shoulders hunched against the sharp wind that had sprung up. Anneke danced beside me, but as soon as she saw her father, she called out his name and ran to him.

Dan bent down and swooped his little girl up in his arms. He was talking to Uncle Orest, nodding seriously. As I came alongside, he glanced at me, stopped talking, and then his eyes slid away.

That didn't hurt. Not a bit. I forced down my frustration. Dutiful wife, I thought. *Dutiful wife.*

"So, what's up for sale now?" This was the classic "ask open-ended questions" portion of *How a Marriage Can Succeed or Fail*. Chapter Three, page seventeen. The part toward the bottom.

I was still trying.

"A couple of terrific appliances up next." The auctioneer answered my question before I asked. "Brand new and hardly used."

He led the bidding the same way he had with the bench, starting high and flowing down until he caught a bid, and away he went. Dan waited, and I watched, trying not to get nervous as the price slowly moved up. I knew shopping opportunities would be limited, and I really, really needed this dryer.

The bidding was random, but steady.

"I think Mrs. Harris had that machine for two months, tops," I heard a woman beside me say as Dan upped the latest bid. "If it doesn't go much higher, you'll get a deal."

It took me a few moments to realize the woman was talking to me. "She hardly used it. Too cheap you know." She gave me a conspiratorial wink. "Hung her clothes on the line, spring, summer, fall, and winter."

The young woman wore a shabby, down-filled jacket over a fitted T-shirt that said "Baby" in pink glittery letters, tucked into snug and faded blue jeans. With her black spiky hair and five earrings marching up each earlobe, she didn't precisely blend.

She rocked on her heels as she glanced at Anneke and Nicholas. "And I'm sure you could use a dryer right about now."

I scrambled for words, trying to figure out what I should or should not say to this complete stranger.

The woman grinned at me. "I'm Kathy Greidanus. Married, two kids." She waved her hand vaguely. "We live just a few miles from your place."

She was short and wiry, with quick darting eyes that flicked from me to Dan to Nicholas, still in my arms, to Anneke crouched by my legs, and finally back to me. "So you got to move into the hallowed home place?" She quirked a laughing half grin at me. "Lucky you."

And in that one gesture, underlined by the hint of sarcasm in those two words, I read a lifetime of knowledge of both Holmes Crossing and its residents.

"I'm Leslie VandeKeere. But of course you already know that."

Kathy shook my hand and turned to Anneke. "Hey, cutie patootie." She casually waggled her fingers.

I peeled Anneke from my leg with one arm, juggling Nicholas with the other, but Anneke froze, staring at Kathy.

"I'm guessing you're Anneke," Kathy continued. "How old are you?"

Anneke rubbed one foot against her ankle, ducking her head slightly. "I'm foah."

"Really? I have a little boy who's 'foah' too. His name is Cardell. He likes worms and jumping on the trampoline. If you want, you can come and jump on it too." She clucked her tongue against her teeth. "If spring ever comes." She glanced at the auctioneer then at Dan. "Looks like you got yourself a dryer."

I saw Dan nodding and realized I had missed the entire event. I didn't even know how much he had paid for it. It was all so anticlimactic.

"Do you do coffee?" Kathy slipped her hands into the pockets of her jacket and shrugged it up around her neck.

"You mean like now?"

Dan drifted away, following the crowd who followed the auctioneer, lured on by the "Bargains, absolute bargains, folks."

"I mean coffee--like the visiting thing."

I gave her a blank look, and she laughed. I hardly knew her, and she was inviting me over already?

"Let me explain." She employed the patient tone specific to use with especially dense people, misunderstanding my hesitation. "I come over, you make coffee, though for me you make tea, we sit down at the kitchen table while our kids fight over Legos, and we talk about the people we know." With her hands still in her pockets, she pointed at herself. "Me. Kathy. Incurable Gossip"

"I think I got that." I gave a light laugh. "I've done coffee." Not as often as I would have liked. I had a couple of friends in Vancouver, mostly co-workers, who'd had the same hectic juggling schedule I had. Coffee was often a quick cup at the local McDonald's while our kids alternately played at the Play Place or cried for our attention. The topic of conversation never rose above the advantages of cloth over disposable diapers. Or vice versa. Depending on which article who read in what magazine.

"I don't want to overwhelm you." Kathy angled me a puzzled

look. "Gloria said you weren't much of the visiting type. But I'm the kind of person who needs to find out for herself."

I felt a pinch of anger at Gloria for talking about me behind my back, transforming me from a person to a topic of conversation. I didn't like it. I'd had enough of "she" and "her" at the family meeting.

"I could come." *Gee, didn't that sound gracious?*

Kathy smiled as if sensing my confusion. She patted me on the arm. "Don't worry about the gossip part. I know how to keep my mouth shut when I have to. I can wait."

"No. That would be great. I don't have a lot of secrets anyhow." I set Nicholas down in the wagon, glad to be relieved of his weight and glad he didn't kick up a fuss.

"Good thing. People in this county can sense a secret quicker than an upcoming sale at the Co-op."

"Co-op? Now you'll have to translate."

"Coming, Sprout?" Kathy held her hand out to Anneke, who, to my immense surprise, took it as Kathy angled her chin toward the crowd and started following. "The Co-op, more formally known as the Holmes Crossing Co-operative, started about the same time that Holmes Crossing was birthed back in the early 1900s. Locals call it The Co-op. Make sure you capitalize the 'The' when you're talking to give it and the ancestors the proper respect."

Kathy flashed me another grin.

"It's that important?"

"Oh, very. We may have a bunch of churches in Holmes Crossing, but we have only one graveyard and one main store, the Co-op. Theology may not unite us, but death and shopping do."

I had to laugh. I could like this blunt, outspoken character. And Anneke, who never went to strangers, tripped alongside her, telling Kathy about her dolls and about Nicholas and how he likes to eat dirt and how his diapers smelled bad, bad, bad. Kathy pulled a face at that and pinched her nose. Anneke giggled.

"Is your husband here?" I asked as we squeezed through the mob gathered around the farm-equipment shed and headed toward Dan. The crowd had thinned out. An aura of intense focus surrounded the remaining group. Clearly I was in the presence of serious buyers.

"He's holding the fort with the kids. It's my afternoon off."

"So you came here?"

"Hey. Out is out. Besides, I picked up some good deals. The tradeoff is that I'm supposed to stick around long enough to find out what the equipment went for. We're not in the market, but Jimmy likes to stay on top of the prices in case we ever are." Kathy pulled a pen and paper out of her pocket, all the while holding onto Anneke's hand and throwing my daughter a question now and again to show Anneke still had her attention. As I studied her, I knew I was in the presence of a professional mother and wondered if I should take notes myself.

"So what's that he's selling now?" I dared to expose my ignorance. Kathy seemed totally non-threatening.

"A John Deere 9650 combine. Not in our league, but obviously old Harris had a few pennies or more."

"Not enough to paint the house."

"Dead investment." She winked at me. "Lesson number one, farmers tend to see houses as a money drain. If you want the kind of farm house that gets featured in *Country Woman*, you have to stake your claim early on in your marriage and defend it against tractors, combines, more land and more livestock."

No problem. I had no intention of creating a farm show home out of the VandeKeere residence.

The auctioneer shouted "Sold!" and moved on to the next item. Bidding shot up quickly, but just as quickly stopped. The people here seemed to know exactly how much they would spend before they came. Kathy scribbled the amount down in her book. As soon as she was done, Anneke reached for her hand.

Nicholas started crying, and I snagged a couple of annoyed glances, even one from my own husband. I might not be able to take charge of my kids, but I could take a hint. "I'll be back," I whispered to Kathy, as if my discretion could offset the angry wails of a little boy who'd had enough of auctions.

Kathy shooed me away with a friendly wave. "No worries. Anneke can stay with me."

"No, I should-"

"Let her stay with me. I won't abduct her. Got my own rug-rats."

She gave me a grin, and I accepted her gracious offer, Nicholas's wails creating an urgency I couldn't ignore.

I quickly pulled the wagon away, hoping the vibration of the wheels over the ruts would lull Nicholas into mellowness. Picking him up would only net me his balled-up fists in my face. Public pummeling wasn't something I liked to indulge in.

It took a few minutes, but he finally settled and slowly slumped to one side, his eyes blinking sightlessly. When I was fairly sure he was burrowed deep in sleep, I laid him down in the wagon and returned to Dan's side to continue my role as faithful wife and good mother. I was doing A-okay so far.

Anneke and Kathy still stood beside Dan as Kathy frowned at the auctioneer.

"Nineteen five, Nineteen five on the Massey!"

I guessed he was coming to the end of the sale. I grimaced at the mangled wreck of the tractor and wondered who in the world would buy that thing. "Going once, twice--" He paused, then pointed to my husband. "Sold to Dan VandeKeere for nineteen thousand dollars!"

"What?" I couldn't stop my involuntary cry. I turned to Dan, who was writing something down in a book he always had tucked in his shirt pocket. "Don't tell me you just bought that tractor?" I hissed aware of the people now watching us.

"You were here." He wouldn't look at me.

"How...what...where are you going to get the money for it?"

Wilma had been pretty adamant that there wasn't a lot of money available right now for any of what she called extras.

Dan sighed, dropped the book in his pocket, but still didn't meet my eyes. "From the term deposit."

My heart leapt into my throat, momentarily choking off any words I might have been able to utter. My hands clenched the handle of the wagon. "You mean the Dream Home Fund?"

"It's just a bank account, Leslie, and I need to get the tractor fixed if I want to get the field work started." He walked away.

But it wasn't "just a bank account." It was part of our future. In Vancouver. It was our investment in our life. In Vancouver.

And with one wave of his hand, he had chosen the needs of the farm over that.

FROM: lesismore@hcrossing.net

To: tfroese@centermail.com

Dan had planned all along to buy that wreck of a tractor. That's why he looked so guilty when I asked if I could come. Twenty-three thousand for something he can't even drive home. Said he was going to take the motor out of this one and drop it in the tractor we have now. And that's why he bought that garden bench. As if that would soften me up. Or the dog. Oh yeah. A dog. My by-the-book, non-impulsive man bought a dog at the sale. I didn't know you could get dogs at auction sales. It belonged to the lady who owned the farm, and she decided at the last minute to sell it, and Dan decided at the last minute to buy it. Anneke is thrilled and promptly named it Sasha. I know that disliking dogs is almost unpatriotic. Dan reminded me that dogs are a man's best friend. A friend that drools and drinks out of the toilet, I tried to tell him. Every time I go outside, Sasha is sitting on the step looking at me like I'm her best friend. I have to confess it's kind of nice to have such unabashed appreciation from someone in this place.

Landlocked Leslie Lenient about the Licking

FROM: tfroese@centermail.com

To: lesismore@hcrossing.net

Okay, I'm getting nervous for U. Taking money out of the Dream House Fund AND getting a dog? That is not playing fair. Sounds to me like U are going to HAVE to get a job. Think on it seriously, sweetums. Taking money out of the DHF is a serious breach of ethics. To me that calls for retaliatory methods. Get a job. NOW. What are U going 2 do with dog when you go back?

To: tfroese@centermail.com

From: lesismore@hcrossing.net

The dog will stay with the tractor and our ever expanding livestock. Yesterday Dan went to another auction sale. Didn't buy a tractor this time but came home with a box of parts for the tractor that is turning out to be more work than he thought. And he bought a box of chickens. Living, clucking, feather shedding chickens. Said my baking inspired him. I had tried to bake cookies the other day and ran out of eggs. The cookies turned out horrible. Dan figured the chickens could serve dual purpose. Give me eggs to make cookies. Then eat the cookies that I make. Great. Our own biological ecosystem.

To: lesismore@hcrossing.net

From: tfroese@centermail.com

U are not a cook either. Go back to work. U will need $$$ to make up for what Dan spent.

* * *

I STOOD in front of the hospital and nervously wiped my hands on the front of my jacket. Ten minutes till show time. I could change my mind. I didn't have to take the interview.

It had been seven chocolates since the auction sale. Seven chocolates since we drove home, each of us sitting on our side of the truck, the depletion of our term deposit creating an uncrossable chasm.

The day after the auction sale, I decided to take my sister's advice and head on down to the hospital, where I filled out an application. Five days later, I got a phone call to come in for an interview, and I knew I had started a process I had to see to the end.

I had agonized longer over what to do with my children during the interview than the interview itself. In Vancouver the kids were in daycare. Here, in Holmes Crossing, it didn't feel right to drop the kids off when they had relatives. But Wilma, Gloria, and Judy all lived in the opposite direction of Holmes Crossing. Judy, who was a twenty-minute drive from our place, lived the furthest, but she was my first choice. I simply couldn't imagine bringing the kids to Gloria's or Wilma's and facing their questions or their censure.

So I phoned around and found a drop in daycare. It would do for today and if I got the job? Would I have to re-think asking Judy? Soon the greenhouse would be too busy and she couldn't take the kids regularly.

But could I bring them to daycare again?

Second thoughts spun their insidious web, tangling my plans, creating complications I didn't have to consider in Vancouver.

Then I thought of staying at home day after day, and I felt a moment of panic. Yesterday I had alphabetized my cd collection, then changed my mind and arranged them by category. I knew other mothers filled their time with various activities, but I was neither gardener nor baker nor seamstress nor true-blue farmer's wife. I was a nurse. It was what I loved to do.

I closed my eyes and opened the door. I didn't have to take the job if I got it.

Ten minutes later I was sitting across a desk from head nurse Sally Richards, feeling as nervous as a teenager waiting for a prom date.

"I'm so glad you decided to come in." She picked up the last of my papers and glanced quickly at her watch. Shift change in fifteen minutes. The atmosphere told me more than the clock did. Tired nurses winding down from their shift had "going home" written all over their faces.

"John told me he talked to you, and I hoped you would apply. Some of the ward nurses have been covering in the Emergency Department, but they certainly don't have your broad area of expertise." Sally tapped the file folder holding my application and test scores and smiled. "You might not see near the drama here that you did in Vancouver, but we have our busy times."

"If it's an Emergency Department, I don't doubt you do." I slowly inhaled the mixed scents of the hospital. Clean linen, waxed floors, the pervasive scent of disinfectant that was the first line of defense against a hospital's biggest enemy, infection.

I missed it. I yearned for it. I wasn't a farmer's wife. This was where I was meant to be.

"I was impressed with the results of your NCLEX scores."

"I test well." Faint nervousness brought out my flippant side.

"And your resume is also encouraging." Sally tapped her fingers lightly. "Though I have to say, I am concerned with how often you've moved around."

"Restless husband." I gave a little apologetic shrug.

"I wish we could offer you full-time employment, but in light of the fact that, as you told me, you are only going to be here a year, I'd like to offer you a casual position. I'm going to be doing another interview in a few days for the full-time position we have advertised."

I didn't let my relief show. Casual sounded pretty good to me.

CAROLYNE AARSEN

The best of both worlds. I would be home enough to satisfy Dan and gone enough to make me feel like I wasn't losing valuable skills. ER work demanded constant upgrading to stay on top of all the latest technology. But my stomach knotted up as I thought of my kids. I didn't want to take them to daycare, but couldn't take them to Judy's. Gloria. Wilma. Gloria. Wilma.

The knot tightened as I tried to imagine taking the kids there every time I worked. Not only did they live in the opposite direction of Holmes Crossing, they thought the opposite of me. Mothers should be home with their children twenty-four hours a day. Ditto for farmer's wives. For a moment, I wished I'd gone to church with Dan the couple of times he'd gone. Maybe I'd dare pray that God would help me figure something out.

I pushed my worries aside for now. I had almost a week. Who knew what would come up? "When do you want me to start?"

"Actually, next week Friday would be great. We can start with the basic procedures, standing orders, that kind of thing. I'd like to introduce you to the staff while you're here, but I have an important meeting to attend."

"I understand. I'll be here Friday. Early." A brisk handshake, and she was off, her feet making only the barest whisper of a sound. I waited a moment, taking in the gleaming floors, appreciating the cleanliness of the place.

A man shuffled past, holding onto his IV pole, his eyes resolutely on the large glass doors at the end of the hallway. Determined face. Square outline jutting through a thin cotton house robe. *Smoker,* I thought sadly.

As I walked slowly past the emergency ward, I caught the palpable change in energy. Nurses tidied beds, restocked shelves. A doctor leaned against the desk of the nurse's station, but instead of trading jokes, his eyes cut to the door. And then I got it. They were waiting.

I heard the faint wail of the ambulance. The doctor shoved off, the nurses stopped, and my own heart started pumping.

Soon, I reminded myself, resisting the urge to pull on a discarded gown and join the action. *Soon I'll be part of this too.*

To: tfroese@centermail.com

From: lesismore@hcrossing.net

There are two words I've come to dread: "Coffee" and "time." Transmitted over the small intercom we have hooked up between the house and the garage, those words can send my heart into palpitations of nervous angst. They mean that Uncle Orest and his two sons are accompanying Dan to the house for coffee. This is the signal to boil water to make coffee, put out goodies, and clean up the counter while kicking toys under the couch and trying to catch Nicholas so I can wipe his face. Then I have to put clean towels out in the bathroom and a smile on my face. All this I can do. The weak link in the equation is goodies. These guys go through a bag of cookies faster than you can say trans-fat. Don't know what Dan will do with Uncle Orest when I start working. I guess that will be his worry. Haven't told Dan about the job. I'm waiting for the right time. Not sure when that will be. I'll have to play that one by ear.

Logical Leslie with the Limited Larder

From: tfroese@centermail.com

To: lesismore@hcrossing.net

Don't play by ear. U are tone deaf! Dan wl get over it. Don't sweat it about the kids. Daycare a couple of times a week won't kill them. U R not a farmer's wife and it wasn't fair of Dan to expect you to quit YR job. Nursing is what U love doing. I still remember that nurse kit I gave you for your birthday. U practically wore that thing out. As for mixed motives, hey. Who does anything out of pure motives these days? U have every right to be angry with Dan for siphoning money off the bank account. Don't apologize for doing what U do best. But U better tell Dan before U put on yr uniform. U know U can't wait for candlelight and wine.

Smart Sibling Sunning in San Fran

FROM: lesismore@hcrossing.net

To: tfroese@centermail.com

I'm being such a radical these days. After I had my interview, I called the assessor. I didn't know which real estate agent to go with, so I chose the one with the biggest advertisement. I'm a sucker for ostentation. He came yesterday. Dan tolerated him, and I had no clue what he was supposed to do except come up with a figure at the end of the day that we would file away with the assessment that was done after Dan's father died. I was glad to know it had been done before. I wasn't a flaming radical after all. But the way Dan treated him, I was tempted to put a disclaimer on the bottom of the paper: No animals were harmed during the filing of this assessment.

Leslie the Liability

CHAPTER 7

"*I* don't want those cookies," Anneke whined as I dropped a cellophane-wrapped package on her legs. She swatted them away and glared up at me.

"Honey, you don't even know what they taste like." I curbed my impatience. Her drama-queen repertoire had been on display all morning. Her blankets were scratchy. She didn't like the cute pink turtleneck I had laid out for her to wear. At coffee time Uncle Orest had teased her, and she snapped at him, which netted me a reproving glance from Dan. As if Anneke's antics were my jurisdiction and my fault.

"I want Oreos," Anneke announced as I consulted the vast array of cookies before me.

I wasn't about to indulge her. In lieu of me baking, we were at minimum going to choose wholesome goodness. She would thank me later when she had strong bones and teeth instead of rickets and dentures and bad knees from overindulgence in trans fat crammed snacks.

As I put the package in the buggy, she crossed her arms and slammed them against her chest, her lower lip dropping in a pout that you could land a 747 on.

No sooner had I made that decision than I suffered the usual moment of self-doubt. Maybe someday she'd be sitting on a psychoanalyst's couch with her perfect bones and teeth, a mental wreck because her mother was so controlling. Trouble was I *wanted* to be firm and controlling. All the magazine articles I read impressed the importance of consistency. But deep down I was still cursed with a lingering teen insecurity. I wanted my kids to like me, but at the same time I wasn't supposed to be their friend.

This raising kids was really about fiddling and adjusting, though, wasn't it?

In the *Parenting Plus* magazine article I read on the fly one day, smart parents were told to simply ignore bad behavior. To focus on the good. So I chose to ignore her and focus on Nicholas, batting the bar in front of him with his pudgy hands as he blew happy spit bubbles. He grinned up at me, and I bent over to kiss his shining apple cheeks.

"You love Nicholas most," Anneke wailed.

Yes, my dear child, at the moment I do. And the guilt I didn't feel was freeing. I gave Nicholas another kiss.

"I don't like you. I don't, I don't, I don't," Anneke shouted.

A woman sidled past our cart, casting nervous glances from me to Anneke, who now stood in the cart and rocking it with all the vigor of a frat house boy. I gave the woman a feeble smile as I teetered between ignoring Anneke and simply taking Nicholas out of the cart and walking away.

"Hey, Leslie, how are you?"

I sucked in an embarrassed breath, then turned to face the unfamiliar voice calling my name. Kathy, the woman from the auction a few days ago. Today she wore a loose T-shirt and blue jeans tucked into cowboy boots. Today her hair looked like a hedgehog on steroids.

I discreetly inventoried her grocery cart. Organic juices and yogurt alongside plastic bags filled with lentils, oatmeal, beans, and various nuts. I glanced at my own cartload, which leaned heavily toward the processed-foods section of the store. *At least I'm getting healthy cookies,* I reassured myself.

Kathy glanced at Anneke, unfazed by her antics. She reached behind her and pulled forward a little girl who had been clinging to the back of her legs. The girl's hair covered her eyes in a tangled mess. A ring of brown circled her mouth. She wore a t-shirt with an orange stain down the front and baggy pants that couldn't seem to decide if they were shorts or capris. "This urchin is Carlene. My youngest. I'm going to make a sign for her that says 'I dress myself' just so people don't get the wrong idea."

"I see." I wanted to make intelligent conversation, truly I did, but my cart still rocked, Anneke informing me and the entire world of her feelings for me.

"So, how are you managing? It must be hard to come down here." Kathy absently stroked Carlene's sticky hair out of her face. She half-turned away from Anneke.

"To the store?" I stole a quick glance at Anneke without trying to look like I was stealing a quick glance at my daughter. To my surprise Anneke had stopped rocking and yelling. She watched Kathy, puzzled.

"No, you nut. To the country. From the city."

Just then a boy slightly older than Anneke hurried over full of self-importance, holding two bags of the self-same cookies I had denied Anneke seconds ago. He dumped them in the cart. "These are the bestest ones I could find."

Kathy stroked his head. "Good job, buddy." She must have noticed my puzzled stare. "Cordell is my cookie and cereal expert. One week he gets to pick which cookies we're going to have, the next, it's cereal."

"That's cute." So I *was* wrong in denying Anneke a chance to pick out her own cookies. Why didn't kids come with a manual? How was a mother supposed to wing it through the myriad of decisions required every day?

"So, how is the dryer working out for you?"

I pulled my attention back to her. "Good. Though I did get the helpful suggestion that if I hang my clothes outside they'll dry faster." Wilma generously gave me this comment, accompanied by her usual patronizing smile.

Kathy clucked her disapproval of Wilma's household hints. "I call that cultural warfare and a direct insult to those of us who prefer to aid the cause of global warming by chucking our clothes in the dryer and enduring the thrill of shrinkage through ever-changing heat settings."

This woman was my new best friend. "Not to mention the fact that our overuse of natural resources will spur the government to increase corporate subsidies to companies seeking alternative energy sources," I countered.

Kathy clapped a hand on my shoulder. "Lady, you are speaking my language. I think you should come over for coffee."

I had told Dan I was coming right back, but I figured it wouldn't do him any harm to wonder where I was for a while. Maybe he would miss me and worry about me, and when I came back, he would enfold me in his arms and tell me that he treasured me and that he was wrong and that we would move back to Vancouver as soon as possible.

Or maybe he wouldn't even notice. He and his uncle had their head buried in the bowels of the tractor ever since the auction sale.

"Sounds like a great idea." I gave Kathy a quick grin.

Kathy's house was only a few miles out of the way, situated close to the highway where the valley was wide open and more populated. As the mailboxes as flitted past I read the names: Brouwer, VandeKam, Huttinga, Flikkema, VanDyke. I sensed a pattern here. Pretty much pretty Dutch. Then we came to Greidanus, and I followed Kathy down the driveway to her house. Kathy's yard and home surprised me, however. From her lackadaisical attitude and tough demeanor, I expected something less, well, froufrou.

The house was an older, scaled-down Victorian, white with green gingerbread trim. It looked like the kind of place a grandmother with an apron would inhabit. Flowerbeds lined the sidewalk, tulips and lilies poking up through tidily cultivated dirt.

She must have caught my expression as I followed her up the walk, holding Anneke's hand, Nicholas resting on my hip.

"You seem surprised." Kathy juggled her groceries and Carlene's clinging hand as she pulled open the wooden screen door.

I knew I couldn't fake it with her and, at the same time, knew I didn't have to. "I didn't take you for the flowers and gardening type."

"It's the hair." She sighed dramatically as she held the door open with one foot, motioning with her head for me to go in. "I should wear it long and loose and drape myself in Eddie Bauer socks, Birkenstocks, and L.L. Bean clothes too." She slipped her boots off on the bootjack and strode into the house. "I've been accused of giving people mixed messages, but hey, in a place like Holmes Crossing with so much tradition, it never hurts to keep people guessing."

"Well, you had me on the run."

As my eyes took in our indoor surroundings, I had another surprise. Dishes sat in precarious stacks on a small, old-fashioned countertop. The table, pushed against a long wooden bench, held a pile of bread crusts and beside it lay an opened pot of peanut butter with the knife still in it. A jumble of clothes lay in a heap on one of the chairs. A plaque above the table caught my eye: "Condition of kitchen variable. Hundreds of people have eaten here and gone on to lead normal lives."

Kathy dropped her plastic bags by a large floor-to-ceiling cupboard and waved her hand in the direction of her kitchen. "Housekeeping and me, not friends. Barely nodding acquaintances." She pulled open the door as Cordell and Carlene heaved cans and boxes out of the bags and put them away.

"Hey, Nicholas and Anneke, you want to help?" she asked my children, whose mouths hung open in wonder at the freedom these children enjoyed.

She didn't have to ask my daughter twice. In seconds she dug into bags, asking where things went and putting them away like she was handling the Crown Jewels.

Nicholas had been squirming to get off my lap from the moment I sat down with him. I looked at the floor, then at the fun the kids were having and set him on the floor in the middle of bags and groceries and kids.

"You put this one away, mommy." Anneke pushed a can in my hand.

Cordell pulled out a bag of tiny boxes of raisins with a gleeful yelp. "Let's make a raisin box tower." He ripped the bag open and spilled the boxes out onto the floor. Kathy didn't even blink.

"Yay, a tower," Anneke called out, though she didn't have the first clue what to do.

"Here, Anneke." Kathy said pulled the plastic bag out of Nicholas's reach with one hand while showing Anneke what to do with the other. "You have to be really careful when you pile them up so they don't fall. Carlene, you help Anneke. Here, Nicholas, here's some boxes for you."

"I've been had," I told Kathy as I helped Anneke balance a box on yet another tower. "All this time, I've been spending a fortune on educational toys when fun and games were right in front of me in the form of boxed raisins."

"Welcome to Groceries R Us." We made a couple more towers, and Kathy clapped her hands. "Okay, Coredell, Carlene, Anneke, let's put the boxes away. You go to the playroom and keep yourselves busy for a while." Kathy's tone suggested that no protest would be forthcoming. And none was. When they were done, Cordell picked up Nicholas as if he had been doing this all his life and carted him down the hallway, Carlene and Anneke trailing along behind him. I looked at Kathy with new eyes. And wonder. How did she do this so effortlessly? An artist, that's what she was.

"Close your mouth." Kathy gave a quick laugh. "You look like a fish."

"I feel like a fish. Out of water. Every time I want Anneke to do something, I feel like I have to convene a tribal council, and even then I'm always afraid she'll vote me out of the house."

"Show No Fear is the first rule of parenting." Kathy pulled a kettle off the stove. "So, I heard that you're an R.N."

"Heard? From who?"

"Wilma and Gloria were talking about it at Coffee Break. I was surprised when they said you didn't want to go back to work."

When did I ever talk about not going back to work in front of Wilma and Gloria? The last conversation we had that even touched upon me working had to do with them assuming I'd sooner be digging in the garden than starting IV's.

"You look confused," Kathy said.

I pulled myself away from thoughts of work and Wilma. "Sorry, you lost me at Coffee Break."

"Sorry. I should explain. Coffee Break is the women's Bible study that's held at the church. There's programs for the little ones and a nursery that run while the moms are busy. You should come."

"First major obstacle. Bible and study. Don't do either. And I'm not so sure I want Wilma to see—" I stopped myself just in time to keep from confessing my lack of Bible knowledge and my struggle with my mother-in-law.

Kathy glanced over her shoulder at me while she arranged muffins on a plate. "I take it you don't get along with Wilma?" Her tilted smile and saucy wink, accompanied by the faint sparkle in her eyes, were clues that she knew precisely how I got along with Wilma.

Not.

But I was trying to be charitable and discreet. I didn't need anything I said held against me at the next convening of the VandeKeere family.

"We have our difficulties," I said carefully. "But she's had hers as well. What with Keith taking off and all."

Kathy snorted. "Honey, that was the best thing that happened to her. Keith was a lazy no-good." She stopped and tapped her fingers on her lips. "And here I said I wasn't going to gossip."

"But it still must be hard for her." I was determined to be compassionate.

"Not so hard now that her favorite child is back. And I'm sure she's happy about you toiling alongside Dan, supporting him and keeping the home happy and healthy."

Was she being sarcastic?

I didn't know Kathy that well and wasn't sure of her place in the community nor her position on the working-mother/stay-at-home mother debate. So I went with the ever popular and seldom out of style, vague. "I'm sorry. What do you mean?"

"Don't worry, Leslie. I know exactly what you're up against with Wilma. She has a good heart but an old-fashioned view of motherhood and marriage." Kathy turned back to the now-whistling kettle and poured the steaming water into a tea pot and brought everything to the table. "So why don't you go back to work? And if I'm being way too nosy, you can tell me to back off." Kathy turned serious now. "My husband says I don't always know when to leave things be. And he's right, but my need to know outstrips my need to be discreet."

I laughed at her blunt honesty and thought of my now sadly depleted DHF and the tractor that Dan and his uncle were, even as Kathy put cups in front of me, fixing up.

"I've actually done that already." I chose my words carefully. "I'll be starting on Friday."

Kathy sat back, her hands cradling her cup of tea. "What are you going to do with the kids?"

"I thought about the daycare in town."

She pulled a face. "Don't do that Leslie. If you need a babysitter, I'll gladly help out. My place is right on the way to town."

I waited, letting the words sink in. "I work shifts."

"That's okay."

I wanted to jump up and accept her generous offer right away but couldn't escape the guilt over not asking Wilma or Gloria first.

I heard the kids playing and turned toward the window. Anneke and Carlene shrieking with laughter and running across the fenced-in yard, Nicholas pouring sand over his feet in the sandbox, supervised by the cookie expert. My heart ached to see my kids playing in a yard with other kids. I didn't go on playdates with other mothers, so I didn't get much advice from other women. Raising the kids was, to me, like driving a car with very, very dim headlights. I could see only the next thing I had to do. Long term, much harder to figure out.

Ever since the kids were born, I'd felt as if Dan and I were two rank amateurs experimenting with fragile substances. My mother was who knows where, and Terra, a single woman, could only cheerlead from the sidelines. Friends at work offered advice, but it never seemed applicable. Now here was a person I barely knew but felt an inexplicable connection to, offering to help me with the crucial job of raising my kids.

I'm not a sentimental person, but that was definitely a choked throat moment.

"Thanks for the offer, Kathy. I might take you up on it."

"You do that." She took a sip of tea. "Now, tell me all about Vancouver. I've always wanted to go but never had the chance."

. . .

From: tfroese@centermail.com

To: lesismore@hcrossing.net

U better tell Dan pretty quick about job or you're going to be in huge doo doo. Gotta run. Big date. Keep you posted.

Tra, la, la Terra

CHAPTER 8

"*W*hy?"

The single-word question hung between us, edged with anger.

"Because..." I could see him stiffen at my standard reply even as the words *tractor, tractor, tractor* echoed in my subconscious and, buried even below that, Missssss Bilingual. Right as I might have been, I wasn't ready to play that card yet. "I tried the cows thing Dan. But I'm not a cow person, horses give me the screaming willies, the chickens give me the creeps. The dog is the only animal I feel comfortable around. I don't know the difference between a cultivator and a combine, and frankly, don't care. I do know ACLS, how to deal with a stroke victim, and how to assess a burn. I'm comfortable in a hospital emergency department, and there have been days since I've moved here that I wish I was back there. Where I know what I'm doing." I clamped my lips together to stem the tide of my run-on babbling. I wanted him to understand. Needed him to understand.

"I want to go back to work because it's the only place I feel like I belong." I stumbled my way through this new situation. "I feel like I should have had my passport stamped before we came here." I drew in a breath, juggling my words awkwardly. I considered bringing up the tractor again and the money Dan had drained out of our house account. But that would take us nowhere. After all, technically, half of our house money was his. If honesty was my new tack, then I had to lay out the rest of my reasons. "I don't feel like I belong here."

"We had been close to farms before?" I could see he was trying to be patient, but he was using up his quotient. Fast.

"I never had to live on them. Nor did I have to try to fit into a place that was unfamiliar to me. And there's another thing. This Christian thing and going to church stuff you've been talking about lately. That's not us. It's not what I signed on for when we got married." I was gaining momentum, and from the faintly sheepish look on his face, I knew I was also gaining ground. And though I wasn't a farmer's wife, I remembered a few things I picked up from working with the cows. I kept my distance, off and to the side, but maintained pressure. "If you're going to be honest with yourself and me, it's new for you too. You never went to church in Vancouver or Fort McMurray or any other place we lived."

His silence underlined the rightness of my cause. But I knew I couldn't claim victory yet. I gently pushed on while I still had his attention and while he was still in a good mood instead of on the run.

"So here I am. Pagan. City person. And everything is new and different and confusing here. So I walk into the hospital, and I hear the clank of med carts, and I get a whiff of hospital cafeteria, and I hear the bleep of monitors, and for the first time since I came here, I relax. I'm in a familiar place. I'm home."

Dan screwed up his face, obviously trying hard to understand. "So it not just about the money?"

"That's part of it." I looked him directly in the eye. "We were going to keep the Fund separate, but that changed didn't it?"

"Leslie, you know why." Dan's lips became two white lines.

"I know you tried to tell me about cash flow and how you access the line of credit, but really it comes down to your mother controlling the farm money, doesn't it?"

"She's had a rough couple of months. I can't expect her to just hand it all over to me. Especially if, as you keep saying, we're only here for a year."

Once again I was caught between the reality of Wilma's humiliating situation and what I had to deal with on a day-to-day basis with Wilma.

"If she's going to hand over the cropping and the managing of the farm, I think she could go one step further. And partly because she won't and because the fund is emptier than I like—" I hurried through that dreaded but necessary territory of the discussion and plowed on. "I'm going back to work. But even more importantly, when I came into the hospital, I wasn't reminded that I don't know the difference between hay and straw, between heifers and bulls."

"Steers."

"See? That."

"But you're learning."

"I don't want to learn--" and then I clamped my mouth shut before I let myself trot down the, by now, old tired road of "this place isn't permanent."

"That's the trouble, isn't it? You don't even give it a chance."

"What are you talking about? I'm giving it a year."

"Give it time, Leslie. You'll come to love the animals, the wide open spaces. Don't you like being home with the kids?"

Direct hit on the guilt zone. "I do. And I wouldn't be working full time. But—" I dug down, searching for a word, a phrase that would connect. "I don't want my kids to grow up like I did. Broke. Wearing crappy clothes while their friends look good. They're going to have the best life I can give them, and if it means working, so be it."

"You don't think I can't provide all that for us?" The hurt in his

119

voice was almost my undoing. I knew what losing the business had done to his pride.

"I think you can. And you have." I paused, trying to find the best way to say what I needed to say. "Dan, we were in Vancouver two years. Before that, Fort Mac for eighteen months. Before that, it was Markham. We've spent a lot of years moving from place to place. This is just another stopover."

Right then Anneke pushed Nicholas into the kitchen and abandoned him in the box while she climbed up on her father's lap. Nicholas let out a wail of disapproval, which I responded to in record time.

"When do you want to start?" The faint tone of resignation in his voice showed me that, while he had accepted it, he still didn't like it.

Here came the next tricky part. I shifted Nicholas on my hips, holding him close to me like a chubby shield. "This Friday." I kept my response short and fast, like a quick needle jab, hoping the speed would eradicate the pain.

"What?" He stared at me, open-mouthed.

Or not.

"How did you get that so fast?" The anger in his voice vied with the puzzlement on his face. "Don't you have to take tests?"

"I did that the day before. I wanted to be sure before I told you." I could see him still puzzling this through and went on the defensive. "I'm not a stay-at-home wife. You knew that all along. I wasn't in Vancouver, and I'm not so sure I can be here." I conveniently left out the fact that I had come here willing to take a chance. But the family meeting, his mother, his sister, the cows, and of course, the tractor that had chipped away at those intentions.

"My sisters manage. My mother managed."

Low blow.

He looked at me then, and I felt a chill begin deep in my being.

"We moved here to help my mother out, to support her. The family needed us. That's why we came."

"My working won't change that."

"What are you going to do with the kids? Obviously you haven't asked my sisters, or they would have let me know."

"I've got that covered already. Kathy Greidanus is going to be taking care of them."

"Why not my mother? Or Judy? Or Gloria?"

"Your mom has enough to deal with, and neither Judy or Gloria are on the way to work."

"Did you even ask them?"

"Kathy offered first. Plus she has young kids for Anneke and Nicholas to play with."

"Mom isn't going to be happy about this."

"Kathy is right on the way to work. Judy lives fifteen minutes the other way."

"She's going to ask me why you didn't."

"And I don't want to add another three quarters of an hour of driving to the kids' day."

"I could take care of the kids once in a while."

"You'll be busy with the field work."

Dan waited a beat, then ran his fingers through his hair. "And what about our marriage? Wasn't coming to the farm about that too?"

The chill spread to my hands and feet. Since that final major blowup back home when I had come back from work early and Dan had shown up late smelling like perfume, Miss Bilingual remained She Who Must Not Be Named. To give her a name would be to give her a place in our life. I wasn't going to cede one second of my time to her. When Dan started confessing, I cut him off. I didn't want details. I didn't want my imagination creating pictures that would forever waver between us. So we only referred to her obliquely.

"What about our marriage, Dan? What about sticking up for

each other and putting each other first? When you used the money from our fund for the tractor, you showed me pretty clearly where what I wanted stood in your life." I clung to Nicholas and thankfully, for once, he didn't protest. I needed an ally and wasn't fussy as to shape, size or mental ability.

"I need that tractor for the farm."

"If that was the case, you should have asked your mother for the money."

Dan's angry glance cut away, and I knew I had scored a direct hit.

But I didn't want to be keeping score, to be shown I was right. Yet I had to keep the vision, or it was going to blur, and once again I was going to lose myself.

"You chose the farm over me."

His gaze swung back to me. "No. It's not always about you. It's not always about choosing one over the other. Sometimes it's about doing the very next thing that's right in front of you. Sometimes it's about making the best of where you are right now instead of always looking ten years into the future and sticking stubbornly to a plan that might not work in the long run."

Our gazes locked. I turned away first. Maybe I was too caught up in what lay ahead, but if a person didn't have goals, didn't have plans, they were vulnerable. You had to take care of your life. No one else was going to do that for you.

"Okay. I'm not going to say anything more about your job. But could you do me a favor? Could you at least try to make the best of being here?"

Considering I had ruined one of my favorite coats "making the best of it," his request seemed a tad unfair. But I wanted peace in our home. I didn't want Dan and me to be carping and fighting.

This skirmish was over, and though nothing concrete had been resolved, at least he was resigned to my working.

"I came here with the intention of making the best of it. This is part of how I intend to do it."

Dan sighed, got up. "Let's go outside, honey." Dan held out his hand to Anneke. Obviously this conversation's shelf life had expired.

Anneke hopped alongside him, chattering about the dog and the chickens, each word, each step carrying them both farther away from me.

Nicholas saw them go and spun around, twisting away from me toward his father and sister. His deafening wails exploded when the screen door slapped shut behind them.

"I know exactly how you feel," I muttered as I tried to console him.

But he wasn't having any of me either. I finally resorted to bribing him with some forbidden chocolate chips and set him in the high chair, freeing myself to get lost in the soothing motions of folding laundry.

"It will be fine," I said to the empty house. "He'll get used to it. His sisters will get used to it. His mother—a" That one was a stumper. I doubted Wilma would get used to it. But that didn't matter. It would all work out.

FROM: lesismore@hcrossing.net

To: tfroese@lakeshore.com

I got rhythm. In my life, that is. Dan is busy in the fields. We don't talk about my work, though he doesn't seem to mind the extra money in the account. He's still upset with me, but I'm busy enough in the house and at work that I can ignore it. And I have a wonderful babysitter. She loves my kids, and she's one of those casual mothers who makes raising kids look as effortless as riding a bicycle. Something I never quite got a handle on either. Remember how many times I skinned my knees?

Loopy Leslie Loving her Life

. . .

CAROLYNE AARSEN

From: tfroese@centermail.com

To: lesismore@hcrossing.net

That church thing Dan goes to. That's not some kind of cult is it? U won't have to pledge your kids to it or wear funny hats? Can't go with the flow if U are going to join a cult.

Terra

* * *

IT WAS TIME. I had found all kinds of excuses to put it off, but I had run out. The windows sparkled, the counters gleamed. The beds were made, and the floors were tidied. My immaculate house was a small penance for working the day before and enjoying it so much.

It was time. I looked outside. Sunshine. Warm, friendly sunshine.

I didn't need to put bulky coats and boots on the kids, which meant Nicholas could walk on his own. I slipped a light coat on, picked up the pail of burnt cookies that didn't make the grade and braced myself to face my nemesis. I knew I had to show Dan that I was giving this whole farm-wife thing my best shot. So I was heading out the door to do "chores" while he headed over to his mother's place to unclog a drain.

The warmth of the sun surrounded us as I closed the door of the porch behind us. I released a lungful of stale air, welcoming the change in scenery. I automatically glanced around, wondering who saw us, then caught myself mid-silliness. There were no neighbors twitching aside curtains to see what I was doing. No one watching us.

Though we'd already been on the farm three weeks (twenty-eight chocolates' worth), I still had to get used to the fact that, if I so desired, I could run outside naked and no one would be the wiser. That was unless Uncle Orest stopped by or Wilma made a

124

sudden stop on her way to town or Bradley VandeKamp, the neighbor, decided to borrow Dan's harrows.

Nicholas didn't want to go in the wagon, so I left it behind. As we started walking down the sidewalk, Sasha came bounding up, her mouth open, tongue hanging out, a doggy grin on her fuzzy face.

"Oh, Sasha, I love you." Anneke grabbed the dog by the neck and buried her face in the matted fur. Nicholas leaned toward Sasha, but I kept his hand in mine. One swipe of Sasha's tail would knock Nicholas on his padded bottom. Usually Nicholas was in his wagon, and Sasha's puzzling canine brain saw the plastic conveyance as a peril and walked wide, suspicious circles around it.

My worries were groundless. Sasha sat quietly while Nicholas petted her head, her tail slowly making a half circle in the dirt of the driveway. Anneke urged her brother on. "Pet the doggy, Nicholas. Nice doggy."

"Doggy." Nicholas's batted Sasha on the head. "Doggy."

My mouth fell open. He was talking. Speaking. Articulating. My amazement was replaced with laughter. His first word was doggy? Not Mommy or Daddy?

"Mommy, Nicholas said doggy." Anneke clapped her hands. "Oh good Nicholas. Good boy," she said, full of maternal pride.

"Hey, little boy." I bent down to pet Sasha as well. "This is a doggy, isn't it?" I pointed to myself. "And I am a mommy."

Nicholas gave me a blank stare, turned back to Sasha. "Doggy." He squealed and tugged on Sasha's ear, knocking over my pail.

I gave up, gathered the burnt cookies, and herded the kids toward the chicken barn. "Hey, kids, let's go. We have work to do."

Sasha sniffed the ground where the cookies had spilled and snorfed up the crumbs I had missed.

I held Nicholas's hand to give him some stability as we slowly made our way toward the barn. A light spring breeze sifted through the cottonwood trees, rustling the leaves that were now fully green. A crow mocked us from the branches, then flew away. Overhead an eagle circled lazily. I watched its progress, pointing it out to the kids.

In Vancouver the sky often hung low, either cloudy or rainy or foggy. Often I was so focused on the car in front of me as I lurched through rush hour traffic, wipers slapping time, I didn't spend much time contemplating the bits and pieces of nature I could see.

This was educational for my children. I looked around the yard that had slowly morphed from dull brown to soft emerald and hoped they would remember this.

A few cows were lined along the fence behind the barn studying our slow progress, their bovine features benign and dull. I couldn't understand why cattle ranching seemed such a romantic pursuit. Cows were big, large and, well, dumb. They took up a lot of space and ate a lot of food. Dan was still feeding them while he waited for the pasture to grow up enough to put them out.

And if cows were lacking in the intelligence department, the chickens we were going to feed rated well below them.

I tugged open the door to the chicken coop. Once upon a time, in some romantic notion I'd had about farm life, gathering eggs brought to mind a hazy picture of plump, contented brown chickens pecking pastorally on the ground while my children and I frolicked amongst them, plucking eggs from soft, straw-lined nests. That romantic notion was whisked away by the ammonia smell that almost knocked me over. Squawks and the muffled thud of flapping wings as the startled chickens took flight shattered that daydream. I sneezed, batting away fluttering feathers, trying to find the chicken feeder in the half light of the chicken coop.

"No frolicking today, kids." I dropped the cookies on the straw covered ground. The chickens at least liked my baking. They usually gobbled up my hapless attempts at the culinary arts, magically transforming them into eggs, which I would use for my next attempt. Which would probably end up back here, thus completing the cycle of life.

I shook some pelleted chicken feed into the feeder and turned to deal with the most complex part of the operation.

Three chickens crouched in the boxes, wings spread over their bounty, glowering at me with beady eyes as they clucked out warnings. Dan had shown me and the kids how to gently slip a hand under their bodies to pull the still warm eggs from under them. He hadn't even flinched when a chicken jabbed the back of his hand with its beak. Not for me. Bravery wasn't my middle name. Actually, it was Annie, but I tried not to advertise that fact.

"The chickens are too noisy." Anneke wrinkled her nose in distaste. "And very, very stinky."

"I agree honey." I eyed the still-nesting chickens. If I made a mad dash, I might be able to pull off a daring egg retrieval and save myself from being called a wuss. I know Dan would laugh if I told him. He would tell his family, and they would laugh. And I would, once again, look like the silly city girl I was.

Let's see. Pride, wuss, pride, wuss.

Nah. Wuss was fine with me. The eggs were safe until Dan got home.

We beat a quick retreat from the chicken coop, closed the door behind us, our onerous task for the day partially completed. Sasha, who had been sitting guard, bounded to her feet, her tail telegraphing her pleasure.

Anneke scampered ahead of me, Sasha loping alongside of her. Nicholas saw the cows grazing in the pasture and pointed one pudgy hand. "Cow. Cow."

I laughed and gave him a quick hug. "You little stinker. You'll say doggy and cow, but not Mom." He looked up at me and blinked, his hand still pointing away. "Cow. Cow."

"Mommy. Try it," I encouraged. "Mommy."

"Cow."

Well, maybe in his mind they were one and the same thing.

We wandered along the fence line as Anneke plucked some dandelions. I let the peace of the scene wash over me, thankful that the open spaces no longer intimidated me. Maybe, by the time I left, I would love this as much as Dan did. Maybe we would come back more often. If he didn't decide that Vancouver wasn't good enough and decide to move across the country again. We really needed to get that Dream Home so we could put down some roots.

By the time we got back to the house, Nicholas was rubbing his eyes and ears. If Anneke could be kept occupied for a while, I might have a chance to send my sister another e-mail, maybe even read another chapter in a book I had gotten from Judy. The thought gave me a tiny thrill of anticipation.

As I hung up the kids' coats, the jangling sound of the phone pierced the quiet. I glanced at the clock as I ran to answer it.

"Leslie, just thought I'd call." Gloria. Her precise words spoken with such scrupulous caring shriveled the faint hope that it might be someone interesting or fun. One of my friends from Vancouver apologizing for not answering my e-mails, my sister maybe, or even a telemarketer asking for donations.

"I heard you started working. And that Kathy Greidanus is taking care of your children."

Nothing like coming out swinging. "I met her in the store one day, and she offered." I tucked the phone under my chin as I lifted Nicholas into his high chair and started buttering bread. Thank goodness for cordless phones.

"Do you think that's wise?"

"I'm sorry?" Jam for Nicholas. Peanut butter all the way to the crusts for her Majesty. No clue what she was talking about for Gloria.

Gloria's silence beat on my ears, but I wasn't going to be the first to break it. She called. Let her talk.

"I realize that you feel the need to work, but I'm just a bit worried about Dan. He's going to start field work in a few days. What is he going to do about supper?"

Supper? The man didn't have two hands? He couldn't feed himself? "He made his own lunches and suppers before."

"Do you think that's fair?"

"Sorry. You lost me." I deftly cut up the kids' bread. Nine pieces for Anneke, cut off the crusts for Nicholas.

"Out here in the country, we farm wives bring supper out to our husbands when they are working in the fields. They put in long days and can't come home for a warm meal. I don't mean to sound nosy—"

But you are.

"—but how are you going to do that if you're working? And, I'd like to say that I would have gladly taken care of your children for you when you go to work."

I dropped into the nearest chair and rubbed my forehead. How to work through this? Sure, Gloria was Dan's sister and the children's aunt. But the kids didn't know her any better than they knew Kathy. And I liked Kathy. And she was supportive of my working. And the kids liked it at her place.

When I picked them up after work yesterday, Kathy had Nicholas on her hip and gave him a kiss before she handed him over. Knowing that he was loved and cared for made his protest at me taking him away worth the moments of self-doubt I'd had about working.

Dan still resented me working, but once I laid out my reasons, he gave grudging approval of my bringing them to Kathy's place. I wasn't used to making my decisions in committee. I thought I'd earned some Good Mother points simply by finding a wholesome alternative to daycare.

"I'm sorry I didn't consult you, Gloria." Big, fat liar. "But Kathy volunteered, and she has young children that Anneke and Nicholas can play with. Besides, she's right on the way to town."

"I would be willing to come and pick the kids up," Gloria said. "We're not that far away." She was the epitome of reasonableness and consideration. So why did it still get my back up?

"I don't want to run the kids around that much. Besides, I'll be working shift work, and it won't always be convenient. Thanks for the offer though."

Nicholas threw the last of his bread on the floor and let out a screech signaling the end of his lunch.

"Sorry, but I gotta go, Gloria. The kids need their nap." And I needed to regroup. "Thanks for calling."

"Well, if you change your mind, you can call me."

I said thanks again and hung up before letting myself get pulled into the lather, rinse repeat cycle of guilt that Gloria could raise in me. While I appreciated the offer, I knew I didn't want to face the unspoken censure that might occur each time I brought the kids to her place.

I cleaned them up and changed Nicholas. By the time his eyes were drifting closed, the phone rang again. This time I checked the call display. This time it was Wilma.

I had used up all my energy on Gloria, so I let it ring. When she called again, I let it ring again.

And one more time for good measure.

CHAPTER 9

"*I* told her that if she doesn't take her medicine, the voices will start, and people will think she's crazy." Darlene Anderson rolled her eyes as if to say "you know what I mean." She angled her head toward the middle-aged woman she was escorting to an empty cubicle. "Then she started running a fever, and I don't know what's causing what."

The woman in question, a Mrs. Rena Tebo, wore a pink hat with a bedraggled feather, a man's woolen vest over a stained white shirt, and a long sweeping velvet skirt. As we settled her on the bed, she kept whispering about a gig she was late for, her fingers twisting around each other. Her cheeks flamed, her eyes were glassy, and I could feel from her arm that she was burning up.

Darlene, who had brought her in, was slightly more lucid. Emphasis on *slightly*. In the time it took us to walk from the reception area to the Emergency Department, she had been chattering steadily about the VandeKeere family, how low the river was, the shameful movie being shown in town, and horoscopes.

She finally lowered her voice and drew me to one side as she glanced sidelong at the woman now settling onto the bed. "I brought her in for the fever, but you know she's right cuckoo, don't you?"

"The correct term is schizophrenic," I said primly.

"Whatever." Darlene dismissed the terminology with a flip of her hand. "Doesn't change the fact that she thinks she's a concert pianist." Darlene sighed. "Absolutely nuts. Thinks she has to go out tonight to play in New York."

It was a Thursday evening. I had drawn the afternoon/evening shift this week, grateful once again for my wonderful babysitter. Kathy gladly took the children this afternoon, promising to feed them supper and bring them home when Dan was done with his field work. I knew they would be all cleaned up and read to and cuddled and snuggled. I had felt a moment of jealousy when I thought of her taking them out of the bathtub all slippery and wet and drying them off, then reading to them. But when I came into the hospital and felt the energy of the place, my emotions balanced out.

I don't know how I managed all the juggling I had to do with daycare and Dan's work before. It wasn't pleasant, but somehow we coped. I would have a hard time going back to that.

"And what is your association with Mrs. Tebo?" I asked Darlene, trying to find my way around this bombastic and rude and yet caring woman as I started a chart.

"Oh, nothing at all. I help her once in a while. Come and clean her house. She throws a fit, but honestly--it's a pig sty." Darlene sighed heavily. "Just doesn't take care of herself. I found her today sitting stark naked in the bathtub. She was shivering even though she was burning up. Silly woman."

I cringed, glancing over at Mrs. Tebo, who, thankfully, was oblivious to all this chatter.

"These old people," Darlene continued. "Hard to take care of. Just like that Mr. Mast. He's a stubborn old coot. Just won't take his insulin. I suppose you need to take her history again." Darlene glanced at the chart. "I don't know why you can't use what you had before."

"It's procedure." I ignored her complaints and got the particulars on Rena Tebo via Darlene and a few muttered responses from Rena herself.

Once I got the woman's sad and all-too-familiar history down, I pulled out the blood-pressure cuff.

"Here. I'll need to help you with that." Darlene scurried over as fast as her formidable bulk would allow her. Amazingly, she didn't knock anything over as she bent to lift Rena's chin up. "The nice lady is going to take your blood pressure, okay?" she yelled, as if Rena were two miles away instead of two inches.

Rena just blinked and stared.

As I put on the cuff and started up the machine, I caught Darlene inspecting me. "You don't go to church with your Dan, do you?"

I blinked a moment, surprised at the question, though after spending even these few minutes with Darlene, the boldness shouldn't have been a shocker.

"No. I don't."

"Why not?"

I ignored her as I noted the blood pressure and took Rena's temperature. Through the roof.

"I prefer not to," was all I could muster. My focus was Rena Tebo right now, not my faith life.

"You should. Be good for you." Darlene nodded, her chins jiggling as if underscoring her comment. "You need to know that God is in control. Especially when those really bad cases come in the hospital."

I thought of the multiple motor vehicle accident earlier this week that had resulted in three deaths--a mother and her two children. I was so relieved I had missed it. Judy had gone to school with the mother and was heartbroken. She and Dan were going to the funeral tomorrow. But I was staying home with my children, blocking my life out into compartments. Work. Home. They didn't intersect. I couldn't allow it or I would constantly be seeing Dan or Anneke or Nicholas on the stretchers that came in.

"I'm sure God has enough people to occupy His time. He won't miss me." I was so smart and glib, hoping I could get her to stop prying into my life. Who was the nurse here after all? Who was in charge?

"He's missing you now." Darlene gave me a knowing look. "Like the one sheep missing from the ninety-nine. He goes after them because He cares."

Sheep? Ninety-nine? What in the world was she talking about?

I shrugged lightly, then moved onto things I did know about. "Dr. Brouwer will want to listen to Rena's chest. Do you think you can get her to put on this gown or at least take some layers off?"

Darlene waved me off. "Not a problem. And don't forget. God is waiting. He wants you to know what your only comfort in life and death is."

I supposed she wanted that to sound comforting. Tell you the truth, it sounded more ominous than reassuring.

"Rena Tebo?" Dr. Brouwer sighed as he finished what he was doing and clipped his pen in his pocket. "That's the second time this week. What is it this time?"

"Elevated temp and b.p. Some question as to what medications she's taken. I've got her ready for you. A Darlene Anderson brought her in."

To my surprise, Dr. Brouwer laughed. "She's a character, isn't she? I don't know how many of the town's down and outers she's tucked under her wing, but it's quite a few. Good thing she's got large wings."

"I got that impression."

To my surprise, Rena was in a gown by the time we got back. Still muttering and still complaining, but in a gown.

Dr. Brouwer checked her over, then pulled out a prescription pad and scribbled something on it. "She'll need to take these twice a day for ten days." He handed it to Darlene.

Darlene nodded slowly, looking over the piece of paper as if she could decipher Dr. Brouwer's handwriting. I knew I couldn't.

Dr. Brouwer talked about ongoing care and follow up, but Darlene waved him off.

"I know how this works." She tucked the prescription in a pocket of her sagging sweater. "I got it under control."

"I don't doubt you do," he said quietly.

We left Darlene chattering to Rena. As soon as they were out of earshot, Dr. Brouwer started laughing again. "I'd imagine you've seen all kinds in Vancouver. But I doubt you've seen too many like Darlene."

"Not too many." Darlene was puzzling combination of generous and strange, but in my mind the generous won out over the rest. Someone willing to cart around a schizophrenic woman and keep tabs on an elderly diabetic man was high up in my books, in spite of her questions about church.

"So what did you do with your kids?" Dr. Brouwer obviously wasn't in a hurry to go. His shift had been over for ten minutes and still he hung around, looking like he wanted to chat, something I had to get used to. In the Emergency Department in Vancouver there was no time for small talk. The smallest it ever got was "You ready for a break?" or "What are you doing this weekend?" usually thrown out as we passed each other in the hallway.

"I took them to a babysitter."

Dr. Brouwer had been gone on vacation when I started and only now, after three weeks of work, had our shifts intersected.

"Who?"

"Kathy Greidanus." I didn't know whether to finish charting or fully engage in chitchat. I picked up Rena's chart, and Dr. Brouwer followed me to the nurses' station.

"How old are your kids?" Dr. Brouwer leaned against the chest-high divider that separated the desk from the rest of the department.

"Nicholas is one and a half, and my daughter is four."

Why was he still hanging around? Most doctors I knew stayed beyond their shift only in case of a pressing emergency or if they were coming down off of a tense code. And then they didn't make with the yik-yak. They kept busy, trying to corral their stress into the farthest corner of their mind where they could handle it.

"Nicholas being the little boy that was with you at the auction." Dr. Brouwer looked like he was settling in for a chat. "And what's your daughter's name?"

"Anneke." Usually I would have brushed off such a blatant and rather clumsy effort at getting to know me. But it had been a quiet evening so far on the ward, and I was in a good mood. Our little family had eaten breakfast together today and, as my peace offering, I tried to make French toast. Though it wasn't completely done in spots, it wasn't burnt either. We'd sat down together and talked in complete sentences. Dan told me what he was going to do that day--fix the air-seeder and work up the back fields. I told him my evening work schedule. Nothing new about my job, whereas Dan's created a steady stream of jargon that was as foreign to me as the church talk he currently indulged in during coffee times with Uncle Orest. *No till, wheat and barley, heat units, desiccation, redemption, reconciliation,* and *sacrifice.*

"How are you coping with the move from city to farm? It must be a bit hard to get used to." He leaned in, not enough to invade my personal space but enough that I caught the barest whiff of cologne...and interest.

"I've had some adjusting to do." My foray into and hasty retreat from cow-moving territory and egg gathering came to mind. "But the countryside is beautiful, and that helps."

His smile slowly transformed his face. Very easy on the eyes. Why hadn't some single woman snapped this man up yet?

"I love it here. I can't imagine moving into the city." He shifted his weight so both his elbows were on the counter now. "I've been hearing good things about your work." Deeper smile. Dimples even.

Pause. Freeze frame. Was I being overly sensitive, or had he made a subtle shift from getting to know me to making a move on me?

Me. With two kids and stretch marks? *Right, Leslie.*

I didn't know how to reply to the compliment or the perceived move, so I made do with an awkward but brief "Thank you." Then quickly concentrated on finishing Rena Tebo's chart.

"I'm sure your mother-in-law is happy to have Dan back here with her."

"She is. She's been lonely as well." *Very good comment, Leslie. Shows sensitivity and caring.*

"Not surprising. Being alone can be difficult." He paused as if for effect, and again I felt myself floundering. Was this a cue for me to express my sympathy?

"Wilma's not the easiest person to be around," he continued. "I imagine it's been difficult for you to establish boundaries." He leaned closer, his eye contact lasting a nanosecond too long.

He *was* coming on to me. I was married. Why?

I had to blink a moment, as if to refocus my eyes. I wasn't used to this kind of attention. I savored the pleasant thought for a brief, fluttery moment.

"Boundaries are important." I used a meaningful tone as I casually brushed a nonexistent strand of hair away with my left hand, making sure the diamond on my wedding band caught the light.

"I know I'm probably overstepping my own boundaries here--"

I'll say.

"--But I want you to know that I understand what you have to deal with as far as Wilma is concerned. I grew up here, and I know her family. Gloria and I went to school together. We used to hang out, and I got a sharp taste of what Wilma could be like. Very controlling. Very manipulative." He paused a moment as if to let this sink in. Which it did once I got over the "I hung out with Gloria" part. Holmes Crossing wasn't that big, I reasoned. If Dr. Brouwer grew up here, then of course he would know most of the people here. Including Gloria and the rest of the VandeKeeres.

And Dr. Brouwer was the first person I had met that had called Wilma for what she was without qualifiers and excuses. I felt the burden I had been carrying slip off my shoulders. I wasn't evil incarnate. I wasn't a paranoid scheming daughter-in-law. I was right about Wilma. His words were like rain on parched ground.

In one corner of my conscience I heard a faint warning.

This is gossip.

Maybe, but it's also the truth.

She's Dan's mother, and he loves her.

Well, yeah, but his mother doesn't love me. And no one seems to get that.

"I know exactly what you're dealing with." His smile deepened as he stayed for another moment, then pushed away from the desk. "I should go. You take care."

He held my gaze a split second longer. A compatriot who knew. I smiled back, and it was as if we now shared a subtle bond.

And when he left, I couldn't help but sneak a quick glance at myself in the glass panel beside me. My features were juxtaposed over a fire hose, but I could make out the faint flush on my cheeks and a heightened sparkle in my eye.

You've still got it. So I winked at myself.

I felt a warning niggle as I thought of one of the reasons we had come back to Holmes Crossing. Marriage maintenance. Dan and I had been making a slow recuperation, hindered by the fact that he spent most of his evenings planting crops lately, but we were making progress back to the relationship we'd had before.

This is nothing, I told myself. Just a lonely guy who likes to chat.

But even as I consoled myself with that, I couldn't ignore the voices gently warning me to be careful.

* * *

"YOU HAVE TIME FOR TEA?" Kathy asked when I stepped onto the porch that afternoon after work.

I was falling into rhythm. Thanks to a couple of nurses who preferred working evenings and a hospital that preferred eight-hour shifts to twelve, I was able to work day shifts. Which meant I often dropped the kids off and picked them up myself. Which had eased off some of the tension between me and the in-laws.

"The kids are in the play room," she continued. "Nicholas had a long nap this afternoon, so he's not going to be ready for bed when you get home."

Most of the time our chats moved from the doorway to the porch to the stairs and finally to her kitchen table if I had time.

"I'd love some tea."

Dan was seeding on the higher land. Wilma had called me at work and informed me that since I was too busy working, she would make sure Dan got a warm meal for once. All of this was delivered with a subtle reproach that made me feel guilty, which then made me resent feeling guilty, which, in turn, I felt even more guilty about. She was, technically, doing a good deed, and I should be grateful. Something else she made sure I realized as I struggled to untangle the confusing emotions she raised in me. So, for now as far as the care and feeding of Dan was concerned, I was off the hook.

Kathy waved me in. "Always time for a friend."

Friend. I liked the sound of that. So I kicked off my work shoes, wiggled my tired toes, and relished the feel of the cool floor on my hot feet as I strolled into her kitchen.

Today Kathy looked like a G-rated version of Daisy Duke with a pair of old blue jeans cut off at mid-thigh and an oversized cotton shirt tied at the waist. "So how was work?"

"Busy." I exhaled a light sigh. "Today was national 'I've-been-sick for-two-weeks-and-now-I-demand-immediate-care' day."

"I didn't see that on the calendar. Is that a holiday?"

"Only for doctors. We couldn't scare a doctor up for love or money. Finally, long suffering Dr. John showed up. He's just great."

"Dr. John? You mean Dr. Brouwer?"

"Yeah." Dr. John had informed me with a conspiratorial smile, that though he would have preferred I call him simply John, he realized the necessity of maintaining professionalism, so could I please call him Dr. John. I did simply because, of all the doctors in the hospital, he was by far the easiest to work with. Always friendly and smiling and helpful.

And all the nurses called him that too.

"Are you sure that's a good idea?" Kathy studied me with a frown of uncertainty on her face.

"What subliminal message are you sending me?"

"Nothing." The frown melted away, replaced by an uneasy smile which, I sensed, had something to do with my casual use of Dr. John's name.

"How were the kids?" I didn't want to talk about Dr. John. Right now he was an ally, and I didn't want to analyze the relationship.

"The kids were great. Anneke helped Jimmy and me plant a garden, and Nicholas played with Cordell."

"You put in a garden with four kids watching? How did you find the time?"

"Are you kidding? Look around and smell the toast burning, honey." Kathy's wave encompassed plates from dinner stacked on the counter and an overturned box of cat food in one corner of the kitchen. "Gardening vs. Cleaning House. Guess which one triumphed?"

"The dilemma of the ages."

"So, next couple of days off. Whatcha goin' to do?" Kathy set the mugs on the table, brushed a cat off her chair, and plopped down.

I didn't want to tell her that I was going to clean my house. Not when my elbows now rested on a table covered with crumbs of cookie, grains of sugar, and a little pile of powdered coffee creamer.

"I don't know. Hang out. Read. Work on my unhealthy cancer-causing tan while Dan goes to church, and try not to let the collective pressure of his family pull me into going as well."

Kathy nodded and I felt a subtle shift in the atmosphere.

"Don't tell me you think I should go?"

"Okay. I won't." She shrugged, then took a sip of her tea.

"It doesn't make sense, you know. I never went before."

Still she said nothing.

"It would just be hypocritical. Right? So don't pressure me, okay?"

"You're the one that brought it up. Now and just about every time I talk to you."

"My guilty conscience prods me to justify my absence." I flashed her a quick smile to show her my humorous side.

"So come and you won't feel guilty anymore. There's not a lot going on in Holmes Crossing, after all. The theatre usually has second-run movies and not much is open on Sunday. Church is kind of the only show in town."

"I've discovered that." I grinned. "First time ever I heard an advertisement for church on the radio. Seemed almost sacrilegious."

"What could it hurt to come? You could test out Pascal's Wager."

"You've read Blaise Pascal?"

Kathy placed a hand on her heart and affected an injured tone. "Some of us here in Holmes Crossing have an edjumacation, you know. Yes, I've read Blaise Pascal. I took two years of a Liberal Arts degree before I met Jimmy and moved back to Holmes Crossing."

I wanted to ask her more about what made her come back here but couldn't abandon Pascal just yet. "So tell me about the wager. Though wagering, I understood, is a distinctly non-Christian thing to do."

"Only if you do it for money." Kathy winked. "It goes like this. If you believe God exists, and he does, you gain everything. If you do not believe He exists, and he does, you lose everything. If you believe God exists and he doesn't, you've lost nothing."

I had to make a mental shift to ponder that one. "Okay. So believing God exists is a 'cover your bases philosophy."

"That's a fairly basic way to look at it and, let's face it, follows the basic principal of medicine too. First off, do no harm."

"You're a treasure trove of trivia."

"One of my spiritual gifts."

I let the wager sink in as I glanced outside again. Anneke was running from Cordell, shrieking. Nicholas toddled after a butterfly, his hands in the air.

"You know, I've always thought of my children as mini miracles. And, if I'm honest with myself, I can't completely dismiss God...or a god. I know enough about human anatomy to be consistently amazed at how complex and intricate it is. How fragile and yet how strong. I guess I believe He exists."

"So why not start finding out a bit more about Him by going to church?"

I tested that suggestion a moment. It couldn't really hurt to go. It would ease the guilt I felt lying in bed while Dan got himself and Anneke ready. Goodness knows I had enough guilt already.

"I suppose I could."

"It would makes things easier between you and Wilma and the rest of the family."

"Is that a good reason?"

"Good enough. Church is all about reconciliation."

Kathy had the same look on her face that I saw on Judy when she talked about church. That peace called to a deeply hidden yearning that surfaced in my own life between bouts of hectic activity. It always caught me at odd times. Once I was kneeling on the living-room floor, phone tucked under my ear as I juggled shifts with another nurse, folded Nicholas's diapers, and tried to ignore the rustling pages of newspapers that Dan dropped on the floor beside his chair. Anneke called from her bedroom for her fifth drink of water, and Nicholas protested his incarceration with intermittent shrieks. When my conversation with my nursing friend was over, I hung up the phone, looked around my house, and a whisper of "is this all there is" hung on the edges of my mind.

Trouble was, I never knew precisely what else there was or how to find it.

"The only time I've been in church were the few Christmas services we attended when we came here. I'm sure it was a shock to dear Wilma and the sisters to discover that they'd been harboring a perfect, or imperfect, heathen in their midst." I tossed the words out with a flippant air to cover the faint hurt I still felt at their censure.

"I know they're not perfect, but they do care."

"You're not allowed to defend them." I injected a pained note in my voice. "You're my ally in the battle against the VandeKeere machine."

Kathy laughed again. "Okay, I know you are having severe

Wilma issues. If it's any comfort, you're not the only one. But even she has her good points."

Kathy poured me another cup of tea, and I didn't protest. In spite of the faint squirmies Kathy's defense of the VandeKeeres gave me and her admonishment to go to church, I wasn't ready to end the conversation.

"Judy can be a lot of fun."

"Judy's great." I took the mug. "She and Dayton were the only ones who came and visited us when we lived in Vancouver."

"Judy is a sweetheart. But you know, whether you want to hear it or not, Gloria is the kind of person you want in your corner when you're stuck."

First Wilma, now Gloria? "I can see that I'm not going to get anywhere with you right now. You are obviously in the Vande-Keere cheering section."

"Hey, I'm trying to make your life here in Holmes Crossing easier for you and Dan's family. Besides, they're good people--warts and all."

"I appreciate the help. I do." I gave my tea an extra vigorous stir. "But we're not going to be here long enough for it to matter."

"So. All the more reason to try to get along with Dan's sisters. And one of the best ways to do that for now is to have one of them over."

I frowned. "What do you mean?"

"What we're doing now? This is called visiting. Sometimes it happens at your house. Then you get to be the hostess. You should try it. Start small and start easy. Invite Judy over and practice on her. Then, when you're really good at it, you can graduate to Gloria and Wilma."

I gave her a "duh" look. "Thanks for the step-by-step instructions."

"I thought breaking it down would make it more understandable."

"It would make Dan happy."

THE ONLY BEST PLACE

"And a happy Dan is easier to live with. It'll make your time here easier." She mentioned that so casually.

"And it doesn't bother you that I'm only going to be here for a short while?"

"Why should it? It's your life. Holmes Crossing isn't heaven, though I know most people here would disagree with me on that point. Besides, you're a city girl. I don't blame you for wanting to go back."

"Well, not right away." A defensive note crept into my voice.

"But someday. And once you've mastered the VandeKeeres, you can move on to other women around here. You'll find out there's an interesting mix of people in this community. At Coffee Break, for instance."

"I'll think about it." I wanted to keep the one step at a time concept. To avoid leaps and bounds into the bonds of community.

"For now, think about the inviting Judy thing. I know she looked forward to having you and Dan move back home."

I nodded, seeing the wisdom in her advice. Family harmony was a good thing to aim for.

As for church, also a small thing to do for family peace.

Besides, it would give me a chance to dress up.

CHAPTER 10

"*A*untie Judy is here," Anneke called out from her lookout point upstairs, just as Sasha started barking.

Thank goodness for a long driveway and Sasha's early warning system. I had a chance to give the kitchen a quick look over. A plate encrusted with toast crumbs tilted toward the kitchen sink. Quick. I didn't have much time. Rinse it off. Where's the tea towel?

All right then, a quick swipe across the stomach of my clean T-shirt would have to do.

Everything else passed nervous inspection. Coffee brewing, cups out, cookies on the plate. House clean and tidy. Leslie VandeKeere, ready to entertain. I had taken Kathy's advice to heart, reluctantly seeing the good in it.

Judy's delight at my invitation made me feel like I had done a Boy-Scout-worthy good deed, which made me look forward to the visit. I liked Judy. I just seldom got her to myself.

Anneke was already thundering down the stairs, and I caught Nicholas before he crawled into the kitchen and into Anneke's path. Anneke's steps never slowed on her way out the door, and I could already see squished fingers and hear painful screams. I wanted Judy to come to a quiet and peaceful home.

"Auntie Judy, Auntie Judy!" Anneke yelled, even though Auntie Judy couldn't hear a thing.

Sort of peaceful, I thought.

Nicholas's hair was a tangle of curls. I had been more focused on the floor than my son, so I gave him a quick finger comb and wiped a smear of jam from his cheek. He swung his head away from me and pushed at my chest, but I held on. One of these days, he would clue into the fact that I was his actual mother.

Anneke was already skipping on the back step by the time Nicholas and I stepped out of the house. The rain shower last night had washed the world clean, and I took a moment to inhale the fresh warm scent. Earthy and, yes, inviting. A bluebird swooped past, and I watched its flight, flashes of blue against the green trees. That bird had been hanging around the house for a couple of days now, fluttering against the windows, desperately trying to get into the house. Dan had set up an old birdhouse, but the bluebird seemed more interested in ours.

I heard the mocking squawk of a magpie and laughed as it swooped across the yard, out of reach of Sasha who was trying to bring it to ground.

A perfect day for a visit.

As Judy parked the minivan, my heart filled with anticipation. Finally, a chance to talk to her on her own and get to know her one on one.

Then the front and back passenger doors opened, and my fragile expectations were squashed flatter than a mosquito. I took a deep breath, pulled out a smile, and walked down the step to meet Judy, Gloria, and Wilma.

"Hope you don't mind that I brought Mom and Gloria along," Judy said as they came up the walk. "They weren't busy today and wanted to come too."

I did mind, but it was too late for that. How was I supposed to get to know any one family member when they always came *en masse?*

"That's great. Glad you could come." I shifted Nicholas more comfortably on my hip as they came up the walk. But he was already leaning away from me toward our company.

Wilma headed the line and easily caught Nicholas in her arms. Once again I felt eclipsed.

I knew Nicholas wasn't precisely bonded to me. I knew that guilt was woven into my relationship with a child I hadn't wanted in the first place. But I was working on it. And that he would still prefer Wilma to me was a small sting every time, a tiny slap to my self-worth.

I wanted to keep one small part of my life where I shone brighter, where I had an ally.

I thought of Dr. John and got a warm feeling. He knew. He understood. I wasn't alone in this.

I invited them in. The house that had looked fine for Judy now took on an ominously dirty note when I saw them through the combined eyes of Gloria and Wilma. I saw a line of dust edging the carpet, a discarded shoe laying behind a door--things I had missed when I was cleaning for Judy.

"I'm surprised you put the couch here, Leslie. Wasn't it along the wall when you moved in?" Wilma looked around with a critical, or maybe critiquing, eye.

In our apartment in Vancouver, I had the couch tucked away in a darkened corner of the living room. I viewed windows as strictly an economic version of electricity. To be used, but not faced.

When we came here, Dan, a creature of habit, automatically relegated the couch to the corner. And I, wife of the creature of habit, left it. Then, a few days after the family meeting, as I was dusting, I heard nothing. Two children under the age of four not making noise are usually cause for concern. So I stopped to listen. I heard the rumbling of a box of blocks emptying onto the floor above me and relaxed.

Then I looked out the window.

We had been in the house two days, and I had treated these multi-paned pieces of glass the same way I had at home. Their sole function was letting light in. But this time I really looked.

First thing I noticed was that they needed washing. Then I saw the bare apple tree in the yard and the empty flower garden beyond the window, and then, as if for the first time, I saw the fields rolling toward a blue sky with puffy white clouds. A calendar worthy view.

It took me about twenty minutes, but I moved that heavy couch so I could look out those windows whenever I had the chance to sit down.

"I always liked the view out this window," Wilma said quietly as I put out coffee and cookies.

I saw her dreamy expression, the faint smile threatening to crack the bright red polish of her lips.

And for the first time since I met her, I felt a faint affinity to her.

She let the smile come to fruition, then blinked, and the moment vanished. As I offered her my lopsided cookies, which had been for Judy's eyes only, I saw by the forced smile that the old Wilma had returned.

I wanted the other woman to make an appearance again. I could learn to like that Wilma.

"You've been baking. Good for you." Gloria gave me an approving look as Anneke wiggled her way onto my chair. Anneke blew kisses at Nicholas, who had switched allegiances to Judy and now sat on her lap, toying with the buttons on her faded and worn cardigan.

"Yes. I thought I would give it a try." For a moment I felt like a traitor for baking Kathy's cookie recipe instead of Gloria's. "They didn't turn out that great, though. They look more like dog crap than cookies."

Wilma's faint gasp, and Gloria's suddenly pinched eyebrows signaled my mistake. Not only had I used mild Emergency Department words in the house, I had performed the nefarious deed in front of the combined decorum of Gloria and Wilma.

Judy laughed. "As long as they don't taste like dog crap, we should be okay."

"Judy. Language." Wilma's reprimand, safely delivered to her daughter, ricocheted off her toward me.

"Oh c'mon, Mom. We're on a farm, for goodness sake." Judy shook her head as she took one of the offending cookies, bit it, and winked at me. "Like I figured, they taste great."

"Thanks a lot." I spoke in a small voice, hoping by keeping a low vocal profile I'd escape causing further offense.

"Hey, did you hear about Belinda Ivor? I heard she broke her wrist." Judy shifted Nicholas, her cup balanced precariously on her other leg.

Wilma perched on the edge of the couch and took a careful sip of her coffee, leaving only a hint of lipstick behind. "She and Connor have four children, don't they?"

"I think the oldest is in the same grade as my Paul." Judy said. "He's a pill. He ran away from home once because Belinda made him eat cauliflower. Didn't come home until he heard the coyotes howling and got scared."

"Remember at the Christmas program? How he hopped around at the back like a rabbit?" Gloria laughed. "Aunt Gerda had the hardest time not giggling"

I wanted to say something about Aunt Gerda and the chickens she brought us to try to make some connection to the discussion, but lost the momentum as they moved on to names that I knew nothing of. So I sipped my coffee, smiled appropriately, kept my mouth shut. Gloria and Wilma passed over a few more names and stories while Judy ate another cookie and entertained Nicholas.

I sat and smiled and let Anneke have small sips of my coffee, feeling like a stranger in my own home as I wondered how listening to Gloria and Wilma chitchat about complete strangers would help me get to know Dan's family. I was going to have words with my dear friend Kathy over her stellar suggestion.

"Hey, we didn't come here to bore Leslie to death." Judy pulled herself out of the chair and swung Nicholas up into her arms. "I don't want those plants to sit in the van much longer, so I figure we should get at it."

"Plants? Get at it?" Once again I was out of the loop.

Judy smiled at my confusion. "We came to help you plant the garden."

"But I don't--"

"Don't worry, city girl." Judy gathered up the empty mugs and plate. "We'll help you through this step by step."

I didn't want a garden. I had no intention of adding extra responsibility to my life. Plants needed watering, talking, caring. I had a hard enough time keeping up with the kids, trying to find out how to maintain our marriage, let alone taking care of some plants that would only wither and die under my watch.

"You don't have to worry about the seeds and stuff." Judy set the dishes in the kitchen sink. "We brought everything you need."

"I'm not much of a gardener." *Actually, I'm not anything of a gardener.*

"It's not a difficult thing to learn." Wilma rose from the couch. "You might even enjoy it."

So I followed them outside. Gloria took charge of Nicholas, and Anneke pranced alongside Judy, prattling away to everyone about the chickens and Sasha and how Mommy was afraid to get the eggs.

Holmes Crossing, Alberta. Where secrets take on a new life.

As I watched Gloria and Wilma laugh at Anneke, then

exchange some more chitchat, I felt a twinge of envy at their relationship. In spite of their feelings toward me, I wished, for a moment, I could have a bit of what they shared. Bonding with my mother, when she was around, meant letting us finish the beer in her bottles or sit quietly with her while she watched *Wheel of Fortune*. Gloria and Wilma had a whole other relationship. Closer to what one might label normal.

"Mom, you can put out the bedding plants in the raised bed." Judy set a tray full of lush green plants on the edge of a long box framed with wooden timber and filled with dirt. The last time I saw that box, weeds had taken it over. Dan must have been busy here. "Leslie, you can work with Gloria and me putting in seeds in the garden."

"Sure." How hard could putting in seeds be?

Actually, very hard.

Carrots went in only one eighth of an inch deep and had to be carefully tapped from the package into a furrow so that only a few seeds came out at a time. Nicholas grabbed my arm, and I dumped half a package in one spot.

Beans were spaced an inch apart and covered with dirt. But not too much or they wouldn't get the proper moisture, and not too little or they would dry out.

Peas, corn, beets, and potatoes also had specific rules. I gave up trying to remember the regulations and instead dumbly did whatever Judy and Gloria told me to do. I was getting real good at that.

"Last row," Judy said as we moved a long string, the heat of the sun now beating on my unprotected head. "This is great, isn't it? Being outside and working in the garden. I just love it."

I wiped a trickle of sweat from my forehead and glanced at the dirt lining my fingernails. My back was sore, and my thighs ached from crouching down. "Yeah. Great fun," I responded with forced enthusiasm. This was an entirely new project for me and, thankfully, not one I would have to repeat.

"Just think, in a couple of months, you'll be eating your own fresh vegetables." Judy looked over the rows we had already put in.

I had been so busy bending, dropping, covering, tamping, and trying to keep Nicholas from sticking bean seeds up his nose that I hadn't had a chance to see what we'd done.

Stakes holding the empty packages marked the rows of tamped-down dirt. As I looked over the large space of ground still empty and bare, I tried to imagine plants coming up.

"That's a lot of garden." I wondered if I would know what to do with the plants once they made an appearance.

"Thankfully Mom kept the garden pretty weed free. As long as Dan didn't throw a huge load of manure on it, you shouldn't have to battle too many weeds." Gloria caught up to me and Judy. "It will be fun to can and freeze your own home-grown vegetables. I have a great pickle recipe you can use."

Can? Freeze? Weeds? Pickle?

I thought of the long rows of vegetables laid in artful arrangements in the coolers of the grocery stores. Seemed to me that putting in an extra hour at work, then buying what I needed for the month was a better use of my time. But I smiled and nodded like bringing in the bounty of a garden was a longing that occupied all my waking hours.

"There. All the bedding plants are in." Wilma brushed the dirt off her hands. "Anneke helped me so nicely."

Anneke squirmed with pride. "I want to do this again tomorrow."

"We only need to do it once, sweetheart." Wilma brushed Anneke's damp hair back from her face.

"What did you plant, Wilma?" I asked weakly.

"Cabbages, tomatoes, cauliflower, and a new type of hardy pepper just for fun."

Fun? She had some crazy sense of humor, my mother-in-law did.

"I like the garden," Anneke said with satisfaction.

"Soon the plants will be coming up, and you can help Mommy and Daddy weed them." Gloria's voice held the same enthusiasm other mothers use to tell their kids about a water park.

"Can I help, Mommy?" Anneke swung Wilma's hand.

"Of course you can. Maybe you can help Mommy figure out which is a weed and which is an important plant." I tried to turn the joke onto myself.

"I have a fail-proof method." Judy surveyed the garden with pride. "You give the plant a tug. If it's hard to pull out, it's a weed. If it comes out easy, it's an important plant."

"In spite of everything, that went well." Gloria brushed the dirt off her pants, and, big surprise, it all sifted off. She caught Nicholas, whose mouth was a huge smear of brown.

"He's been eating dirt." I tried to keep the panic out of my voice. Dirt and who knows what else.

"He'll be fine." Judy pulled out a Kleenex from her pocket and wiping his mouth. "It's good for him."

The last time I checked the Good Health Eating Guide, dirt wasn't on the food pyramid.

"The ground has extra moisture," Judy said. "Something we haven't seen in a while."

"It will be a good year." Wilma smiled down at Anneke as she spoke, and in the expression on her face and the soft tone of her voice, I caught an echo of the emotion I had seen a few hours ago.

In those unguarded moments, I caught a glimpse of the Wilma who I knew Dan loved. And I wished she would show that self to me more often so that I could learn as well.

"So, Leslie, I hope you can keep the garden weed free," Wilma said. "You need to work at it regularly, you know."

Her little salvo declared an end to the truce I had mentally declared.

"I guess all I can say is that I'll try." I gave her a weak smile.

"Do, or do not. There is no try." Judy gave a female imitation of Yoda as she dropped an arm around my shoulders, waggling her eyebrows at me. "So, cookies have you left? Hungry are we."

"I have to get back to the farm." Gloria glanced pointedly at her watch. "Sorry."

Judy gave me a look of regret. "Maybe some other time?"

"For sure. I'll see if I can scare up an even scarier cookie recipe." I dragged my gaze away from Judy and included Wilma and Gloria in the invitation. "Come again."

They nodded, got into the van, and drove away.

Well, that was one visit down. At least I'd have something to report to my husband. Something that would make him smile.

And the garden was in. Let's not forget that.

I TOOK a bite of my toast, caught Nicholas before he climbed out of his high chair, poured Anneke a cup of milk, and picked up a piece of gummed-over toast that Nicholas threw on the floor all without missing a beat. Extreme Mothering, not for the faint-hearted.

"I don't want my egg." Anneke wiped her mouth with her sweater cuff and pulled a nose at the boiled egg she had insisted on minutes ago.

"You asked me for it. Now you have to eat it." I felt a hint of pride at the firm tone of my voice. The sound of a mother not to be trifled with.

She gave me a suspicious look, as if wondering where the body of her other mother was. The one she could push around. I gave Anneke a knowing smirk. I had been watching Kathy. Getting pointers. Anneke's life as she knew it was changing.

Dan sat hunched over some farm journal. Thanks to last night's rain, the fields were too wet yet to work, so he was biding his time over breakfast. I had to work one shift tonight, then the blessed peace of an entire weekend off lay ahead. I had bought a fun game that I wanted to play with Anneke tomorrow. I needed to mend some of Nicholas pants. Maybe we could do something wild and crazy like take the long trip to Edmonton. Dan's birthday was coming up. I couldn't bake a cake. I couldn't knit him slippers. But shopping for that hard-to-buy-for person on my list, I could do with my credit card tied behind my back.

My mind flitted over the past week and caught on an errant thought that had been hanging around ever since Darlene's visit with Rena Tebo.

"Dan?"

"Hmm?"

"What would someone mean when they say they know where only comfort in life and death is?"

"And you want to know this because—?"

"A lady named Darlene mentioned it. Is that some kind of local saying?" I glanced sidelong at Nicholas. He was straining at the harness that clipped him to his high chair.

"Down!" If he gained one more inch, gravity would fulfill that succinct demand.

Dan slowly scratched his chin, his fingers rasping lightly over his whiskers as he stared off into the middle distance. "It's in the first question and answer of the Heidelberg Catechism."

I got up to stop Nicholas before he became Emergency Department material. There was nothing lamer than coming into work when you didn't have to work.

"And what is that?" I grunted as I managed to get Nicholas back into his chair long enough to unclip him.

"The Catechism? It's, well, teachings. Of our church. Of course other churches use it as well." He leaned back in his chair and folded his arms over his chest.

I lifted Nicholas out of his high chair and tried to wipe his face as he fought to pull away. I managed a few swipes before giving up and setting him on the ground. Prisoner in Cell Block

Nine was free. He scurried as fast as his pudgy hands and dimpled knees could carry him toward his father.

Dan snapped his fingers as Anneke quickly wormed her way onto his lap, then taunted Nicholas from her perch. "I remember now. I think it goes, 'That I am not my own but belong body and something or other in life and death to my faithful savior Jesus Christ." He stopped there, frowning. "Then something about blood. And that's all I remember." A note of regret edged his voice as he looked from his children to me.

"And just when I think you can't surprise me anymore," I said with forced humor. Right before my eyes, my husband had transformed from Dan the mechanic-slash-farmer to Dan the theologian.

"Mr. DeWaal made us repeat that answer again and again until we knew it cold." He rested his chin on Anneke's head as a gentle smile played over his lips. "Except I can't remember the rest of it. That question and answer is like a basic confession of everything I believe."

My heart hitched as I watched Dan hold his children and talk about what he believed, an unfamiliar note of yearning in his voice. He cut his gaze in my direction, then smiled my favorite crooked smile that signaled he had something funny to share. I was ready for a lighter topic of conversation and thankful for the small connection we had created.

"I remember one girl I really liked. I was only twelve, I think. It was one of those innocent boy-girl things. Then one day at supper, Gloria was teasing me, and she asked me if this girl knew what her only comfort was. We laughed about it, and it got to be a bit of a joke."

"Gloria and teasing. Not a combination that flies off the top of your head." I spoke before I had a chance to filter the words.

To my surprise, Dan didn't even catch it. He still had that thoughtful look on his face. "When I was dating you, Gloria asked me the same question. I laughed it off then too."

"But you went out with me anyway." I laughed to cover up the momentary hurt I felt.

This was his cue to get up and give me a hug and tell me he loved me exactly the way I was. The same thing he would do whenever I made one of my "fat" comments.

But he held Anneke and Nicholas, his expression serious as he looked away.

And a faint misgiving began edging around the periphery of my paranoid mind. The same misgivings that had taken hold the first time he talked about coming back to Holmes Crossing. To family that I knew didn't approve of me. Was it happening already?

Did Dan regret marrying me?

I stacked the bowls on top of each other, then the plates, retreating into the busyness of dishes and cleaning up, the question assaulting every wall I had built the past while. *Was that why he had been attentive to Miss Bilingual?*

I shut that line of thinking down. MB had been slowly morphing into a hazy memory I was determined to beat into submission. Dan had apologized. It was over even though the wounds were still tender.

It's just this place that is making him look that way. He's in the house he grew up in. Of course some of the traditions and ideas he grew up with are going to come back. Haunt him.

"Leslie, would you consider coming to church with me?"

Dan's question slipped past the noise of cutlery on china. He shifted Nicholas on his lap and flashed me an uncertain look. "I know you always said you don't do church. But I wonder if you would reconsider."

"Why?" I defaulted to the Anneke's favorite question. One that often stopped me in my tracks.

"Anneke likes going." He turned to our daughter, tilting her head up with his forefinger. "Don't you, pumpkin?"

Pulling offspring into battles to reinforce arguments was

playing dirty.

Anneke nodded vigorously, her hair bouncing on her shoulders. "I sing songs in church. And have a story and a snack."

"Would you do me a favor and think about it?" Dan lowered a wiggling Nicholas to the ground.

Nicholas padded over to me. Thankful for the distraction, I bent over to pick him up and give him a motherly shnoozle, but he thrust my hand aside. A gentle blow that was a direct hit in the Mommy zone. I hadn't been around the past few days, and this was his punishment on the one day I was home.

I looked from a son who was growing more disconnected from me to a husband who was trying to push me in unfamiliar directions. I had thought things were slowly moving to a point where I was regaining measure of control. Work. Save money. Stay minimally involved in life here so as to make our exit and re-entry into our real life smoother.

However, the ground of my plans was shifting, disorienting me. I didn't know what was expected anymore. I looked at Dan, wondering where our relationship was moving. Or drifting. The longer he stayed here, the more he sounded like the rest of his family, and the harder it had become to find the common ground I had hoped to stake our relationship on.

"I'll think about it." This was a change in strategy, and I had to retreat to reformulate my battle plan. "Do you want me to take the kids to Kathy's tonight, or can you keep them?"

Dan considered. "I'll take care of them. What do you want me to feed them?"

I thought of the empty day he had ahead and tried not to resent the fact that meals were still my department. "There's a few leftovers in the fridge."

"Sure. I can do it."

Dan gave Anneke a kiss before he left. My world was ordered for the next twenty-four hours. I had hoped to ask him to come in this afternoon so I could grab a nap, but figured I was already pushing things with my supper request. I hoped it would be a quiet night at work.

But as I washed kids and cleaned house, I couldn't get Dan's request off my mind. Nor his recitation of that catechism slipping so easily off his tongue.

Coming to Alberta had caused him to shed a disguise. Hard not to feel disoriented and unsure in the face of this "other Dan." The Dan, I was sure, his family preferred to see.

I can't go to church. It's not who I am.

What could it hurt? Maybe just my pride?

And what would my sister say? She was the one who thought Dan's church was some kind of cult.

Well, I hadn't been feeling strong lately. Dan and I had reached some sort of detente, but it was as if we had reverted to the side-by-side living we had made for ourselves back in Vancouver.

I knew danger lay that way.

CHAPTER 11

"*I*s her dress okay?" I asked Dan as I leaned across the back seat of the truck and re-clipped the barrette in Anneke's hair. "Not too fussy?" Asking Dan was a waste of breath. He was no arbiter of fashion, but I was shooting in the dark here. No fashion or parenting magazines had any hints on what the well-dressed toddler wears for worship, so I was winging it. Though he had taken Anneke before, what she wore didn't concern me as much until this Sunday. I was along now and would see firsthand any reaction to her outfit.

I had done the back and forth, reasoning with myself, trying to justify and find the right reasons.

Finally I figured I would just go to church already. It wasn't a hard thing to do. At least that's what I thought until I started figuring out what to put on our kids. Or myself.

I settled on a dress for Anneke and Business Casual for myself. Hair pulled back in a demure ponytail, minimal makeup and sensible shoes. Here's hoping.

Dan gave Anneke a cursory glance in his rearview mirror. "She looks fine."

I smoothed a hand over Anneke's gleaming hair.

Anneke, check.

I noticed a piece of toast crumb hovering at the corner of Nicholas's mouth. A quick swipe with my finger got rid of it before he could spin his head away. His dampened hair still held comb tracks and his apple cheeks shone with health and vitality. His grey cord pants were still clean, his yellow shirt tucked in and crisp.

Nicholas, check.

I pulled down the visor and took a few extra seconds to check my lipstick, tuck a strand of hair back into place. Was the lipstick too much? Did women even wear makeup to church?

Me, not so check.

"Is there something special going on today?" I asked as Dan maneuvered the truck between two minivans. "There seem to be a lot of people here."

"The parking lot is only half full yet. Last time Anneke and I came, we were late, and there were even more vehicles."

The nervous fluttering in my stomach grew. Though I was in Holmes Crossing at least three times a week for work, my drive never took me past the church. The only time I saw this many vehicles in one place at the same time was at the mall.

I had thought churchgoing was out of fashion. At least that was the impression I got from the occasional magazine article that bothered to deal with the churchgoing segment of the population. Obviously the families exiting the vehicles were misinformed.

Dan got out of the truck and swung Nicholas out of his car seat. As I helped Anneke, my eyes were drawn to the church building. My stomach twisted and spun.

The church stood on the edge of town, the highest ground for many miles. Beyond the church and the houses tucked around it, looking away from town, I saw open fields and, beyond, the hills that rose from the river valley to the fields above. God's house nestled in nature's cathedral.

The church was white, solid, with angled roofs and rows of stained-glass windows. From outside, it was hard to see the pattern. They were meant to be viewed from the inside, to let the light shine through them into the church. I knew the building had been put up in the heyday of the twenties when prosperity was on everyone's lips and in everyone's bank account. It replaced an older, smaller version that Dutch immigrants had put up at the turn of the century. It bespoke of solidity, community, and the unchanging nature of faith in Holmes Crossing. Dan's family had been a part of it since the very beginning.

I reached out and blindly caught Dan's hand, feeling a sense of vertigo at this succession of generations. He squeezed back and squared his shoulders, and we started walking toward our now-shared destiny. I guessed from the faint film of dampness on Dan's hand that he was as nervous about bringing me as I was about coming. I wanted to tell him that I wouldn't mess up, but we were already approaching the church, and I could feel waves of reverence lapping at our feet, drawing us in.

We went slowly up the steps into the main foyer. I caught buzzing conversation, a few heads turned our way, polite smiles, some frowns.

Don't look at your clothes. They're fine. I forced my lips into a smile and held on.

A bank of boxes filled the back wall, each box labeled with a name. When I saw how many VandeKeeres there were, I felt the weight of the history of Dan's family and community. Dan's father and grandfather had stood in this entrance waiting to go into the sanctuary beyond the large oak doors. I was walking across the floor that had been trod by Dan's ancestors and now his aunts, uncles, cousins, mother, sisters, friends, neighbors, classmates. A great cloud of witnesses, some now buried in the cemetery down the road from the church, some still very much alive, all anchoring him to this place. The sheer volume of his family, the community, the size of this building...I couldn't begin a tug of war with such an impressive arsenal.

Who wouldn't be feeling a tad jumpy right about now?

At the entrance to the sanctuary, a young couple handed out papers to the congregants. I got one, along with a polite smile. But as the woman looked at Dan, her smile shifted, and her eyes crinkled with pleasure. "Hey, Danny. You coming to Mom and Dad's open house?" She looked from Dan to me. "Is this your wife?"

"Leslie, this is Barry and Lorna Nichols." Dan introduced us. "My cousins."

"From Uncle Orest and Aunt Gerda?" See? I could do the Holmes Crossing connect-the-dots thing.

"No. My parents are Tenie and Jeff Smith."

Huh?

"Sorry." Lorna laid a friendly hand on my shoulder. "My mom is a sister of Dennis and Orest. She married a Nichols."

Spin went my head. "Okay." I'd have to get Dan to draw up a family tree so I could be ready for the next family confrontation. I thought Lorna said something about an open house? I was about to ask her, but she bent over and shook Anneke's hand. She looked up at me. "Your girl is such a little VandeKeere. And this little boy, why he looks exactly like Gloria's oldest."

Okay, wasn't staking a Holmes Crossing claim on Anneke enough? Couldn't she at least give me Nicholas, who, I knew from my own baby picture, was a miniature me?

"Wilma's sitting with Judy and Dayton and their kids, but I can see there's space for your family." Lorna glanced through the double doors to the sanctuary, of which I had, until now, only caught a quick glimpse.

Anneke tugged on my hand. "I want to see Grandma," she whined. Her voice caught Dan's attention, and he quickly ended the discourse on crops and spray he and Barry were having and escorted me and Anneke down one of the aisles of the church. As we walked, I caught snatches of conversation, whiffs of perfume, and scores of unfamiliar faces bathed by diffused lighting filtering through the large stained-glass windows. I didn't know what to take in first, the people, the windows, the ceiling, the large pipe organ in the front of the church.

A symphony of light and color overwhelmed me, combined with smells and people all gathered in one place for an event that had nothing to do with celebrities or sports. I caught a sense of anticipation and community. I could see from the heads bent toward each other, the gentle murmuring of conversation all around us, that these people knew each other. From the quick smiles that people gave me and Dan as we passed, they all knew us as well.

Community, I thought. I had never really been a part of any group of people other than at work, and that was a fractured group at best. But as we made our way toward the front, I caught a glimpse of Delores. Though she was half-turned away from me, her voice carried like a mess sergeant. I saw another couple who had come into my department. I had my own little connections, I thought, as we came to the pew where Wilma and her children were sitting.

As Dan stepped into the pew, his mother looked at him, then past him to me. The pleasure that lit up her face made all the agonizing over my decision to come worthwhile.

Nicholas promptly wiggled his way onto Wilma's lap and granted her his most beguiling smile. My brief flash of resentment may not have been the most suitable emotion, considering my surroundings, but why did he always play the charmer with her?

Judy leaned forward in her seat and blew a kiss at her brother and waved at me.

Anneke sat between me and Dan, the toes of her best black shoes tapping out her happiness on the pew in front of us.

As I settled in, my gaze flitted from the gold and silver lines etched on the pale pink and silver painted pipes of the massive pipe organ to the intricate patterns in the stained-glass windows to the plaster work on the ceiling to the antique wooden pews curved in a semicircle facing the front.

I saw age and beauty mingled with the reality that this had all been here longer than I had, longer than Dan's parents had, longer than his grandparents had. *A heritage,* I thought wistfully. A bedrock of history I had no experience with.

Dan had been baptized in this church, had grown up surrounded by these walls, these people. Though I had heard the stories and felt the weight of his legacy at the farm, this church, this unique community, brought into startling clarity the stability of Dan's past life. And his present life?

Did I dare dwell on that? "Give it time," Dan was lately fond of saying, as if the depletion of my chocolate account was buying us the peace and stability we had been looking for since we got married.

Slowly the empty spaces around us filled, and people greeted Dan and Wilma, smiling at me and Anneke and Nicholas, who blithely ignored them all.

It was as if everyone knew Dan and, by extension, knew me and our kids and where we had come from and what Dan had done in Vancouver, and how Dan's business had failed thanks to that man who had cheated us out of all that money.

My smile hid a swift flash of fear. If they knew this much about us in the short time we'd been here, how much would they know in a few more months? My weight? Our bank account balance? Where I hid the chocolates so the kids couldn't find them?

Judy leaned past Wilma and Dan. "Leslie, how's the garden?"

I gave her a careful smile. Once Wilma and Judy and Gloria left on that fateful day, I thought it best if I simply let nature take its course in the garden department. Nature had a better handle on what to do with all those seeds than I did. I had no idea what condition a garden was supposed to be at by this stage. "It's...growing."

"Well, that's what gardens are supposed to do." Judy added a quick wink to her comment, which made me feel even more uneasy. She knew I hadn't even so much as pulled a weed.

Just then a group of kids walked to the front of the church and picked up the various guitars that were set out on the stage. I recognized Tabitha as she sat at the electric piano. She glanced our way with a self-conscious grin. A young man settled himself behind a drum set that had been hidden by a screen. Everyone turned to Tabitha. She nodded once.

And music the likes of which I never thought a person would ever hear in church started up. It filled the building with pounding rhythm. A screen rolled down from the front and words flashed onto it from a projector somewhere in the building.

I wonder what John Calvin's impression of this would be. I rose to my feet with the rest of the congregation. Everyone started singing, Anneke and Dan singing right along.

Of the gathered people, it seemed only Nicholas and I didn't know this song.

I kept my eyes on the screen, listening intently, determined to make my own spot in this place, however temporary it might be. Amazingly enough, the melody was simple and the words easy to sing, and by the third verse I caught right up.

At the end of the song, I chanced a sidelong glance. Wilma's benevolent expression was a pale imitation of the one she usually lavished on her beloved offspring, but hey, I took it for a cautious peace offering.

I think I can do this, I thought as we settled into our pews after the third song.

The minister came to the front. He was a middle-aged man, slender with thinning blonde hair and wire-rimmed glasses. He had a friendly smile, and I noticed him glancing our way and then hold my gaze. For a terrified moment I thought he was going to "out" me and make me stand up and introduce myself. Then his eyes moved on, and I breathed a sigh of relief.

As he read the Bible, I became distracted by Anneke squirming onto my lap, fiddling with my necklace, then wiggling off again. But when the minister was finished reading the Bible, he said, "This is God's Holy Word," with an authority that caught my attention.

He then clasped the sides of the podium and looked around again, smiling. He started talking about what he had just read. About God as invincible. As raw power whose spoken word created life. "Yet," The minister said, "His greatest victory was when he became weak and vulnerable. When he kept all the angels that would have leapt to do his bidding at bay. He overcame darkness by letting his light be snuffed out."

I tried to follow along, but he was kind of losing me with the light thing.

"When Jesus hung on the cross, when he gave up his life, he became a powerful force that broke the power of Satan forever. It was his weakness, his letting go because of his great love for us, that gave us our greatest strength. We too must learn, in love, to let go." I glanced sidelong at Dan, his chin resting on Anneke's head. She had slipped into his lap during the service, and now had her head tucked into Dan's neck, her hair falling over her face.

Let go. Become weak. Foreign concepts to me. Dangerous concepts. Being weak was what got my mother diving into a sea of alcohol, blearily trying to swim to the other side while my sister and I watched from the sober shores.

Being weak was something I avoided at all costs. You had to be strong to survive this life.

"Before giving us everything, before giving us all his love, all his grace, all his peace, God requires everything," the minister was saying, pulling my attention back to him. "All our love, all our lives, all the things that we scramble so hard to achieve. All we have is from him, and so, to return it to him is an act of faith. Of falling gracelessly into the arms of grace. Of letting God's love hold us up."

I closed my eyes as his words wound around my soul. Falling into the arms of grace. These poetic words touched a hunger buried deep in my soul. Grace. Falling. Letting go. It sounded so easy. So peaceful. I liked the idea of God's love holding me up.

But that would mean letting go. Letting God take control.

Be careful, Leslie.

I heard Terra's voice of warning like a clear bell sounding *dangerous waters ahead.*

I was pulled back to reality. I couldn't give this God what he demanded. Everything? Dan? My children? My dreams and plans?

Something inside me closed fist hard.

I concentrated on my hands, letting my mind slip away to other things. The house cleaning I had been putting off and should have been doing this morning. The laundry that was piling up. And I *should* weed the garden.

Soon he was finished, and we started singing a song that had an older tune. The words were vaguely familiar. I think I'd heard them on the Christian radio station I listened to from time to time on my way to or from work. It was about the Father's love. Vast. Beyond measure.

I sang along but couldn't connect with the words. In my mind I was already driving home, planning the work I had to do yet.

But as I looked at Dan, I caught a glimpse of that hunger I'd seen on his face before and I felt like he was slipping away from me again.

To: lesismore@hcrossing.net
From: tfroese@centermail.com

U know where I stand on this whole weakness thing. Don't become like mom – blaming everyone else – weak and afraid. I told U church was 4 weak people. Doesn't this prove that? U are woman hear you roar. Hear me roar. U need to come and see me. Cut loose. Be my sis again.

Terrible Tempting Terra

CHAPTER 12

"Wilma picked up the kids?" I clutched my cell phone, staring out at the parking lot where Kathy was supposed to have been in a few minutes with my kids. I was going to take them shopping after work and had looked forward all week to do it. Last year Dan and I were so busy keeping our heads above water that his birthday simply floated by, one more casualty of trying to keep things going. This year things were going to be different. I was even going to attempt the impossible. Dan's favorite chocolate layer cake.

"When did she do that?" I asked.

"Earlier today. She sounded like she ran it past you." Kathy's voice had a note of surrender. "She said she wanted to take the kids shopping."

My heart downshifted and tightened. Shopping. Right. Way to steal my thunder, Wilma. "She didn't tell me a thing." Had I said something on Sunday that gave her *carte blanche* to push her way further into our lives? Maybe she assumed we were now best friends because I went to church? I pressed down my frustration as I leaned against the cold brick wall of the hospital. "Then I guess I get to drive home all alone."

CAROLYNE AARSEN

"Sorry about that. Next time I'll call you first."

"I'm hoping there won't be a next time."

"Hey, it's the kids' grandma. It's no big deal." Kathy sounded reasonable until she heard my sigh. "I know I'm supposed to be on your side, but she is your mother-in-law and God loves her too."

Anneke's song of the month bounced into my head. "...he loves me too, he loves me too, I know he loves me too." God loved Anneke. God loved Wilma. What about me?

"She has her good points." Kathy continued. "It's just that she has a take-charge attitude."

"More of a takeover attitude." I felt abandoned. Just when I thought I had an ally in Kathy, she stood up for Wilma. These were not the rules we had been playing by up until now. I had understood that Kathy had a hard time with Wilma so, *ipso facto*, she would be my sounding board on all things Wilma.

"You're right," I conceded, "but in the VandeKeere family, she's still the odds on favorite. I could use someone on my side."

"Don't worry, I still like you the bestest."

"And you'll invite me to your birthday party and not her?" I glanced around to make sure no one was listening in. Working in town made me hyper aware of the fact that everyone knew everyone, and in my dark delusions, I thought someone, some-where would report what I said back to Wilma.

"No, but I'm the neighborly sort. I might give her a candy bag." Kathy laughed. "Are you stopping by for some tea?"

"No. I should go home and pretend to be a responsible and loving mother, instead of a money grubbing healthcare profes-sional. That's code for nurse, by the way."

"Don't talk like that, Leslie. You are a loving mother. But you're also trained to be a nurse. Doing that honors God as much as if you stayed home every day with the kids."

Honors God? What did that have to do with being a nurse?

172

"Thanks for the vote of confidence. I'll take you up on the tea another day."

"I'll hold you to that."

In spite of my momentary pique with Wilma, I did appreciate the peaceful drive home. I also couldn't help reviewing what Kathy had said about my mother-in-law. I knew I put Kathy in an awkward position with my reversion to childhood tactics.

As a kid, whenever I came to a new school, I picked out one girl and slowly felt her out. Then, as soon as I knew which girls she didn't like, they became my enemies too. It was how I cemented the relationship. When you changed schools as often as most people change their minds, this desperate alignment became a means of self-preservation.

Somehow I had to figure out a way to get along with Wilma. I recognized the gentle reprimand in Kathy's words, and the adult part of me knew she was right. Surely I could find a way to make peace with Wilma in the short time we were going to be here.

As I drove, I watched the fields flow by, their furrows showing a flush of green. One more turn in the road and I would come to the top of a hill, and the road would follow the edge of the valley a ways. I slowed down, and even though I'd seen it over a dozen times by now, each time the play of the sun over the valley brought out different features. The sky was a clear Alberta blue, wide open and beckoning. I slowed as I crested the rise and pulled over to the side of the road.

If this was a calendar picture hanging up in the hospital in Vancouver, I would have stopped, taken a second look, and wondered what it would be like to live there.

Well, I was *there*. Right now. I thought of my family waiting for me back home, of Wilma who could so easily get under my skin. I thought of learning to like where I was. Right now, I was making a memory. Why not store these moments up to treasure later on? Sure, living here was not my dream, but there were things I could take away from here, things I could appreciate.

I sighed, remembering my mother's frequent moves. In each place Terra and I had tried to find the positives. Too many moves to too many dingy apartments and bleak neighborhoods had worn down that skill. As a teenager, after enduring yet another school, yet another round of trying to fit in, I had promised myself with Scarlet O'Hara intensity, when I grew up, never again. Without the 'God is my witness' part. God hadn't been a part of my life then, though between Dan, Kathy, and church, He was slowly making inroads on my life now.

I stacked my hands on the steering wheel and rested my chin on them looking over the valley, watching the shadows of the clouds scudding across the valley floor and the sun glinting on the river rushing through the valley. I turned the other way, toward the fields that flowed away from me. I thought of Dan and the kids waiting, but in spite of my eagerness to see Nicholas and Anneke again, I waited, letting the moment imprint on my mind.

A vagrant thought, ethereal as smoke, drifted through my mind. Home. My family waited for me there. At home.

It's not your dream home.

It wasn't, but I had to concede it was a lovely stopping place.

Does it have to be temporary?

I stifled that thought. I wasn't ready to let go of the dream that had kept me going through so many years.

Letting go is not always a bad thing.

The sermon from Sunday came back to me again, as it had the past few days. Letting go. Becoming weak and vulnerable. These were the polar opposite of the lessons Terra and I had ingrained in each other from the time we were young. We'd had to be strong to survive, to keep going. I'd had to be strong to make it through nurses' training. To hold down two jobs.

And what are you holding on for now? Why does it have to be Vancouver?

Anxiety pricked at me like a mosquito. Of course it had to be

Vancouver. I couldn't stay here. I'd have to share Dan with Wilma and Gloria.

But Dan is much happier here. The kids love it here too.

But I didn't. Did I?

The question buzzed and wouldn't leave.

A car slowed down as it drove by, the driver, a young man that I vaguely recognized as the son of one of the neighbors. He looked at me, his eyebrows raised in question as he pointed at the hood of my car. I smiled my reassurance and shook my head, circling my finger and thumb in a gesture to show I was okay.

He nodded, waved, and drove off.

Neighborly of him. Nice to know that if something was truly wrong with me, I could count on someone stopping. I put the car in gear and headed down the road toward home.

Half an hour later I parked by the garage and turned the car off.

As I got out, I saw Nicholas bobbing and weaving toward me from the direction of the garden, something long and dark trailing from his chubby hands, Sasha right beside him.

The smile in my heart reached my mouth at the same time Dan caught our boy around the waist. Dan spun him around and tossed him up in the air, then caught him and planted a kiss on his grubby cheek as the dog danced around them both, his tail sweeping back and forth. Dan tucked Nicholas close in a man-hug. When he turned and saw me, I caught a glint of pure, unadulterated happiness in his eye.

My husband stood there a moment, looking as solidly planted in the earth as the trees behind him.

I felt a twinge of envy. He belonged here. Was a part of this. It was in his upbringing, in his blood and bones. If this were a movie, the wind machine would start up now, blowing his hair away from his features as he stared off into the distance, music swelling, creating a mood of triumph, of dominance. A man. His son. His dog. His land.

"Mommy, Mommy, Mommy!" Anneke ran past Dan toward me, her arms outstretched in welcome. I met her halfway and was almost bowled over by her onslaught.

As her warm, sticky arms tangled themselves around my neck, I stole another look at Dan to anchor myself in reality. No music and no wind. Just my husband with his crinkly smile, faint white lines emanating from the corners of his eyes. It was as if each week here sloughed off some of the desperation that had haunted his eyes those last months in Vancouver when he struggled to hold onto the business. Each day brought some new lift to his face.

Good looking guy. My heart lifted in that funny little way it used to when we were first married. Before the kids came into our lives. Before life and necessity and circumstances and whatshername had thrust us apart.

"Mommy, you have to come and see the garden." Anneke caught hold of my face and leaned away from me.

I passed Dan, then on a whim, held back a moment, leaned toward him, and managed an ungainly kiss hello that landed somewhere on the region of his left cheek. Dan looked surprised at my sudden display of affection.

Had it been that long?

He caught me by the back of my neck, his fingers tangling in my hair as he steadied my head.

He looked deep into my eyes, then lowered his head and caught my mouth with his. His lips were warm, tasting lightly of salt and promising further intimacy.

And just like that Miss Bilingual was back.

I pulled away, trying not to see the hurt on his expression.

"Mommy, come on. You have to see."

I drew away from my husband, drawn inexorably by the pull of a child who presumed she was the center of her world and who would brook no competition.

"Come and see!" she called out as Dan fell into step beside us.

He used to always put his arm around my shoulders when we walked side by side, but we kept enough distance between us that it couldn't work.

I hated Miss Bilingual. Hated how she would show up at the least opportune moments. Hated how she made me feel about my husband. I clenched my hands, wishing I could simply eradicate her from our lives.

"See, Mommy? See?" Anneke, still holding tight to my hand, leaned away from me, pulling me onward. "See the plants?" A pile of wilted green plants lay in the top corner of the garden, harvested, I presumed, from between the rows that now showed themselves. Straight and tidy.

"Look at the plants," Anneke demanded.

As I bent down to inspect a row of rounded stalks pushing themselves through the crumbling dirt, a sense of wonder overtook me. Only a few weeks ago Judy, Gloria, and I had dropped hard white seeds into the ground in neat orderly rows. I knew that for things to grow, seeds needed to be planted, but knowing it in your mind and actually seeing the results was another story.

"They came up." I touched one that was uncurling.

"And see the corn, Mommy?" Anneke, my impatient guide, pulled me farther along. One row over, tiny blades of what looked like grass were coming up. The carrots were a pale fuzz of green only discernible if you put your head level with the ground, which I had to do, according to Anneke. The crinkly leaves of the potatoes were making an appearance, as were the fat, round leaves of the cucumbers.

"I need to put up a pea fence," Dan said as we stopped by a double row of plants. "They need something to climb up. Otherwise they sprawl all over the garden."

I glanced at him, then back at the garden, wonder spiraling through me. All these little miracles came from the few packages that Judy and Gloria had brought. And this was only the beginning.

"How long before the plants start producing?" I bent down to touch a pea plant already sending out tiny tendrils of green.

"About six to eight weeks. Depending on how much moisture we give them and what kind of season we have. We're lucky we had enough moisture to start off with. That doesn't happen every year."

I glanced up at him, the damp coolness of the dirt giving way to the heat from the sun overhead. "This is amazing. I've never had a garden before."

Dan pulled me to my feet. "You might not think it's so amazing when you have to start picking beans."

I heard the faint humor in his voice and on impulse hooked my arm around his waist, determined to move on. "I'm glad we did this."

"Trust me, hon." He added an extra squeeze to his one-armed hug. "Once you've tasted fresh vegetables, you'll be putting in a garden every year."

I looked back over the huge expanse that had been planted, leaning into Dan, enjoying this moment of closeness in spite of the ghosts hovering over our marriage.

This huge garden would never fit in a city backyard. Why did that thought give me a moment of regret?

"I want to eat, Mommy." Anneke grabbed my hand and swung it. "I'm hungry."

"Sure, honey. Let's go make supper." This time I was prepared. I was going to make an awesome supper. I had chicken defrosting in the fridge. All the ingredients for a stir fry recipe that Kathy solemnly promised me was Leslie proof.

"You don't need to worry about supper," Dan said as we walked up to the house. "Mom brought a casserole when she brought the kids."

Blink. Think. My stomach dropped a bit as my little moment of triumph slipped away.

"She thought we might like some home cooking for a change."

Dan's cute smile didn't even approach canceling the innuendo of that particular statement.

"I was going to do home cooking." Disappointment put a note of petulance in my voice. First she takes away my shopping trip. Now my supper? *Nuts.*

"Well, maybe tomorrow."

All that was missing from this conversation was a patronizing pat on the head. There, there, Leslie. Be a big girl now.

My previous pique with his mother bobbed to the surface. "Why did she pick up the kids from Kathy's place to go shopping without asking me?"

"She asked me." He gave me one of his patent, slightly exaggerated, shrugs, shorthand for 'You're overreacting, and I can't reason with you right now, so I'll ignore you until you can act more mature.'

"Don't do that. I hate it when you do that."

"Do what?" He gave me a tired look.

"Brush aside what I think is a problem."

"Les, there's no problem. Anneke and Nicholas happen to be my mother's grandkids. Nothing's wrong with her taking them out to buy a few things." He yanked open the door and let the kids and me go in, then let it slam shut behind him.

"There is a problem if I, the mother, isn't consulted." I sat down with Nicholas and pulled his dirty jacket off.

Dan's face grew grim. "But, I, the father, was." He turned to Anneke. "Here, baby. Put your boots on the boot rack." He hung up her coat. "I wish you didn't have these issues with my mother. She's just trying to help."

I couldn't think of what to say. First Kathy, now Dan. I was trying to like Wilma. But she balked me on every turn. As a woman and mother, I expected Wilma to know the unwritten rules of mother and wife-hood. Uninvited movement into another's territory was considered either a hostile move or an insult. Close friendship or illnesses nigh unto death were the only time these rules didn't apply, neither of which were the case. "How is taking the kids shopping helping?" I had looked forward to helping them pick something special out for Dan, and I had been robbed of it now.

"You don't seem to have time."

Warning, warning. No-win situation approaching.

I could almost see the red lights flashing, the sirens sending out scary alerts. But I said it anyway. "I'm working, Dan."

"You don't have to. At least not as often as you do."

"You don't seem to mind that half of my paycheck goes into our bank account." And away I went, flailing down the slippery slope of an argument that I knew would not end well.

"And the other half?"

I gave him a narrowed look as I slipped Nicholas's other boot off of his foot and dropped it on the porch floor. "The other half is for our house fund. The one that got severely depleted when you bought the tractor."

"We've already discussed that."

I gently pulled Nicholas coat off, trying to ease away my growing frustration. I felt as if I were fighting an unstoppable foe. The farm. His family. His community. Memories I desperately wanted out of my mind. "I know that. But the house was for us. For our family."

"And saving for that house, that future, means you're gone all the time." If ever there was a red-flag word, *all* was it.

"I don't work *all* the time." I spoke quietly, but my teeth were clenched. I thought he had accepted that.

"Not here, and I love it. But back in Vancouver you'd be back to full-time work. At least here we get to see you during the day. Admit it. Staying here could be just what we need."

"Like we need your mother breathing down our necks all the time?" Encroaching on my territory. Taking my kids shopping for their father's gifts.

I wonder what she bought Dan. Would she know that I hoped to give him some decent pajamas? A Swiss Army knife?

"She's trying to help."

"She's trying to control you." I dropped Nicholas's other boot on the floor with a muffled thump as it hit his jacket.

Dan picked up Nicholas's boots and handed them to Anneke, who dutifully put them away. "And what are you trying to do?" He snatched Nicholas coat up from the floor.

"I'm trying to put our marriage back together."

Dan's eyebrows snapped together. "You're not going to forgive me for that, are you?"

"I have forgiven you, and I want our marriage to work..." my sentence trailed off as the truth of what he'd said struck me. Maybe I hadn't forgiven him as readily as I said. It had been a large hurt and betrayal. Another woman encroaching on my territory as surely as Wilma was.

"I'm not as strong as you, Leslie. I need help and support to get through stuff. And I feel like I'm getting that here. I'm tired of moving around. I'm tired of trying to find out who I really am."

"So when we go back to Vancouver, we can stay there. Settle down."

"We can stay here."

He spoke so quietly, I almost didn't hear him. His words underlined what had gone through my own mind just up on the hill. I swallowed, my stomach feeling like it had fallen into a crevasse, dark and bottomless.

I sucked in a breath, swallowed down my panic and spun toward our son.

"Oh, Nicholas, look at you," I said in a shaky voice as I brushed the dirt off his clothes.

Dan swung Anneke in his arms and, without a backward glance, strode out of the porch into the kitchen.

Nicholas declared his independence and elected to walk on

his own. So I followed more slowly. Had Dan really said "stay here?"

Try as I could to get rid of them, the words echoed in my mind as Nicholas and I made our way into the house.

Dan already had a tablecloth on the table by the time I came into the kitchen. Anneke crouched by the cupboard, pulling plates out and setting them on the floor. Nicholas scooted over to her and started slapping his dirty hands on the dishes, which initiated a skirmish settled as quickly as it began when Nicholas beaned Anneke on the head with a plate.

By the time I had the kids settled and Nicholas changed, supper on the table.

Food trumped discussion, so we ate quietly, limiting our conversation to "pass the salt," tacking on belated "pleases," and admonitions to the kids to eat. The homemade casserole was hot, spicy, and creamily delicious. Nicholas decided to eat it by osmosis, mashing food into his face and hair.

When we were done, I got up, but Dan put his hand on my arm. "Gloria gave me this Children's Story Bible. I thought we could read to the kids at suppertime."

What could I say to that? Gloria had given, and Dan had taken. But his comment about wanting control, though thrown out randomly, had stuck as firmly as the pasta now decorating Nicolas' hair. This home was Dan's as much as mine. If he wanted to read some story Bible, then I could go along with it.

He beckoned to Anneke, who scooted over to her father and his lap. He set a worn and dog-eared book on the table in front of them and opened it to the first page. "In the beginning, God made the heavens and the earth..."

Once upon a time, I thought irreverently. But in spite of my slightly cynical bent, I caught myself listening. Getting caught up in the simple language of the story that, I knew, was ages old. It was still around. It had lasted through generations. Might be worth paying attention to. Nicholas crawled out of his high chair and wiggled his way onto my lap. Might rebuild some tiny connection between Dan and me.

As Dan read, his voice grew softer and the Leslie-induced frown on his forehead slipped way. Anneke leaned forward, engrossed in the colored pictures.

This might be what Dan's youth had been like here in this kitchen: The sun slipping below the horizon, drawing the dark across the sky. The room growing cozy, safe, secure. His father reading, his sisters sitting around the table, his mother maybe holding Dan on her lap like I now held Nicholas.

My baby rubbed his face with one hand, but lay quietly in my arms, a warm package of little boy wrapped up in stained overalls and t-shirt. It hadn't seemed that long ago that he was just a tiny bundle of flannelette. Now his head lay pillowed on my shoulder, his dimpled feet, minus the socks he had pulled off, rested easily on my knees. I nuzzled Nicholas head, inhaling the smells of little boy and food laced with a hint of dirty diaper. I glanced at Anneke, pretending to read along, her bow-shaped lips forming the words after Dan.

He closed the book, then moved directly into a short prayer. When he said "Amen," Nicholas repeated it. I couldn't say anything, but I had lots to think about.

* * *

"C'MON, HONEY. WAKE UP." I shook Nicholas gently, preparing myself for a full-scale onslaught. This early in the morning, the only light came from the glow of a Winnie the Pooh night light. I heard the hiss and spit of rain on the windows. I was already dressed for work and now had to go through the ordeal of getting the kids up to take them to Kathy's place.

Anneke sat on the bed across the room scratching her tummy. When we first moved into the house, I gave each of the kids their own room, thinking I did Anneke a huge favor. Anneke, who always complained that Nicholas was manhandling her Barbies and eating her Shopkins, that Nicholas cried too loud, that Nicholas smelled bad, bad, bad, was now sharing with the same little brother because she couldn't handle the bounty of a room all to herself.

"I'm tired, Mommy." Anneke sniffed, letting her hands drop to her sides. "I don't want to go."

"I know you don't." I gently commiserated with her like the parenting magazines told me to. "I understand that you're tired and that you would probably sooner stay here, but we have to get going, or Mommy's going to be late for work." Oh, very well done. Verbalizing the child's frustration to show that you under-stand, then telling her what's going to happen anyway. This seemed like a lot of work but, apprentice that I was, I was always rooting around in parenting magazines. The magazines should come with a warning, "serving suggestion only," just so a mother doesn't get fooled into thinking her children might actually resemble the perfection of perfectly posed child on the cover.

"I want you to stay home," Anneke grumbled as Nicholas started twisting like a snake, his face scrunched into deep lines of disapproval.

"Warning, warning. Move alert to code red. Boy is waking up," I heard a voice still raspy with sleep say.

I glanced over my shoulder at Dan, standing in the doorway scratching his stomach. Like father like daughter. His hair was a tangle of blond that still needed cutting, his chin shadowed with whiskers, and his ragged pajama bottoms hung just below his waist. He really needed new pj's.

But it was his smile that caught my attention. That slightly crooked lift of his lips that signaled that all was well with his world. It was this smile that attracted me to him the first time I saw him with his friends. It was the same smile he had when I walked down the aisle toward him. A smile I saw more frequently of late.

I felt the low-level pull of attraction and, in spite of Nicholas, now squirming under my restraining hand, grunting his displeasure, and preparing for a full-scale assault on our senses, I couldn't look away from my handsome husband.

He moved toward me, and his warm hand caressed my back and rubbed a gentle circle. "How did you sleep?"

"I slept good."

A gust of wind threw raindrops against the window. "It's raining. Unbelievable." A trace of awe edged his voice. He walked to the window and placed his hand against the cold pane, as if touching the water that now ran down the glass outside.

He turned to me, his smile taking on a note of fun. "I have a great idea. Take the kids to our bed. We'll all cuddle together for a while."

I felt the pull of deep temptation and for a moment imagined myself and the kids curled up in together, a little nest of a family all warm and cozy while outside, the rain came down. A moment of pure connection and family time.

He caught my hesitation and looked from Nicholas to Anneke, then blinked as if realization finally dawned. "You working today?"

I nodded.

"I thought you had it off?"

"I did, but yesterday Roberta called, frantic. She needed to switch with someone and couldn't find a replacement."

Dan's face slipped into displeasure, taking with it my faint moment of happiness. "But we were going to Aunt Tenie and Uncle Jeff's open house today."

Surely I wasn't going THAT crazy? "I didn't know anything about that." I barely knew anything about his Aunt Tenie and Uncle Jeff other than they were connected to him through the young couple we met at church.

"They mailed us an invitation. I was looking forward to introducing you to more of the relatives."

"I don't remember getting an invitation."

He sighed, pressed his lips together and nodded. A long-suffering nod. My least favorite nod. "Obviously not important, is it?"

I turned away from the no-win discussion as my mind raced over the past few weeks. The junk mail consortium hadn't been alerted as to our whereabouts, so we hadn't received any offers for low-interest credit cards or Publishers Clearing House prizes. Yet.

I wouldn't have missed addressed mail. Would I? Was I slowly going crazy living out here? But if I knew I was going crazy, then I'm not crazy. Am I?

I picked up the now-squirming boy throwing his head around in frustration. "No up, no up." I managed to make it to the bathroom, get the diaper off, and get the majority of the mess cleaned up before Nicholas started thrashing in earnest.

While I performed my diaper-changing calisthenics, Dan silently hovered in the doorway, waves of disapproval crashing over me as his young son made his own similar disapproval clearly known. Nicholas flailed his arms, one little fist connecting solidly with my arm, a fat foot thumping me in the stomach as he screamed.

"Leave those poor kids at home today." Dan raised his voice above Nicholas's cries. "I'll take them to the anniversary party myself."

I cringed as I thought of Dan showing up sans spouse. I imagined Wilma's and Gloria's surreptitiously exchanged glances, then sighs. That Leslie.

As Nicholas's screams stabbed repeatedly through my Nicholas Defense System, I also imagined driving twenty minutes to Kathy's house with this thirty-five pound bundle of fury and dropping him off. "You sure you don't mind?"

Dan's long-suffering look normally would get my hackles up,

but with Nicholas still screaming, the anniversary party coming up, I was at his mercy.

"Just wanted to make sure." I raised my voice so he could hear, then manhandled Nicholas back to his bed, his haven. But he wasn't that easily pacified. I had pulled him from his beloved sleeping place, and he wasn't going to let me off without a fine.

He screamed some more, but then grabbed his blankie and pulled it toward him, rubbing it over his face with jerky movements, his sobs decreasing in intensity.

"I'm going back to bed." Dan still held Anneke. "I'll hold the fort and keep the family intact. You go to work and make your money." He yawned, a jaw-cracking, slow yawn, and then slouched back to our bed, Anneke's head tucked into his neck.

His comment, delivered so casually, had barbs that clung. It wasn't just about the money. I worked so we could have a future. I worked so I could keep up my skills. I worked because it was as much a part of me as farming was for him.

But neither he, nor his family, seemed to recognize or understand that.

I heard Nicholas ramping down his anger, Anneke's muffled giggle, Dan's deep voice teasing her.

A few moments ago, I wanted to cuddle in bed with my husband and my daughter. Now all I wanted was get to the hospital as soon as possible. Keep the family intact indeed. As if his one day of babysitting was worth more than the dozens of days I had already spent with the kids. Dan was the kind of man who would take out the garbage once and give the impression he had just cleaned the entire house.

I slipped out the door and almost tripped over Sasha, who lay huddled against the door. She jumped up, her mouth open in a happy, doggy smile, her tail waving a welcome greeting. I took a moment to pet her. At least someone in this house loved me today.

She followed me to the car looking hopeful, then, when she realized there was no trip in the offing, her tail slowed down, her head drooped and, disconsolate, she trotted back to the house, dropped down in the lee of the overhang and stared morosely at me.

"I know how you feel," I muttered as I shivered in the car, waiting for it to warm up.

I glanced up at the house. The lone square of light from our bedroom winked out, cutting me off, and as I drove away, I imagined Dan and Anneke cocooned in a pile of blankets as they drifted off to sleep.

And me? Well, I was off to work to make that money that Dan so quickly denigrated but didn't seem to mind when it showed up in our checking account. I didn't understand why going to work made me look greedy and why holding onto the bank account made his mother look cautious.

I got angrier as I drove. Thankfully I didn't have to navigate past snail-paced tractors pulling huge implements or fuel trucks that usually took up half the road. The quiet roads still surprised me. In Vancouver, driving to work meant scooting between hundreds of cars, wondering why all these people were on the road, juggling through radio stations to avoid depressing news, and worrying about what the owners of all these cars were going to do when the oil ran out.

I've always been good at multitasking.

But now my commute was quiet and, because my anger always manifested itself physically—in this case via my foot on the accelerator—short. Which meant I had almost an hour to kill before the sun came up and my shift started.

I got some coffee at the staff cafeteria and picked up a muffin for breakfast, looking forward to a few moments of absolute peace. One other nurse dawdled over a newspaper and didn't even look up as I passed.

An empty table called out to me, and as I dropped into the chair, I yanked the paper off my muffin, anger with Dan battling with guilt that I would miss his family get-together. Other than Wilma and Gloria, the few members of the extended VandeKeere family I had met were friendly and pleasant. I hadn't met Dan's Oma, who lived in Edmonton, over two hour's drive away. She was going to be there, and I would liked to have met her.

I had a grandma of my own stashed away somewhere. My mother lost her when she turned eighteen and was pregnant with Terra and hadn't bothered to go looking for her again.

Once in a while Dan would ask me about my family. I kept telling him there wasn't much to say, which was true. He never really understood. Now, as we were spending more and more time in the bosom of his family, I knew he never really would.

As for our own family, I was getting nervous. Dan had taken to glaring at me each evening as I unwrapped another chocolate. Every week created some new shift in our relationship. I wasn't sure if we were shifting closer together or if Dan was slowly sucked into his family and away from me.

Not thinking about that right now, I warned myself. I pulled a pen and notebook from my purse. My dream book had all the details of Dan and my dream home. The size, the number of rooms, the style of the cupboards, the brand of siding, the colors of the paint. Sometimes I rearranged the house plan, moved the rooms, added features that I found in home and gardening magazines.

I flipped through the book, coming to the back section. The finances. I examined the final figure Dan and I had estimated our house would cost us. My heart sank as the dream wavered. Was I being realistic? Would we ever be able to afford it? And if not, then what?

Stay here. The phantom thought reared its head again.

"You busy?"

Dr. John. Yay. Distraction.

"Do you live in the hospital?" I closed my dream book. "Weren't you on call last night?"

"Just finished and needed some down time. I don't like going home. House is too empty."

He sounded so lonely, and I felt a flash of pity. "How was last night?"

"Steady, though I managed to get some sleep about four o'clock." He brought me up to speed on a few of the cases even though Roberta would be giving me a rundown at changeover. "Amelia Castelman brought her baby in again. Poor thing is going downhill, but she won't let me refer her to either a pediatrician or a social worker. I was tempted to keep the baby in the hospital so we could feed her, but I didn't have a strong enough reason, and Amelia wouldn't allow it."

Amelia's baby's chart was long and illustrious, as was Amelia's. Single mother, living on welfare. Her little girl was borderline malnourished and, we were sure, developmentally delayed. But Amelia wouldn't let us refer her to a specialist. Social Services had gotten involved, but again, their hands were tied. Not enough evidence.

It broke my heart. Each time that baby came in, I wanted to kidnap her and bring her home.

That's why I didn't read the papers. Why read about misery abroad when enough of it came through the doors of the hospital?

"All in all, another night in Holmes Crossing." Dr. John rubbed his chin, his whiskers dark against his skin. I thought of Dan's whiskers. Mentally compared the two. Then wondered why I has. Married women shouldn't be comparing their husbands to attractive men. It wasn't fair. I got to see Dan in sickness and in health, in dirty clothes with grease under his fingernails and first thing in the morning when both his hair and his moods stuck up in all directions.

Dr. John's smile made his eyes crinkle with warmth. "You're looking lovely this morning."

After my fiasco at home, his compliment was like gourmet

chocolate. Smooth and soothing and easy to take. "Thanks." The kindness in his voice made me feel trembly. "Not feeling too lovely."

"Why not? Your in-laws making you feel inferior?" John's hand skimmed over my arm in what was probably just a gesture of sympathy.

But I clung to it, feeling like I had an ally. "I missed an anniversary party today that I knew nothing about. Big problem."

"If it was a VandeKeere function? Sorry, my dear, you are in it deep."

"I can just imagine what Wilma and Gloria will say." I shook my head. "Or look like." I could just imagine perfect Gloria with her perfect figure, clothes, and hair. Which usually made me perfectly envious. Which I didn't want to be because envy of Gloria meant she had something I wanted, which meant she had something over me, which meant I was lacking.

Jealousy. Not as easy as it looks.

"You don't want their life," Dr. John said quietly. "All that pressure to keep up the facade. I'm sure Gloria spends hours getting the eye shadow right."

This comment struck me as a little harsh, but at the same time I felt a niggling satisfaction that someone somewhere didn't see perfection in Gloria. "I guess I won't be asking her for makeup tips."

"You don't need makeup tips from anyone." He leaned a little closer, smiled just a little deeper, and then his hand covered mine. "Especially not from someone like Gloria. You are a very beautiful woman in your own right."

He's coming onto you.

I knew it, and I knew the danger, but I let myself linger in the light of his appreciation for a little longer. The insecure part of me welcomed his flattery, his attention. Like eating that extra piece of cake you know you shouldn't. This morning I needed the boost more than ever.

He yawned and rubbed his eyes with his other hand. Lines of weariness etched his face.

"You'd better go home." I felt a moment's sympathy for him. "You look exhausted."

His smile warmed my heart. "I am tired. But it's nice to sit with you a minute."

You're playing with fire.

This time I listened and slowly drew my hand away from his. Then I checked the clock. "Time to go." I stood as he pushed himself up with a sigh. He was so tired, he almost swayed into me. I had to take a quick step to avoid him.

"Sorry about that. Exhaustion makes me clumsy."

"That's okay." But as I walked away, I couldn't resist a glance over my shoulder.

He was watching me! His scrutiny made me uncomfortable, but I am a weak woman, and the second glance from him was as tangible as a touch.

FROM: tfroese@centermail.com

To: lesismore@hcrossing.net

I wouldn't fuss the Dr. John thing. Sounds like U can use a friend. As for Dan, U need to set some boundaries sister. Dan is changing the rules and U shouldn't put up with it. Sure Alberta is beautiful, but so is Vancouver. Do you really think you'd manage to survive there? BTW I'm probably going to be moving up there. Lost my job here. Boss was a jerk, so it's all good. So U have to move back, little sis. Be like old times again.

FROM: lesismore@hcrossing.net

To: tfroese@centermail.com

I don't know what I want anymore, Terra. Josie, my last friend from Vancouver hasn't been returning my calls or my e-mails. I feel like I'm slowly losing my identity, my husband, my family. I'm getting confused. Dan and I have been living past each other the past few days. Judy called, said she was sorry I missed the party. I felt bad for letting her down. Gloria phoned too. Said she had forgotten to tell me about the party. Said she was sorry. I felt like hanging up on her. Then I felt like hanging her. Not the kind of emotions a person should be carrying around.

CHAPTER 13

"*R*oberta just called. She's going to be about half an hour late. Had her own emergency at home." Arlene leaned against the partition that gave me some privacy from the rest of the ward.

I felt a stab of annoyance with Roberta, but knew that it could as easily have been me trying to find a babysitter.

"Lucky for her, things are pretty quiet for a Friday night."

I looked up at the receptionist, horrified. "Are you asking for trouble?"

Arlene shot me a puzzled look.

"You never, never, say that out loud." I gave her a stern look, hoping that by warning her I had possibly staved off disaster. The same thought had crept around the edges of my mind, taunting me, but I knew better than to give it even a whisper of attention for fear it would create its own energy. "Every time someone says that, things go haywire."

She laughed. "Sorry. I was just making conversation."

I was about to reply when I heard the roar of a car pulling up to the entrance, tires screeching, and horn blasting.

"Like I said," I muttered as she left to see what the problem was tonight. I got up to prep a room just as the doors swooshed open and the unbridled sobbing of three teenage girls filled the entrance. I couldn't help the faint up tick of my heart, the little adrenalin rush that prepared me to face this so-far unknown.

"She's not talking. She's really sick," the girls wailed.

I strode quickly out to the reception area and repressed a sigh at the typical Friday-night sight that greeted me.

A boy who didn't look old enough to drive half-carried, half-pulled a young girl whose long blonde hair hung in a stringy mat over her face. Her head hung almost to her stomach; her bare feet dragged over the floor. She wore standard-issue low-cut blue jeans and a skimpy T-shirt, her clothing almost identical to her two friends who were sobbing and hugging each other.

The sour stench of regurgitated alcohol and food rolled ahead of her, and I tried not to sigh. I could handle blood a lot better than vomit.

Arlene glanced up at me. "Guess you got work. I've paged Dr. John. He'll be here right away." She called one of the girls aside to get what information she could. Her next step was the unenviable job of calling the young girl's parents.

The young man turned to me, desperation in his eyes. "I don't know what happened. We were at a party."

I glanced at the girl's stained blue jeans and the vomit streaking her T-shirt and clothes. And as I brushed her hair aside, my heart skipped its next beat.

Tabitha. Dan's niece and Gloria's pride and joy.

Her pert little face and beautiful shining hair was smeared with dirt and puke, her head lolling to one side, like a doll with a broken neck.

"What's your name?" I asked the boy.

"Deke."

"Help me get her on this bed, Deke." I glanced over at the hysterical girls and chose the most lucid one. "You come with me. The rest of you go back to the reception area."

"She's not going to die, is she?" the other girl sobbed, weaving as she stood.

"Go wait in reception," I said firmly. I didn't have time for handholding.

Once we got Tabitha into bed, I propped her up so she wouldn't choke, then brushed her sticky hair away from her mouth and checked her breathing, trying to reconcile this girl with the sweet young thing I saw laughing with her mother.

"What happened?" I asked Deke as I pulled open both eyelids. Pupils normally dilated, thank goodness. I slipped up her sleeve to check her blood pressure. Her icy skin made my own heart rate jump. *Possible hypothermia.* I needed to start an IV, but I needed more information first.

To my surprise, my hands were trembling as I pressed the button to inflate the b.p. cuff. I had never had to work on someone I knew so well, and it created an extra tension.

"We were at a party and then, well, I don't know." His voice trailed off, and guilt emanated from him in waves.

"You know. Tell me." My don't-mess-with-me nurse voice was colored with an edge of ticked-off-auntie.

"Well, we had some liquor there."

"How much did she have to drink?" My glance ticked from Deke to the girl. "Did she have any drugs?"

"Do you remember, Cassie?" Deke asked the girl, who steadfastly refused to look at me.

"Don't mess with me, kids," I said sternly as the machine read off her b.p. I clipped an oximeter to her finger and turned back to Cassie. "I don't care what you did. I'm not going to report you to the police, but I need to know exactly what happened so that I do the right thing for Tabitha. We don't have a lot of time here."

Cassie turned wide eyes to me. "Are you going to tell my mom?"

"Right now that's not important. What else did Tabitha have to drink?"

I glanced at the monitor. Steady and normal. Heart rate slightly decreased.

"No drugs. Right, Cassie? She didn't have any drugs. And she only downed one cooler. I swear."

"Don't swear. Tell the truth." I glanced down at Tabitha, hating the way she smelled and looked.

The scenario was so cheap. So common. "She had way more than one cooler."

"Okay. Maybe it was more."

I started a chart, scribbled a few notes. Standing orders in this case were to start an IV to rehydrate and dilute the alcohol, so I prepped the site and started the drip. Cassie wavered at the sight.

I checked Tabitha's oxygen levels and her heart rate and put my hand to her cheek as I double checked her physical appearance.

"How much more and how quickly did she drink it?" I pressed as soon as I got Tabitha hooked up. I caught another quick consultation between Deke and Cassie and resisted the urge to grab the young girl by the shirt and shake the information out of her. My niece lay on the bed between us, with who knows what kind of alcohol cocktail spinning through her veins, and these two were trying to protect themselves.

But if I pushed too hard, they would clam up, and if Tabitha had taken drugs, this would be a whole different scenario. I doubted it, based on Tabitha's appearance, but it was too early to rule anything out.

Deke started. "She might have had a couple of coolers. I think." Another quick "cover for me" glance to Cassie.

"And some Jack Daniels and vodka," Cassie added sullenly.

I heard Dr. John's welcome voice, then he whisked the curtain aside. He glanced at Tabitha, then at Cassie and Deke. Now that the doctor was here, the atmosphere became more serious.

"How long has she been like this?" Dr. John glanced at the chart, then stepping between Deke and the bed to have a closer look at Tabitha. He took a moment to glance at me. Smile. I felt a flush of warmth, then pulled myself back. Focus.

I gave a succinct rundown of what I already knew and how Tabitha was responding, my voice clipped as I struggled with my anger with these kids.

My niece reeked of alcohol and bodily fluids, and I wanted nothing more than to strip her down and wash her up. Clean away the filth that dirtied her body and my image of her. But we had procedures to follow, and we still had to get what information we could from these teenagers.

"Has Arlene contacted her parents yet?"

"I believe so." Hadn't I often wondered what kind of parents would let their kids go wild like this? Even after I met the parents, their protestations of their child never doing something like this before would, at times, strike me as false or naïve in the extreme.

Now I knew what kind of parents let their kids go wild like this. Parents that did their best. And really, truly, didn't know every detail of their kids' lives.

Dr. John examined her, then scribbled some orders on the chart. "I'd like to keep her overnight. I'm concerned about her alcohol level."

I adjusted Tabitha's shirt, pulling it up around her shoulder. Sweet, loving Tabitha, who happily carted my kids around, had been hanging around with a guy who reeked of alcohol himself, sporting a ring in his eyebrow and a tattoo on his neck, gravity fighting with his skinny hips for his baggy blue jeans, his T-shirt ripped and stained.

What would Gloria think?

I felt a flash of guilt and shame for her. Getting blindingly drunk with Deke and Cassie on a Friday night was hardly on Gloria's wish list for her daughter.

"You kids should go." Dr. John signed off the orders on the

chart. Then he caught Deke by the shoulder. "Don't even think about driving, kiddo. You smell like you're way over the limit."

"I only had a couple of beers." His gaze flicked toward me, then back at Dr. John and held up his hands in surrender. "Okay, okay. I'll get a cab."

Dr. John sighed. "Fourteen. What possesses these kids to be so incredibly dumb?"

I wanted to defend Tabitha. To explain how sweet and sensible she could be.

"We'll keep her overnight." He stripped off his gloves and glanced at Tabitha and sighed heavily. "I'm sure Gloria is not going to be impressed." He sent me a conspiratorial look, and as he passed, a faint brush of his warm hand over my back, right between my shoulder blades. "Thanks, Leslie." His hand came to rest on my shoulder. "I'm beat and I'm heading home. I think Dr. Williams is on call next." He smiled at me, tightened his hand. "I'll see you tomorrow."

I swallowed at the promise in his voice and couldn't help a quick glance over my shoulder as he left. He was looking at me as well. A flush warmed my face as I turned back to the work at hand.

I got a basin of warm water and started cleaning what I could of Tabitha's face. Other than monitoring her vital signs and keeping her hydrated to dilute the alcohol, there wasn't much else we could do. Arlene would notify one of the ward nurses to come and get her, but for now I wanted to get her clean. To remove the mess that coagulated on her face. I didn't want the ward nurses seeing my niece like this.

Normally I wouldn't know the kids who came in in this shape. Normally I would clean up, and when I got home, tell Dan how incredibly stupid some kids would be.

Could I tell him about tonight?

I did what I could, then stayed by her side, doing my charting while I waited for the ward nurses. I didn't want to leave her alone and so far no one else needed my help.

Then a sound of hurrying feet and I heard someone call out, "Where's my girl? Where's Tabitha?"

I stepped outside of the cubicle and came face-to-face with Gloria. She blanched, stared at me a moment. "How is she?"

"She's in the cubicle. She's okay for now," was all I could say.

Gloria nodded and rushed past me to her daughter.

I decided to give them a few moments peace and returned to my desk. I felt surreal as I made notations I'd made countless times before. But the person I write the information on wasn't an unknown person I could create my own scenarios around. This was a sweet young girl who sang in church, who had a cute smile and a cheerful attitude. This was my niece.

"Leslie." Arlene popped her head over my desk, her face flushed. "Got a lady here with chest pain."

Tabitha was set aside in my mind as I ran to the reception area in time to see a young woman supporting an older woman who had her hand pressed against her chest.

"It's my mother. She's been complaining about her chest," the younger woman said, her frantic gaze flickering from me to Arlene.

I felt an uptick of adrenaline. *Possible heart attack?*

"I'll need you to answer some questions." The clerk pulled the younger woman aside to the admissions desk.

I grabbed a wheelchair and put the older woman in it. I recognized her as the woman who had the farm auction where Dan bought the tractor that started us on a not-so-nice trajectory.

"Call Dr. Williams," I said to Arlene. "Then get the lab. I'll need an ECG stat and a cardiac workup." I left Arlene still asking some questions of the younger woman, daughter I presumed.

As I wheeled toward the trauma room, the usual questions came back to me like riding a bike.

"When did the pain start, Mrs.--"

"Harris. Margaret Harris. I was, well..." she hesitated as I helped her into bed.

"Were you working? Resting?"

"I was getting up to get some coffee."

"How did it feel?"

"Like a cow landed on my chest." She stopped. Breathed again, as if making sure she still could. "I couldn't get any air. My left arm tingled. I thought I was going to throw up." Another grimace of pain flitted over her face.

Sounded like classic cardiac symptoms. While I went through the automatic questions about her allergies and medical and family history, my mind scrambled.

OIL--Oxygen, Intravenous, Leads. OIL. The acronym I'd memorized long ago beat an insistent rhythm in my mind as I put her in bed and elevated her to a semi-seated position. I slipped on the O2 mask, high flow, attached her to the vital signs monitor and cardiac monitor from the crash cart. Too much to do, not enough hands. I pulled in a breath, slowing myself down. OIL. Intravenous. Where was Dr. Williams?

I slipped the canula in. *Nice and smooth,* taped it down and adjusted the flow. My mind ticked over my list again. *Oxygen. Check. Intravenous. Check. Leads. Check and Check.*

I scribbled a few quick notes on a clipboard on the crash cart as a lab tech came. I turned my attention back to Mrs. Harris.

Her b.p. wasn't bad, but I gave her a shot of nitro, made a quick note, and glanced at my watch. I felt slightly outside of myself, watching myself going through the routine that so easily came back to me. In charge. In control.

A clatter of wheels announced another lab tech with the ECG machine. And right at that moment, the daughter appeared by the bed. She didn't even ask, just went straight to her mother's side. It was getting crowded in here, and Dr. Williams still hadn't shown up. I could use his help.

"I'm sorry, ma'am, you'll have to move," the Lab tech snapped as he pulled out the leads for the ECG machine.

"I have to be here," she said firmly.

"You can move to the head of the bed," I said. "You won't be in the way there."

She gave me a thankful glance.

I checked the cardiac monitor. Classic wave form of an acute heart attack.

"How is your pain?" I asked her again as the tech pasted the leads to her chest.

"About a seven." She gave her daughter a weak smile. "It's going down, Linda."

Linda stroked her mother's hair. "That's good, Mom. You hang in there. We still need you around."

"Shouldn't have sold the farm."

"If you had kept it, you might be lying on the kitchen floor all alone right now."

"Maybe. But maybe I'd feel like I had a purpose."

"You have a purpose, Mom. That's to be with us yet." Their conversation registered in one part of my mind, and I felt my own heart tremble with yearning. I thought of my own mother and, for a fleeting moment, wondered where she was.

"Sorry I'm late." Dr. John rushed into the room, slipping his latex gloves on. He gave me a tired smile, then turned his attention back to the patient. "What do we have here?" He pulled the ECG readout as it rolled off of the machine, glanced at the patient, then at me. "Morphine."

I drew it up and gave Mrs. Harris a small amount of morphine through the IV, my eyes constantly monitoring her blood pressure, oxygen saturation levels, and heart rate. I didn't have time to grab the chart and quickly scribbled what I could on the back of my hand.

The lab tech came back with the results. Dr. John scanned them before looking up from the paper at the patient. "Looks like you're having a heart attack, or what we call a myocardial infarction. We're going to give you a drug to break up the clot that's causing this. Before we do, we need to ask you a few more questions."

Linda gasped. "Heart attack."

"Thankfully we caught things in time." As Dr. John went over the screening questions, I saw a faint track of moisture drift down Mrs. Harris's cheek. She pressed her lips together but made no move to wipe her tears away.

The words *heart attack* had such a deadly connotation for the average person. Such strong terminology striking at, well, the very heart of a person.

I sympathized, but as I injected the clot buster, I glanced at the clock and couldn't help but feel a flush of accomplishment. Twenty-two minutes from the time Mrs. Harris came into the hospital until we injected the clot buster. Not bad.

Dr. John must have caught my look because he gave me a quick wink of understanding. I hoped the Harrises didn't catch it. This quick rush of adrenalin was what emergency nurses lived for. It was our drug of choice, and every time we handled an emergency smoothly or cheated death, the charge came. The more complicated the situation, the stronger the rush.

I tried to explain this to Dan once, but I may as well have been speaking Urdu. Sometimes when a bad case had gone well, when once again I had helped snatch a patient from greedy death, I wished he could see so he could share my thrill, understand why I needed to be here as much as with him and my children at home.

For now I had Dr. John, and as he surreptitiously squeezed my hand, I felt a connection I never did with my own husband.

Mrs. Harris was stable for now, and her daughter held her hand. Their eyes were closed, and Linda's lips were moving. "Thank you, Lord," she whispered over and over again, smiling as she did so.

Whatever gives her comfort. At the same time I felt a flash of envy. She at least had someone to talk to when all was said and done. Well, she could keep talking to God. I still kept my eyes on the vital signs monitor.

Dr. John laid his hand on my shoulder. "And again, nice work. Glad you're on my team."

I was still coming down from my adrenaline rush. "Thanks." I smiled. As he returned it, his eyes singing into mine, I heard a faint niggling voice.

He's coming onto you. Keep your distance.

I chanced a sidelong glance, surprised to see his eyes holding mine. A little too intensely. I knew I should listen. My rational self told me to be careful. But the lonely self, the one whose self-esteem had been battered by a woman who had, for a while, held my husband's attention, not only continued to hold his gaze but lifted her hand up, covered Dr. John's hand with hers and gave it an extra squeeze.

It's innocent. Means nothing.

He should be watching Mrs. Harris as closely as I am.

Confusion and professionalism fighting with the too basic need of any woman to know that she's attractive to another man.

So why do I have to remind myself of that? And why is this man so appealing?

The ward nurses came to take Mrs. Harris away and, in the confusion, Dr. John and I ended up standing close.

"If things slow down here, we should go for coffee." As he held my gaze, I saw raw longing and yearning in his eyes. "I need to talk to you." He lifted his hand from my shoulder to my face, his fingers trailing over my cheek. I couldn't stop a shiver, unsure of my reaction. Excitement? The knife edge thrill of teetering on the brink of a forbidden abyss? I had always been afraid of heights. I would get shaky standing on deep pile carpeting. But each time I stood on a high building, I would inch to the edge and look down. And each time, some perverted part of my psyche would wonder what it would be like to jump.

That was what I felt now. This steady, inexorable pull toward a place I knew I shouldn't be, but I felt drawn by a person who had already made that fateful step past boundaries and borders and now invited me to do the same.

Unprofessional, my mind cried, even as a very female part of me was drawn to the simple fact of an attractive single man desired me, a married woman. A man who understood what I had to deal with.

I couldn't look at him anymore, and as my eyes slipped past him, I noticed a figure standing in the open door.

Gloria. The surprised look on her face convinced me she had seen everything.

"Is something wrong, Gloria?" I wished my face wasn't so flushed.

"No. I had a few questions." Her gaze ticked from Dr. John to me. "They can wait."

Fear clawed at my belly. How had this looked to her? What had I done? What had I allowed?

CHAPTER 14

"Can I come in?" I tapped on the open door of Tabitha's room, taking a few steps in. The only illumination in the room was the light at the head of Tabitha's bed and the faint glow from the IV readout.

I had finished my shift over an hour ago, and during that time, I hovered between going straight home to my husband and my children and wanting to talk to Gloria, who, I knew, was with Tabitha in the ward. I wanted to see how Tabitha was doing, but I dreaded facing Gloria and her censure.

I should never have encouraged Dr. John. Should never have given him even the vaguest hint that I was willing to take the same steps he would.

This is how it happens. I hovered outside of Tabitha's room, still wavering. This was how Dan got drawn into his relationship with Miss Bilingual. So easy. A smile, an argument with a spouse whose faults had accumulated over a period of six years, creating an unfair comparison.

It would have been so easy to carry on, to slowly break down one barrier after another until there were none left to cross, no place left for retreat, no place left to hide.

I closed my eyes and leaned back against the wall, my heart stuttering in my chest as realization chilled my soul.

I was no better than Dan.

I stayed there a moment, shame and guilt and fear washing over me in waves of self-recrimination. How had I come to this place? How had I allowed this to happen?

Step by step. By keeping Dan at arm's length. By punishing him for what had happened.

Yes, he had done wrong, and yes, there were repercussions. But this was how it happened. Lonely people seeking comfort in all the wrong places. Did it really happen this easily? Was it so simple to slip into unsuitable relationships? A glance. A shared laugh. A spouse who was so busy with other things and other people that you felt a seismic shift of loyalty in your own relationship and desperately needed confirmation that you were desirable. Wanted. Needed?

I gave myself a few more moments of self-accusation, then pushed myself away and went into the room to face Gloria.

She sat beside her daughter, reading. She wasn't wearing makeup; her hair wasn't curled. I hadn't noticed that when she came into the Emergency Department. But now, in the reduced light, she looked drawn, tired, and vulnerable. I had passed Gerrit in the hallway, and he had stopped me for a quick hug, quietly thanking me for what I had done for his daughter. I didn't know what to say. Normally I wasn't involved with the aftermath of an emergency procedure. In Vancouver, the ER was often looked upon as a sorting house. Critical goes here, surgery goes there, others get a prescription and are on their way. Once we triaged and treated, we seldom saw our patients again, unless they were "regulars."

Now I looked at the clean and tidy face of a girl who had been much, much worse only a few hours ago.

"How is she doing?" I spoke quietly to Gloria, shame edging my voice.

"She's fine. Still sleeping."

Tabitha's hair shone, and the faint sprinkle of freckles over her nose stood out against her pale skin. But, thankfully, she looked as innocent as she had the day she and Allison had first burst into my kitchen.

"Did she wake up at all?"

Gloria nodded.

"That's good." I walked over to the opposite side of the bed and checked Tabitha's pulse, taking refuge in my job as a nurse during this awkward moment. Normal. Temp. Normal.

"Will...will..." Gloria's voice faltered. She took a deep breath and tried again. "Will there be any long-term damage from this?"

"I believe we caught it in time. The fact that she woke up is good. Means she's not too deeply unconscious." I gave Gloria an encouraging smile. "She'll be fine."

She nodded, then gave me a furtive glance. "I...I don't know what to say. Thank you for...for...what you did. It was a hard...situation."

I could see that Gloria was stumbling, and I wasn't sure what I was supposed to say. I was uncomfortable with her hesitancy when I knew I was at fault.

But she was reaching out to me, and in spite of the jokes I had made at her expense, in spite of my frustration with her and, yes, my jealousy of her, I had to say something to make the connection.

"It's not that abnormal." I stroked a strand of hair away from Tabitha's face. "I've seen it happen lots. To all kinds of kids from all kinds of homes. And it doesn't mean she's a bad daughter." *Or that you're a bad mother.*

Her hand rested on the cover of her book. A Bible. Not a book I knew a lot about. Since Dan started reading the Children's Bible in the evening, I had picked up ours up from time to time in the evening, trying to make a connection with a man who was changing on me. I discovered I liked reading the Psalms and I liked some of the stories Jesus told, but a lot of the rest was hard going. All that finger wagging from the prophets. I couldn't figure it out.

Dan didn't know I read it. I didn't want to get his hopes up in case the whole Bible thing was simply a passing fad, something I did in Holmes Crossing and dropped when we moved back to Vancouver.

I tried to imagine myself in Gloria's place. Tried to imagine what it would feel like to be sitting by the bed of a daughter who had messed up so publicly. Not only publicly but in front of the one person that you personally disapproved of.

"You didn't put the alcohol in her mouth." I kept my voice quiet. I was in no position to make any judgment of her.

She flicked another curious glance at me, then sighed. "No. But I taught her better than this. We raised her to be a good Christian girl. I don't know what we did wrong."

I fingered Tabitha's hair again, so nice and clean now, all traces of what had happened washed out. Cleansed. "I don't know much about raising teenagers, and I don't know much about being a Christian, but I do know that kids are going to try things out no matter what their parents teach them. They come to an age when their peers are more important than their parents. I've seen this kind of thing again and again." I paused, searching for something I could use. "I also know that the kids we seldom see again are the ones who have parents who keep caring. Who keep loving their kids regardless of what they do. And if Anneke did the same thing, I would be horrified and hurt."

I noticed the faint glint of tears on Gloria's cheek, and in that brief moment of vulnerability, I felt a faint throb of caring for this woman. She reached out and touched her daughter's cheek. Tabitha was the bridge between Gloria and me.

I didn't want to leave. I wanted to maintain this fragile connection.

"Thanks for telling me that." She sniffed and swiped at her

cheeks, glancing across the bed at me. "I do love her. But right now I am struggling between anger and plain, ordinary humiliation. She smelled so terrible. So common. She reeked of alcohol. And I'm supposed to be a Coffee Break leader." She laughed, then shook her head. "Pride. What a mistake."

Her admission and her faint laugh did more than any Bible lesson she could have taught me. I smiled at her and took a huge chance by touching her arm.

"She's a good girl. Give her some time. Her behavior is not a reflection on you."

"I'll give her a good talking to when she comes out of it." Gloria shook her head. She squeezed my hand lightly, tweaked out a faint smile. "Thanks. This means a lot."

We shared a look, then she let go of my hand and fiddled with the sheet covering Tabitha. "Leslie, I know..." She stopped, bit her lip, and shook her head. "Leslie, please be careful with Dr. John. He's ...he can be..." I caught a glimpse of confusion and regret. "Just be careful."

Her words reminded me of what she had seen and how the situation must have looked from her point of view. I had let myself be drawn to a dangerous place, and her gentle suggestion drew me back. Guilt fought with shame and relief. I had come so close to doing something truly stupid.

And I understood how Dan had almost done the same. I could no longer accuse him from a point of self-righteousness. I had toppled as easily as he had.

I nodded, understanding the suggestion subtly woven through her words. "Thanks, Gloria." And I meant it.

I had lots to think about as I drove home that night. As I got closer to the yard, I pulled over, looking at the house from the road.

Lights winked at me through the darkness from various farm yards beyond ours. I could see ours and the VandeKams down the road. One of the many Brouwers whose names showed up above mail slots in the back of Holmes Crossing church. I thought of the smiles I got when I accompanied Dan to church. Delores had given me a hug the second time I had gone, loudly proclaiming how glad she was that I had come. As if I had given her a gift.

I turned off the car, killed the lights, and got out of the car. The silence, now familiar, didn't hurt my ears as it had that first time. In fact, I even welcomed it.

I rested against the warm hood of the car, leaning back to look up at the sky. Stars shone back at me, like crushed diamonds tossed over a velvet sky that stretched from horizon to horizon. A wave of dizziness washed over me as my tiny mind tried to grasp the vastness of our galaxy and the universe beyond. If I looked any longer, I would shrink down, disappear like a gnat.

And then I saw them. A wave of light that confused me at first. It wasn't the moon behind a cloud bank. There were no clouds. Then it moved, shifted. I saw green slowly emerging at the bottom as the light meandered across the sky, shooting upward and undulating in waves of green edged with a surprising pink. The silent show went on and on.

The Northern Lights.

My breath caught momentarily, and I felt my throat close up in awe. I had heard about them but had never, ever seen them. And here they were, billowing and surging like a curtain caught by a wind filling the northern sky with a splendor that I couldn't begin to take in or express.

Snatches of verse from an old song was all that came to mind. "Oh, Lord my God, when I in awesome wonder...I see the stars, I hear the rolling thunder..." And the Northern Lights, I wanted to add. *"How great thou art."*

After twenty minutes the light seemed to fade into a faint, white glow, and my heart slowed.

I looked back at the homes beyond me, unassuming beneath all that glory and majesty, and the people I was slowly getting to know. "Do you really care about all these people, God?" I whispered into the evening silence. "Do you really see them and love them like the minister said you do? Do you see all the things we do?" I shivered, then pressed myself closer to the car. "Did you see what happened with me and that doctor? Did you know how, for a small moment, I wanted to be with him? That I wanted to feel special to someone?"

I waited a moment in the cool silence for some kind of revelation to my whispered confession. Some judgment.

A small breeze teased my hair and tugged at my sweater, but other than that, nothing.

Well, it was worth a try. I slipped back into the car.

As I drove down into the valley, I thought of Dan and my children, and suddenly I pushed my foot harder on the accelerator. I wanted to be home.

FROM: tfroese@centermail.com

To: lesismore@hcrossing.net

U sound confused, sis. Stay the course, hand on the tiller. Don't get sucked into the cult. God is just a fantasy made up by people who can't explain things. Course, I can't explain things either but at least I admit it. Come to the light, sis and not those Northern Lights - though that would have been kewl to see. Come back to Vancouver

CHAPTER 15

"$\mathcal{I}$'m glad you had fun." Kathy gave me a self-satisfied smirk as she helped me load the large plastic dollhouse into my car.

It was late afternoon. Kathy had called me at work and asked if I wanted to go to a garage sale. I got off at four, and Dan wouldn't be home until later on that evening. I had gotten used to having my husband around more often and didn't always like being home when he wasn't.

My little side trip with Dr. John had made me more cautious, less judgmental, and a bit more careful with my husband. We were making tentative movements back toward being a married couple. I hadn't said anything about Dr. John to him, figuring that nothing had happened, so nothing needed to be said.

I had taken a week off work, needing to center myself and find a way to re-knit my life with Dan. To pull myself away from Dr. John and his flirtation. I knew where to put what I felt for him, and as I faced the reality of how truly close I came to making a monumental fool of myself, I found myself slowly retreating from that dangerous place.

The past week my shifts hadn't coincided with Dr. John's. It helped that I made sure they didn't. I was keeping my distance. Wary and vigilant, devising ways to make things better between me and Dan.

Today was a quiet day and, again, Dr. John hadn't been working, so my day held an ease that I was beginning to enjoy.

"You had fun today, didn't you?" Kathy repeated, as if needing to hear my words of surrender.

"Okay. You got me." I smiled as I set a large box of dollhouse accessories beside the dollhouse. "Pawing through someone else's used stuff was more fun than I thought it would be."

"It's the adventure. You know exactly what you're going to get when you go to Wal-Mart or Costco. Garage sales are all about adventure. The thrill of the hunt."

In addition to the dollhouse, I'd found a cute push-toy for Nicholas and a goofy farmer hat for Dan that the garage sale lady had thrown in for free. But the best part was a couple of lily plants that had been hiding in a corner. The lady who ran the sale told me they were perennials, and if I wanted them to do really well next year, I would have to cut the blooms off. I had no intention of doing that. The lilies were beautiful and starting to open up. I had the perfect spot for them right outside the back door. If I could keep Sasha out of the bed, they would add a wonderful splash of color.

Kathy had bought a couple of lawn chairs, some clothes for her kids, and a large beach umbrella that Cordell dragged down the sidewalk

"Good job, buddy." Kathy took the umbrella from her son and gave me a teasing smirk. "And are you sure you're done?"

I glanced back at the house, remembering the other toys I looked at but put back, the cute shirt I had found with the price tag still on it, and the funky lamp that would look so cool in our bedroom. "I have to be."

"And did Madame have a good time?"

I didn't change my expression. "You're liking this, aren't you?"

She nodded, her glance cutting to the amount of stuff I could barely fit in my car.

"I told you already, I had a lot of fun."

She yelped and made two fists. "Ladies and gentlemen, we have a convert." Her eyes sparkled at me across the truck bed. "Whaddya say? Hit town again next week? There's two happening in the new subdivision. Should be pretty good."

"Give me a chance to make the cultural shift." I laughed. "I'm still getting used to paying for things with a personal check." It still surprised me that the woman holding the garage sale took a check from a complete stranger with only my last name as security. "VandeKeeres are good for the money," she'd said when I told her I had no cash.

The vehicles were loaded, the kids settled and bribed with some candy Kathy had brought along. As I closed the car door, I looked back at Kathy. "Thanks for bringing me."

"What shifts are you working next week?"

I told her, and we chatted some more about inconsequential, drowsy subjects. It was easy talk, even though hovering over our chitchat was a desire to confess.

Confess what?

The words made me feel as if I had done something wrong, which, I had reasoned with myself, I hadn't.

But another part of me wanted to speak the words of the situation aloud. To hear them through the ears of a nonjudgmental listener.

And then what?

I pushed the questions aside. Nothing had happened and, I knew, nothing would. Dr. John was a mistake that would never be replicated.

A few flies buzzed lazily around our heads, and in the distance I heard the buzz of a lawnmower, the hissing tick-tick of a sprinkler. I wanted to hold fast to this glorious summer day. Me, spending ordinary time with a friend after a fun afternoon.

Life was good, and as I got into my car and waved goodbye to Kathy, I felt a sense of warm wellbeing.

I glanced over at Nicholas, fast asleep in his car seat, his cheeks bright red with sun and fatigue. He'd been uncharacteristically quiet and patient with me as I poked and prodded and snooped through the sale items. He'd probably be up most of the night in payment for these few moments of peace, but I didn't begrudge him the rest.

The warm sun shone through the windshield as I drove, the purr of the car engine making Anneke drowsy. I saw her head slump to one side as she drifted off as well.

I hummed the song I remembered from church. I had gone again the past two Sundays. Nicholas was in a good mood both times, and I wasn't working. Dan was happy, and Wilma was smiling more at me.

I recognized a few people who had come through the Emergency Department and a few more from my shopping trips at the co-op. I didn't feel as much a stranger as I had the first time. Each time the minister spoke, I discovered more about God. But I kept my guard up. No sense in jumping into this all the way without knowing where it would take me. And yet I found my resistance wavering.

I made the last corner out of town, then headed down the road toward home. Soon I came to my favorite part of the drive. Up and up through wooded hills, then cresting a ridge and then, suddenly, ahead of us lay our place.

I saw the patchwork of fields in the valley, some bright green from irrigation, a hint of yellow already starting in the canola fields. The fields higher up looked as if a giant comb had raked through them, creating green furrows alternating with cultivated brown fields. It didn't seem that long ago that Dan had worked the higher land, planted it, and now it had been up for over a month, growing more every week.

I felt a beat of expectation as I headed toward our yard,

thinking of Dan and looking forward to telling him about the garage sale. He'd get a kick out of the hat.

As I drove into the yard, I slowed down by the garden. I had weeded it yesterday, taking peculiar pleasure in sorting out the bad from the good. Restoring order to the neat rows. The carrots were finally recognizable, and the peas were starting to crawl up the fence.

I parked in the yard and got out, a feeling of accomplishment flowing through me.

Dan came out of the house and walked toward the car. Why was he home already?

"How was town?" He glanced at our sleeping kids as I got out of the car.

"Kathy and I went to a garage sale. I didn't think you would be back until after supper."

"That's why you didn't come straight home from work?"

"Yeah." I gave him a puzzled look. He sounded angry. "Is something wrong?"

"Why isn't Kathy home yet if she went with you?"

"I don't know."

"And you really went to a garage sale?"

What was with the good cop-bad cop routine Dan was pulling off all by himself? "The evidence, Mr. CSI, is in the car." An edgy tone entered my voice at the mistrustful one in his. "One doll-house and three lily plants."

He looked from me to the car, his eyes narrowed, an unwelcome slant to his mouth, and a question clenched my heart with an icy fist.

"Where did you think I went?"

Dan blinked, then shook his head. "It doesn't matter."

"It does." I tried to hold his gaze, but he shoved his hands in the back pocket of his blue jeans, not looking at me. "You're angry, and I haven't done anything wrong."

"I don't know about that."

"Enough with being vague. Something is bothering you. What is it?"

Dan sighed. "What's going on between you and Dr. John?"

I endured an instant of guilt so intense and familiar, it felt like a friend. Behind that came a mocking soundtrack, the velvet voice of Elvis singing "Suspicion" thrumming through my mind. I mumbled out a non-dramatic, "Nothing."

"Really? Then why did he have his hands all over you the other night?"

I swallowed a surge of anger that was chased by a wave of self-condemnation. "First off, that sounds gross. Second, that sounds *really* gross." He made Dr. John seem like a lecherous old man who couldn't keep his hands off me.

But other than the lecherous part, he does touch you a lot.

"That's no answer, Leslie. Is there something going on between you two?"

You two. Like we were a couple.

I knew I had been skirting along the edge of trouble when I encouraged Dr. John. Yes, he understood what I was dealing with. Yes, Dan didn't. Yes, Dr. John was caring and considerate.

But nothing really happened, I wanted to say, even as a small voice mocked my self-righteous protestations.

You liked his attention. You encouraged it.

Not much.

Enough to let him think he could carry on.

But I didn't want him to carry on.

But behind all my self-talk came another question. How did Dan know?

I looked at him. Really looked at him. Saw the hurt in his eyes and felt my world twist and spin as the very things I had accused him of now faced me.

"You're not saying anything. He called here today. Have you and he--"

I swallowed my pride, took a breath, and started down the

same road Dan had taken over half a year ago when he tried to explain to me how he got tangled in his own particular web of attraction. "He was being nice. Helpful. And yes, maybe I let things get out of hand. But nothing happened. I was in a bad place, and he was just...just being kind."

I had wanted to talk of the situation, to hear it through someone else's ears, but hearing them through Dan's and seeing the hurt in his troubled gaze, the same hurt I had felt with Miss Bilingual, made me realize how cheap it sounded.

"If I talked too much to Dr. John, it was because I could vent to him about Wilma and Gloria. Because he knew what I was dealing with. Because he sympathized with me, and I could tell him things I could never tell you."

"Gloria said he could be like that." Dan's voice held a sorrowful note.

"Gloria? When did you talk to her?"

"She was the one who told me. Warned me actually. About you and Dr. John."

My mouth opened and shut like a fish as I tried to find the right thing to say, the right thing to do. I never truly understood the full meaning of the word *flabbergasted* until this moment.

The irony of it all. The deep injustice. I say nothing about Tabitha, and Gloria has the bald-faced nerve talk to Dan behind my back about me.

"I can't believe this," was all I could come up with. "I can't believe she would have the nerve...after what I had to clean up ...what I had to do..."

Dan stood rock solid, his arms across his chest. "She told me about Tabitha. Told me what you did. She's grateful. Don't think she's not." He glanced at the kids in the car. They were stirring. The statute of limitations was running out on this discussion, and I was trying to encapsulate my confusion, my anger, and, yes, my guilt, into something resembling a coherent sentence.

"Why didn't she talk to me first?" I thought Gloria and I had come to an understanding. That gentle soundtrack moment in the hospital room had been wiped away by her self-righteous attitude. One step forward two back. "Doesn't she care?"

"I know my family's not perfect. But you can't accuse them of not caring. They're involved in our lives. They care about our marriage. And I do. I had hoped that moving here would help us. I thought you wanted the same."

"I do..."

"Then why were you spending time with this doctor?"

"Why were you spending time with Miss Bilingual?" Guilt made me lash back.

"Her name was Keely. And I spent time with her because I was weak and because I was confused and because she was around and you weren't..."

And back we went to ancient history as words pushed us apart again.

"I was trying to keep our family financially afloat," I protested.

"Like I am now. And I apologized and apologized for Keely. And I apologized for trusting Lonnie. That was a mistake I am trying to fix by moving here. And you may not see it, but I appreciate the help we get from my family. I don't see your sister helping out. Or your mother."

My face stiffened as the blood drained to my chest and pain lanced through my very being. "Low blow, Dan. You know as well I do that I haven't heard from my mother in months." My voice broke. Did he think I liked how dysfunctional my family seemed compared to his? Didn't I get to see enough disapproval from Wilma and, yes, Gloria? Had he moved so firmly over in their camp that he could no longer see my point of view?

"If she ever stayed in one place long enough, maybe you would hear from her."

"Don't you think I want that?" I cried. "Do you think Terra and I chose to have an absent mother? Do you think I enjoyed wondering if she was going to be home when I got home from school, wondering how we were going to make it through the week? Do you think it's easy for me to be surrounded by your family who have always been here and probably always will be, a reminder of what Terra and I don't have?"

I pressed my lips together. Dan knew about my past, but I seldom spoke about it. The past was, well, the past. I didn't want to spend too much time comparing memories. Dan's would always eclipse mine. "Your mother is far from perfect either, Dan VandeKeere. And each time I see your family, I see a family so different from mine, but yet not so different. Your mom may go to church, but she sure hasn't made much of an effort to make me feel like a daughter-in-law. From the first time she met me, she made up her mind about me, and she doesn't seem to want to change it no matter what I do. Yes, my mother is a failure in the mother department, but I would be careful how you throw around accusations. They can come back and smack you in the face."

And I should know. Dr. John's face suddenly superimposed itself on Miss Bilingual's. Our combined failures.

"My mother has had her own difficulties." With those words, Dan aligned himself with Wilma's side.

"Your mother had a husband who loved her and gave her a home. That was your father. That her second husband was a snake is hard. But she had and still has people around her. A community and people who care. My mother had no one. And maybe I'm not perfect, I've never claimed to be, but I hope that if Nicholas ever gets married, I won't treat his future wife the way your mother treats me."

Dan blanched as my words spun like a cyclone, gathering speed as I spat them out in anger and self-defense. But I couldn't stop now. "And if you're going to blame everything that's wrong in your mother's life on the fact that some man recently left her in the lurch, then you're only making it easier for her to be unkind and uncaring and controlling." And I should know. But I wasn't going to give him any more ammunition.

"She's not controlling, Leslie."

"If she's not, why does she insist on controlling the farm accounts?"

"Because we were only going to be here awhile."

Were. He said were. "And now?"

"Things change." He drew in a deep breath. "In spite of what you've just said about my mother, I don't think I want to leave."

A wail from Anneke scattered the conversation. I blinked, trying to ground myself back in the present. I needed to retreat and regroup. Regain control.

"I can't talk about this now, Dan. I just can't." Too many emotions churned around us, too many words had been thrown on the ground. We needed some time and space before we took them up again.

The next few hours were painfully silent as we ate. Dan read the story Bible again, but I couldn't listen. My emotions were a patchwork quilt of guilt and pain stitched together with anger. Not comforting at all.

Afterward Dan carted the dollhouse into Anneke's room and helped her set it up, a job I had been looking forward to doing.

Instead I planted the lilies, watered them, and stood back to garner what precious enjoyment I could. The woman at the garage sale had told me that if I clip them off, they would grow better next year. I didn't care about next year. I wanted to enjoy them now.

Stay here?

I know my kids loved it here. They loved their grandma, correction, Oma, even if I didn't. They loved their aunties, the chickens, the dog, Dan's horses.

And you don't?

I closed my eyes as my once ordered future shifted and

changed. I couldn't fit my head around that yet. Didn't know where to put it.

What would I lose? What would I gain?

I put the kids in bed while Dan retreated to his shop. We maintained a quiet ceasefire, neither talking. We neither of us knew what to say, how to regain lost ground.

I tried to read a book, but gave up and went to bed, lying between the freshly washed sheets, trying to find sleep. Dan joined me much later, but he turned away from me, presenting his back to me across the expanse of our bed, which now seemed as broad as the Atlantic and as uninviting. In minutes I heard him snoring.

I woke up in the horrible early morning hours, unable to sleep and made my way back downstairs. Two o'clock in the hospital was usually a chance to catch up with some of the other nurses, catch up on paperwork. At home, it was an empty, lonely time with no one to connect with. I checked my e-mail. Nothing from Terra or Josie. Somehow it didn't matter as much as it used to.

I wandered around the house, restless, unsettled.

Then I saw the Bible sitting by Dan's chair. I snapped on the light and picked it up. I had read it a couple of times before, not sure of where to start. A piece of paper stuck out from the pages, so I opened it there. Psalm 23. I dropped into Dan's chair and started reading. The rhythm of the language and vaguely familiar words drew me in. " ...he leads me beside quiet waters. He restores my soul." I drew in a long slow breath as I read, letting the cadence of the words wash over me. Comfort me. "...You anoint my head with oil. My cup overflows. Surely goodness and love will follow me all the days of my life and I will dwell in the house of the Lord forever."

I dropped my head on the chair and stared at the ceiling. The house of the Lord. Did God really want me? Would he really restore a soul that had been tainted by wrong?

Could Dan and I possibly find our way through this dark valley we had dropped into?

Somehow I didn't think it could happen.

I felt as if my life was unraveling, and I didn't know how to put it back together again.

FROM: lesismore@hcrossing.net

To: tfroese@centermail.com

I am confused. I need to talk to you. Need to figure things out. Call me or write back. Haven't heard from you for awhile. Right now I need my sister.

CHAPTER 16

"And when did you say you injured your back?" I asked my patient as I whisked the curtain closed around the bed. The day had been busy, thankfully. I didn't have time to spin through the endless circle of what I had said the day before yesterday, what I should have said, what I shouldn't have said. Dan hadn't brought it up yesterday or this morning.

I didn't know how to proceed from here, and I couldn't mention it to Kathy or ask her advice. There was no article on the internet or any magazine I read that covered How a Marriage can Succeed with uneasy truces.

"Ten years ago. I was working as a roofer. Slipped on a shingle that some idiot had laying around and *wham*." He smacked his hands together. "I was sliding down that roof and on the ground before I knew what hit me. Saw more stars than the Walk of Fame." He gave me a quick grin, then, as if realizing that he was supposed to be in pain, winced. "I need to see the doctor."

Mr. Francisco wore scruffy blue jeans and a tattered jean jacket, and his hair was pulled back into a greasy ponytail.

"Before I get the doctor, can you do a few things for me so I can judge the extent of your pain?"

This netted me a sullen look and a shrug. "Sure. As long as you don't make me throw my back out. I'll sue, you know."

Of course he would.

"Can you lift your arms over your head?"

This was done with much groaning and moaning as I watched for any telltale signs. I knew that the motto of the justice system was innocent until proven guilty, but I had a vibe about this guy.

I gave him a few more small exercises which he performed mindlessly, his begrudging air slowly fading as I took notes.

"Can you touch your toes?" I asked the question casually, and when he easily bent over to do this, my vibe grew stronger. He should have been in agony.

"So when is the doctor going to see me?" His voice grew quieter as he straightened. "I really need something for the pain 'cause I lost my other prescription."

Of course he needed a new prescription. And as we went through the list of his allergies, big surprise, he named every common pain killer that could be acquired without a prescription.

With patients like Mr. Francisco, training and intuition collided. My training taught me to be sympathetic, to listen and to be non-judgmental. My intuition thought *drug-seeker*.

"Are you on any medication now?" I injected a pleasant tone into my voice. It was work, that injecting. I knew this guy's type all too well. We came across them day after day in Vancouver, and it was always a struggle to deal with them professionally and courteously when you knew they were using and abusing the system.

He lifted his hands just a fraction. The pain, of course. "Well, I had some medication, like I told you. But I was with some dudes, and we were hanging out at my place. One of the guys went into my bathroom. He's a big time druggie. Loser." He gave a slow, knowing nod, trying to pull me onto his side. "I'm sure he's dealing on the side. Knows I'll squash him like a bug if I find out he's doing that stuff. I'm sure he took the stuff from my bathroom 'cause as soon as he was done, he told this other guy they had to leave real quick. I was going to go to my regular doctor, but he's gone on some fancy trip to the Bahamas. You know doctors." He lowered his voice and angled his head with a quick jerk toward the cubicle where Dr. John was busy with another patient. "I had to come here anyway to see some guy about a truck that I was going to buy. I was gonna try to go without the pills, but the pain, it just got too bad."

"That's too bad." I forced sympathy into my voice.

"Anyway, when can I see the doctor? I'm dying here."

I smiled politely as I carefully wrote out some notes on his chart. I'd seen dying, and Mr. Francisco was a long way from hearing the angels sing.

"I'm in pain, nurse. You have to pay attention. You have to treat me."

Don't roll your eyes. Don't even make eye contact. Just keep writing.

"You hearing me, nurse? I got rights, you know." His voice rose with each declaration.

Relax. Don't take it personally. Don't let your emotions intrude on your patient-nurse relationship.

"I'll get the doctor." I gave him a careful smile.

As I left, I massaged my temples, trying to push away the pain that had been steadily building since my confrontation with Dan. I couldn't push aside the angry words thrown down between us. What he'd said about my mother, what I'd said about his. What Gloria had said about Dr. John.

I worked the night shift after our fight, unintentionally underscoring his accusation that I put work before family. But I couldn't be at home with all that tension boiling beneath the quiet façade we kept up for the sake of the kids.

Once again our lives slipped past each other. I hated it.

227

In spite of my pique with her self-righteous gossiping, I set my own pride aside long enough to realize that Gloria was right. I had been edging around dangerous territory encouraging Dr. John. And I had encouraged him for the wrong reasons. Pride. Selfish gossip. In spite of what Gloria and Wilma had done and said, I had no right to bring down their characters just to prop up my own weaknesses. What had been worse was realizing how easily I had slipped into the same territory Dan had been. I had come here with a sense of pride and superiority. All lost. Swept away.

So I created a distance between me and Dr. John the few shifts we'd worked together. I kept our conversation professional and didn't rise to the bait when he made a comment about Gloria. And I kept my distance.

I checked on the woman with the croupy cough beside Mr. Francisco. Thankfully she didn't ask when Dr. John was going to see her. I didn't have an answer.

As I stepped out of her cubicle, a noise at the front desk caught my attention. My heart sank when I saw the man carrying a child, a woman hurrying behind him. All the beds were full. Mr. Francisco had been triaged to the end of the line and was our last patient. If we had a real emergency, he'd be bumped back to the waiting room, which would make him even more cranky.

Then the frantic looking man by the front desk glanced over his shoulder and ice slipped through my veins.

It was Dan, and he carried Nicholas.

Wilma was right on his heels.

Questions skittered through my mind. Why was Wilma here? Kathy was supposed to be taking care of the kids. But right behind those questions a larger one loomed, heavy and threatening.

What was wrong with Nicholas?

Go. Now. Hurry. Your baby. Your little boy is in trouble. You should have been at home. You knew he wasn't well. Dan was right. You do put your job first, and now Wilma gets to see firsthand.

Nicholas had been fussing all last night and was a feverish that morning, but I had put it down to teething. Had I been so terribly wrong? Me? A nurse?

Guilty fear tumbled through my mind as I made my rubbery legs hurry to Dan's side.

"He's burning up." Dan looked to me as if I had an answer. All I had at the moment was a flash of guilt that I hadn't been home to prevent this. Whatever *this* was.

"Bring him into the trauma room." I held back from pulling Nicholas out of his arms and instead hurried ahead, Dan and Wilma right behind me.

Relax. Assess. Triage. Treat.

I ran through the litany that always helped me during the harder cases that came into the emergency room in Vancouver.

The words usually calmed me and pulled me back from the emotions of the situation. I had a job to do.

But I had forgotten about Mr. Francisco glaring at me through narrowed eyes as he sat on the bed we needed for Nicholas. "Where's the doc? I thought he was going to see me next."

"We have to move you back to the waiting room," I said firmly. "We have an emergency."

He didn't budge.

"Please get off the bed." I couldn't stop the edge in my voice. My son needed that space.

"I'll sue."

"I know a good lawyer. We have a very ill child." I didn't have time for this. "Now get off that bed."

I didn't know where this fit in nurse-patient procedure, but the anger in my voice must have gotten through. He shifted off the bed. I was there in a nanosecond of his butt slipping off the sheets, whipping them off, replacing them as he stormed out the door. He moved surprisingly fast for someone with severe back pain.

When Dan and Wilma came in the room, I saw Wilma look from me to the retreating back of Mr. Francisco, then back at me, puzzled. No time to explain.

"Lay him on the bed," I told Dan. "Take off his coat and shirt."

My heart stuttered in my chest as Dan undressed him and handed the clothes to my mother-in-law. I pulled the crash cart close, clipped a new cover on the thermometer, and checked his temperature. Sky high. His breathing was fast, pulse erratic.

"Dr. Brouwer!" I called out, knowing he was somewhere on the ward. "I need you *now*." Again, no time for niceties. This case now had priority.

Nicholas' chest was clear.

In spite of my training and my previous experience, I couldn't pull back far enough from this case. This body burning with fever, lying so still on the bed was my son. My baby boy. I called to Arlene to get a lab tech down here.

"What happened?" I started a chart.

My mind clicked through the possibilities as a faint whisper of a memory teased the back of my mind. The mother who had come in the other day talking about a suspected case of meningitis at the daycare. We hadn't treated the child here, so I never thought of it again. Until now.

"Kathy said Nicholas was cranky when you left for work," Wilma said. "Then he started shivering a couple of hours later, and he threw up. She called Dan, who called me, and we met at Kathy's place. When we picked Nicholas up, we noticed that he was all stiff."

Febrile convulsion?

Habit and training pushed away the emotions for the moment as I scribbled rough notes on the chart. I would translate later. I hooked him up to the vital signs monitor, slipped the oxygen mask on, snapped a tourniquet on his arm, and swabbed the spot where I would start the IV. I was pushing things. O2 and IV were not on the standing orders for a young child presenting with a fever. But I couldn't get rid of the doubt scratching repeatedly at the back of my mind.

Why was that cannula shaking so much? Why couldn't I hold it still? I swallowed and tried to relax.

Oh God.

I took in another breath.

Oh God.

The expression had always been simply that. An expression. A cry to a deity that I had conveniently sidelined, only to call Him out when things went wrong. God's name was an expression of fear, a cry for help.

It was only in the extreme situations of my job that I used His name. But now, as I gently pierced my own son's soft skin with a needle, I felt as if I mentally whispered to Him. Drawing on His power and strength.

"When he got drowsy on the way here, I knew something was really wrong," Wilma was saying.

Nicholas's eyes fluttered open. I didn't want to make eye contact. He was a patient. If I saw his eyes, if I saw tears or pain, he would cease to be a patient and suddenly become my son.

Check oxygen levels. Increase saturation. What would the doctor order from the lab? I started a requisition form.

Where was Dr. John?

I checked the vital-signs monitor, my mind still flipping through possibilities.

Chills. Fever.

Treat the fever.

I slipped him to his side and gave him a Tylenol suppository, then noticed how his legs were drawn up. That puzzled me as the whisper in my mind amplified.

CAROLYNE AARSEN

Mother panic clawed at my nurse persona. I couldn't separate them. My little boy lay on the table, deathly ill.

Where was that lab tech?

I glanced at the clock again and made a snap decision. I couldn't wait another second. I wrapped a tourniquet around his other arm, tightened it, and once again slipped a needle into my son's soft skin so I could draw blood. A faint gasp from Wilma pierced my concentration, but I couldn't lose focus. Every second counted to my fevered brain. Once the vials were full, I carefully set them onto the crash cart.

"What's wrong with him?" Weariness and concern edged Dan's voice. "Why did you take his blood?"

I looked across the bed at him and forced a reassuring smile as I pulled off the latex gloves. "The lab will need to run some tests."

I looked down at Nicholas and ran my finger down his soft cheek. He held his head funny. The whisper gained volume. I was about to extend his knee to check my suspicions as Dr. John swept into the cubicle. Dan's eyes narrowed when he saw who it was. Please, no time for this, Dan. No time.

"What do we have here?" Dr. John asked.

"High fever. Did up the blood work." I listed symptoms, turning my son's pain into something clinical. Detached. Simply another patient.

Just as I spoke, a tech came into the room.

I angled my chin toward the crash cart. "You drew blood already?" she frowned, and Dr. John picked up on that.

"That's not part of standing orders." He checked the chart.

"I couldn't wait." I kept my focus on my son. "I think this is serious."

"I know you may have done things differently in Vancouver, but here we follow policy and procedure." Dr. John snapped on a pair of gloves and waited a moment, as if to let his words sink in. I realized what he was doing, and I felt another flicker of panic, followed by anger. We had so often been warned about doctor-nurse relationships. I understood the full implications of it now.

"We don't have time for this," I said. "I'm suspecting meningitis."

Too late I realized what I had done. I had not only criticized Dr. John in front of other people, I had also stepped way out of the bounds of my job and delivered a premature diagnosis.

"I think you might be overreacting." His quiet voice told me more than either Dan or Wilma could pick up. He reached for the otoscope and checked Nicholas's ears himself.

I bit my lip and imagined myself grabbing the front of his lab coat and giving him a shake. Why was he dawdling? Every moment counted.

Keep your mouth shut, Leslie. Don't say anything.

"His ears are red. He might have an ear infection." Dr. John ignored me and gave Dan a patronizing smile.

I couldn't stay quiet. I threw away any shred of pride I had and looked him directly in the eye, pleading with him. "Please, John. This is my son. I know he has more than an ear infection."

Dr. John frowned again. "Is this going to be a problem?"

"I think we should do a lumbar puncture."

Dr. John's eyes narrowed. "Last time I checked, that was my call to make."

I had already rebuffed advances from him that I knew I had unwittingly encouraged. Now I had chosen to go toe to toe with him. If he wanted, he could fire me on the spot, could reduce my hours, could make my life here at the hospital miserable. But I was now nurse *and* mother.

"I know my son. He has never thrown up. He has an elevated heart rate. Nicholas is not teething, doesn't have an ear infection, and doesn't simply have a cold."

Down girl. Keep your voice down. You're exhibiting classic signs of a hysterical parent who wants the entire health care system to move heaven and earth to fix her child.

But it was my son who lay on the table, not my pride or my job. And I knew how quickly we had to act.

Then, with a sigh as if to show he was still in charge, he turned back to Nicholas and lifted his head.

It barely moved. *Nuchal rigidity.* My heart skittered like slippery shoes on ice.

"We'll need to do a lumbar puncture," Dr. John said. "If positive, we'll have to call an air ambulance."

"Lumbar. That's the back, isn't it?" Panic filled Dan's voice. I didn't like to hear that. I wanted Dan the way he always was. Calm and in control.

"We need to drain some spinal fluid to confirm the diagnosis of meningitis." I could barely speak the words as I reached for the lp kit. This was my little boy they were going to do this procedure to. My chubby little Nicholas. Dan's wild gaze snagged mine, and I tried to give him a reassuring smile even though I knew more than he did what the potential complications for Nicholas were.

The next few moments were a flurry of busyness as I unwrapped the lp kit and laid it out, the lab tech returned to collect the fluid, and Dr. John prepped the site. A wave of fear pressed relentlessly against the thin wall of resolve I had erected. I couldn't let it get in. Couldn't let it wash over me.

Dr. John inserted the needle into his spine and, as the fluid came out, the wave grew. Cloudy. My knees wobbled, and ice splintered my heart.

Dr. John called to Arlene to order in the air ambulance, ordered intravenous antibiotics. My hands weren't shaking as much as before, but even so I found myself concentrating fiercely on my job and then, while we waited, writing everything carefully down on the chart as if writing down the precise time and exact measurements would make all the difference for my son.

Son.

I looked down at Nicholas with his one arm strapped against

the bar, his leg immobilized, the IV cannula sticking out of both like an obscenity.

As a father has compassion on his children. The Bible passage slowly filtered past the flickers of fear, eased them away. God loved Nicholas. I had to cling to that.

Finally, remembering that Wilma was here, I looked at her. She stood at the bedside, her eyes firmly on Nicholas, her fingers resting lightly on his leg. His grandmother.

"So what now?" Dan's voice hadn't lost its panicked tone.

"We wait for the air ambulance."

"That's it? That's all we can do?"

I nodded.

Waiting was an agony for parents, and even for nurses. As long as we had a job to do, as long as we were intervening, we felt as if we were pulling the person toward life. I needed a job to do. Something so I could feel like I was keeping my son alive. Keeping him healthy.

"If it's okay with you, I'd like to pray," Wilma said quietly.

I glanced at Dan, who was looking down at our son, his hand clutching Nicholas's. He nodded slowly and closed his eyes.

I guessed praying was doing something, so I closed my eyes.

"Dear Lord, we know that You are a Father and that you love your Son." Wilma's voice was surprisingly calm. "We know how deep Your love is, that You know if even a hair falls from our head. Lord, we plead with You for this child. Be with the doctors that will take care of him. The nurses..." Her voice wavered, which almost made me lose it. She loved my son as well. And she loved God. She was a worthy intercessor.

Wilma cleared her throat. Continued. "Keep him in Your care, Lord, we pray. Keep him healthy. Let us enjoy him again. Amen."

I took a long slow breath, my eyes on Nicholas. He still looked flushed, still lay deathly still.

Nothing had changed, no bright lights accompanied by stirring music, angels singing. No miracle, yet I felt a whisper of peace sifting around the edge of my fear. Nicholas had family around him, interceding.

Then Nicholas stiffened, and vomit spewed out of his tiny mouth. And the peace exploded, thrusting us violently out of the moment.

CHAPTER 17

"*N*o answer at all?" My sweaty hand clutched the headset of the phone in the parents' room of the hospital.

Where are you Terra? I need you.

"I'm sorry, ma'am." The disembodied voice gave standard issue condolences. I whispered an equally fake thanks and dropped the phone in the cradle.

I had dragged myself here after spending most of last night standing guard over my son, keeping death at bay. I had fallen asleep on the couch, had just woken up. My first thought was a desperate need to connect with my sister. But nothing. Had she moved already?

"Hey, there."

I jumped, then felt a hand on my shoulder. Dan crouched down beside me.

"Hey, yourself." I wiped my tired eyes.

Images of last night scurried through my mind. Flashing lights, the drama of the quick transfer, and then the helicopter lifted off, propellers whup-whupping, taking our son away. Then our own mad dash to Edmonton in the night and the long vigil by Nicholas's bed in pediatric ICU.

Dan had left toward morning while I stayed behind. Finally, one of the ward nurses practically pushed me to the parents' room. The last thing I remembered was wondering if I could sleep while my son lay in critical condition.

"Have you seen Nicholas?"

"I just checked on him. He's sleeping." To my disappointment, Dan didn't come and sit beside me. Anneke had slipped in and found the toys. I called her name, and she got to her feet and walked slowly over.

I must look a wreck. I pushed at my hair now nested around my face, finger combing it. I held out my arms to my little girl. When she finally came, I pulled her into my arms, clinging tightly. Then I pulled away and looked her over, almost hungrily.

If it wasn't so pathetic, I would laugh.

She looked like a little refugee. She wore her favorite polka-dotted skirt, the one that was far too large for her, a plaid coat over a stained T-shirt, and rubber boots. Her hair was pulled into some semblance of a crooked pony tail, and I saw a smear of jam on one corner of her mouth and dirt under her fingernails.

I cleaned the jam with a dab of Magic Mommy Spit but was helpless about the rest of her new look.

She had obviously dressed herself, and Dan obviously didn't care.

Obviously, because his ensemble was hardly GQ material. Oblong oil stains decorated his pants, and his shirt had a darker spot on the chest where a pocket had once been and had since been ripped off.

If my family looked like this after two days away from me, I couldn't imagine what my house looked like. *Dan* and *neat* were not two words that dovetailed.

"How are you doing?" He sat beside me but kept his distance.

"I'm tired." I wanted to cuddle into his arms and let his

strength wash over me, but I didn't know how to behave, what to say. Before this emergency, we had been walking carefully around each other, our actions, the words I had spilled out filling a space between us that kept us apart.

He touched my shoulder lightly, then withdrew. He pressed his hands against his knees and got up. Paced the room. Turned to me, his truck keys jingling in his hand. He wasn't leaving already, was he?

"Dan, what's--"

"Leslie, I need--"

I waved my hand at him the same time he told me to go ahead. An uncomfortable pause followed. He spun his truck keys around his hand. And again.

"I'm trying to find the right way to say this." He stopped, his keys still jangling, a nervous habit I hadn't seen in a long time.

He sighed and dropped the keys in his pocket. "You know, *sorry* isn't a big enough word for this." He spoke softly. "But I don't know what other one to use." He stopped, giving me a careful smile.

"What are you sorry for?" I prompted, not sure where he was going.

Dan gave me a cautious smile, lifted a shoulder in a shrug. "Lots of things. I've had time to think the past many hours at the house, without you." He scratched the side of his face with one finger, as if drawing out his thoughts. "I feel like I need to go back and apologize. Way back. Past what I said yesterday, past what I thought we needed, past thinking that what I wanted you should want, past not appreciating all the work you did for our family before, past…" he paused and, to my surprise and shock, his voice broke. He looked away as if ashamed. "I've not been the husband and support I should have been. I've put so much of my needs first."

His words flowed over me, a gentle slide of struggle and confession.

He pulled in a shuddering sigh then looked at me again. "I'm just so very sorry. I don't blame you if, right now, you really don't want to be with me."

His words were a jolt. I needed him now. The past thirty-six hours had revealed my rant against his mother for the petty thing it was. Down the hall our son clung to life. Everything else was swept away as inconsequential.

"I've never wanted to be with anyone else and I can say that truthfully." I matched his quiet tone. "I'm sorry for what I did. I want you to know that thing with Dr. Brouwer never went any further than what Gloria saw. But I was wrong to even encourage that." I rubbed my forehead, wishing I could ease away the pain tentacled around my head. "I'm sorry for judging you. I had no right to take the moral high ground."

Dan slipped his arm around me and gently pulled me close. "Don't. Please. What you did wasn't so bad. It just sounded bad because I thought you went as far with the relationship as I did." He sighed and laid his head on mine. "I have so many things I regret more than I can tell you. I always loved you. Just you. You need to know that."

I looked at him, and older, deeper emotions wound themselves around my heart. "I love you too," was all I could say.

He smiled at me, sorrow edging his mouth. "And I'm sorry for what I said about your mother. That wasn't right. And, believe it or not, I'm really sorry I bought that tractor without talking to you. I put my needs ahead of yours then. I think I've done it more."

A knot of unbearable pain that had pressed on my heart slowly released its hold as he spoke, as he touched me. And with the release came the reality of what I had said.

"Well, we may as well keep going." I leaned into him, his arm warm on my shoulder. "I was wrong about your family. Wrong to resent their involvement." I thought of Wilma praying earnestly for Nicholas. She loved him too.

Dan laid his finger against my lips. "I don't want us to fight. I don't want us to be strangers. Our boy is sick, and I want us to be together. Supporting each other. I love you. I always will." He stopped, his voice breaking. "I love Anneke and Nicholas. And you all need to be the most important people in my life. Not my mother or my sisters or the farm or the rest of my family."

My throat thickened, and I couldn't stop the quiver of my lip. But as I reached for him, he held up his hand. He had more to say. "I asked my family to stay away. To give us some space. And I want you to know that when this is over, when Nicholas is better, we're going to sit down and talk about what is going to happen in our lives, in our future. Whatever we decide, I'll stick with it. If we go back to Vancouver, I'll try the garage thing again if that's what you want. The farm, well, it was really just a dream, wasn't it?"

I could read nothing in his eyes, but the muted yearning in his voice cut me like a knife. I knew how much he loved it here, how much of himself he put into the farm. For the first time since we got married, I saw my husband smile every morning. I saw him enjoying his work, playing with his kids. Home every night and sometimes during the day, a rarity even during his down times with the business.

"Moving to the farm wasn't so much a dream as a plan."

Dan gave a short laugh. "A plan that isn't turning out too great. Keith came just before Nicholas got sick. That's why Mom was over. He wants money, and he's entitled to some. Not as much as he thought, thanks to the assessment we had done, but some nonetheless. I've used up the line of credit to put the crop in, and he doesn't want to wait. So we'll have to look at selling something. Of course, if we move back to Vancouver, that will have to happen anyway."

My mind flashed back to the auction. I imagined people digging through stuff from the farm. Bidding on Dan's equipment. His cows. Maybe his horse. I thought of Mrs. Harris in the hospital and how futile her life seemed now that she didn't have the farm. I never realized how connected you could become not only to property but to the land itself and how it fit in with community and life beyond the farm. I had lived in a large city, but here, my world had expanded far beyond the confines of my own home.

"We don't need to talk about anything now." I gently shifted our conversation away from a decision I was unsure of at the moment. But I was thankful for the gift of freedom he had given me. "Right now our focus is Nicholas."

He gave me a careful smile and I sank further into his embrace, letting his warmth and strength hold me up.

And then, for the first time since Nicholas had been diagnosed, I started to cry.

"Is Mommy sad because of Nicholas?" Anneke's flutey voice slipped over my sorrow, making her presence known.

Dan kept one arm around me and held out his other for our daughter. "A little bit," he said as she insinuated herself between us. But he slipped her to one side so that he sat between Anneke and me, holding us both. He gently kissed my temple, his breath warm against my hair.

My sniffles subsided. I heard a nurse paging a doctor, and I straightened, listening. Thank the Lord, it wasn't Nicholas's doctor.

"We should go."

Dan nodded, kissed me again, and together we got up and walked back to our son's room.

CHAPTER 18

A faint snuffle from the bed pulled me out of the dull sleepiness that dragged at my eyes.

Nicholas lay on the bed beside me, the oxygen mask still covering his face. His IV dripped slowly into a tiny body that lay unnaturally still, the only movement the rise and fall of his chest. Two days without change.

On those days when his relentless busyness wore me out, did I think I would ever wish I could be back home vacuuming sugar out of the dog's hair? That I would yearn to be cleaning up food coloring, sponging pen marks off the linoleum, wiping out dirt from the inside of his mouth and hands?

I wasn't used to being a medical bystander. Emergency work was all about doing. Fixing. Immediacy. Results. The day-to-day maintenance and slow recuperation took place out of our sight, here, in the ward.

It was wearying beyond anything I had ever undergone before.

I stretched, trying to push the fatigue out of my body, trying to corral my stampeding thoughts. Silly pictures resonated through my head. Anneke's horrid clothes. The faint musky scent

CAROLYNE AARSEN

of old clothes from when Dan hugged me. I didn't know if I still had a job after my confrontation with Dr. John. Keith was pressuring Wilma for a settlement. I couldn't fix, plan, or work around the events of the past few weeks.

Beyond that welled a fear of what my house looked like even though I could do nothing about it. Once in a while, when I was alone, it would loom in my mind like a dark cloud, but I couldn't allow it to take over. I had the next hour with Nicholas to think about.

A movement beside me caught my eye, and I spun around.

Dan stood at the foot of the bed.

"How is he?"

The deeply familiar voice pulled me toward him. He laid his hands, warm and strong, on my shoulders, his health and vitality pushing away sickness and fear.

He dropped a quick kiss on my cheek, then pulled me tight against him. I clung to him.

Sniffed.

The gown he wore masked but did not eradicate the fresh scent of clean clothes. In spite of his declaration that things were going to change, I knew it would take aliens and a body swap to get Dan to do laundry. And then I smiled, guessing that it was either Wilma or Gloria. Interfering in-laws. Thank goodness.

"Is there any progress?" Dan's voice rumbled under my cheek. I burrowed deeper, resisting the pull back to the lynch point of our lives.

"Tomorrow they want to do an MRI to see if his brain--" I faltered, took a breath, and tried again. "To see if there's been any brain damage."

Dan held me tighter, and I stopped talking. For now I wanted to enjoy the warmth of my husband's body, the strength of someone stronger than me holding me up. Supporting me. The nurses were wonderful. The counselor suitably concerned.

But they didn't care as intensely about the tiny body in the bed behind us as the man holding me did.

We had made this child together. Dan had clipped his umbilical cord. Dan had been the one to hold him beside me and announce his name. Nicholas Daniel VandeKeere.

He caught my face in his hands. "And how are you doing?"

I carefully probed my emotions, trying to pull out the ones I could describe. "I'm okay. Tired. Scared." That last word wasn't supposed to have slipped out. I was a nurse. Trained. I knew exactly what was happening with Nicholas's blood counts, his oxygen saturation, his intracranial pressure. Fear wasn't supposed to enter into the equation.

Dan looked surprised. "I didn't think you were scared of anything. You would talk about things that happened at work so easily...." he let his sentence fade away, and I filled in the blanks.

"I care. It's just that I can't care too much." I stopped, my throat thickening as my gaze cut to Nicholas, a small body with tubes and leads snaking out from him. Oxygen hissing, monitors bleeping, IV slowly metering out exact dosages, catheter draining. All so familiar, but so wrong. "Whenever emotions get engaged, I can't do my job."

"But watching you in the hospital, working on Nicholas...I've never had a chance to see what you do." He touched my cheek lightly. "I never realized how critical your job is. I tended to treat it like my job. Fix and walk away. It's not the same at all." His embarrassed smile showed me the revelation had been more than his macho self would admit.

He pulled me close in another hug. "Anneke is outside," he murmured into my hair.

I nodded, not wanting to say anything, not wanting to dispel this moment.

"Is she allowed to come in?" Dan asked.

Each time Dan and Anneke had come in the past couple of

days, we had visited in the family lounge. I didn't want to take any risk of her contracting meningitis as well.

I looked sideways and caught a glimpse of my daughter standing in the hallway, clutching a brand-new teddy bear in one hand, leaning toward me, an expectant look on her face. She was being restrained by Wilma.

Over the past few months, a barrage of emotions and changes had bombarded our family from every direction, bringing us to new and different places.

Now our family's world had narrowed down to this small place. Dan, me, and our children moving carefully through the days, hardly knowing what we could expect. But we were still together. That had to count for something.

And, added to that, a family who was working in the background. Supporting. Helping where they could. I knew that Wilma or Gloria or Judy were feeding Dan. Taking care of Anneke. Probably cleaning the DayGlo floor as well.

"Mommy. Where's Nicholas?"

The plaintive note in her voice was my undoing. What could it hurt? She'd already been exposed to him. Already been dosed with antibiotics and sterilized and checked over until I was sure the only thing wrong with her was probably ear wax buildup.

"She'll have to gown up." I pulled away from my momentary haven. "And when she leaves she'll have to wash her hands. She can't touch him, only look at him."

"That's all she wants," Dan whispered. He motioned to the Wilma, who drew Anneke away to gown her up. It was then I noticed the corduroy jumper, the clean ruffled shirt, and the smooth braids in her hair. She looked like my little girl, not a waif, and one of the tight coils inside of me loosened. Wilma was taking care of her, keeping her looking the same as I had.

I walked to the doorway and motioned to Wilma. "You have to gown up too."

She looked from me to Anneke, then gave a brisk nod. I knew

this wasn't going to be a Hallmark moment. Wilma was still Wilma.

But she had prayed for my son and was probably still praying for my son. He wasn't just mine and Dan's. Nicholas belonged to a larger group. Family. Community. It might not take a village to raise a child, but it sure helped.

As Wilma and Anneke entered the room, Anneke ran to me smiling, her arms held out. "Mommy, I miss you." She clutched me around my neck.

She planted a wet kiss on my cheek, then grinned at me, then Nicholas, her world complete. *How bare bones children's lives can be.* All she needed was her mom and dad and little brother, and her contentment quotient was filled.

"Why does Nicholas have wires on him?" she asked in a matter-of-fact voice.

"You remember what Daddy told you," Dan said. "Nicholas is sick, and the doctors need to do all these things to him to make him better."

Her gaze ticked over each item, and she nodded as if granting her approval. "Can I give Nicholas his teddy bear?"

"Sure you can, honey," I said. We kept our voices quiet. Anneke didn't know how tenuous our grip on normal was. We were all together, and that was enough for her. I glanced at Wilma in time to see her press her lips together tightly. Holding back even as she adjusted the mask on Nicholas' face and rearranged his sheets. I wanted to tell her it was okay to cry, but thought I would be overstepping a boundary that had shifted, but still lay between us.

Anneke bent over and kissed Nicholas, her mask touching his cheek. Then she looked at him, as if waiting for a reaction from her little brother. When none came, she wriggled loose out of Dan's arms. "I want to go to the playroom."

Already? She had just gotten here. "Don't you want to sit with me for a little while?" I wanted to hold my healthy child and smell her and feel her wiggling on my lap, life and vitality and everything that I wanted Nicholas to be again.

"I want to see the toys." Her lip started to droop in a pout.

"I'll take her," Wilma said.

"I can go." I looked back at Nicholas, momentarily torn.

Noise and a sudden movement in the hallway caught my attention. Judy stood in the doorway, Allison, Tabitha, and a couple of Gloria's boys behind her.

"Hi, there. I know we can't all come in, but the kids wanted to see Nicholas." Judy caught sight of her mom and her glance flicked from Wilma to me, her eyebrows lifted in a question. I nodded as I hurried to the door.

Judy hugged me and murmured her sympathy. I felt a gentle connection, an opportunity to release my tension to someone else. She stroked my face and smiled, one hand still holding my shoulder.

"I'm glad you asked us to come," she said. "We all wanted to come and see him, but we didn't want you to feel overwhelmed. Goodness knows we've done enough of that to you since you came here."

"Thanks," was all I could say through a throat thickening with grateful tears.

"You're okay with Mom being here? She's not rearranging Nicholas bed or bossing the nurses or anything like that?"

"It's okay, Judy. She's his grandma...Oma, and she does care."

"A lot."

My happy gaze touched on the kids gathered behind her looking solemn and concerned. So many of them here? It was a Friday night in a city a long ways from Holmes Crossing, and they had foregone giddy teenage plans to see our son. *Their cousin,* I reminded myself.

"How is he?" Tabitha asked.

"He's had a couple of rough days. We're taking things one day at a time." I stopped there. I wanted so badly to assure them that everything was going to be fine, but the lack of progress had milked dry my own optimism. I knew the guarded looks the doctors exchanged with the nurses. I had read the charts. I knew the odds.

Douglas, one of Gloria's sons, flashed me a shy smile. "I'm sorry about Nicholas, Auntie Leslie. We've been praying for him."

"I got a card." Tabitha handed me an envelope, her movements quick and self-conscious, as if she remembered the night she had spent in the hospital. "I know it's kind of lame. Mom and Dad told me to tell you they want to come tomorrow if that's okay."

"The kids really wanted to come tonight," Judy said. "The rest of the family would like to come too, but we wanted to stretch it out. Kathy and Jimmy want to come. We had to tell other members of the congregation that for now, it was family only."

The list of names, the group of faces looking at me with concern, slowly loosened another coil inside of me.

Dan and I weren't alone.

"Shotgun on going first," Allison said with authority, grabbing a gown from the cart beside the door. The kids argued over who would go next as Douglas, Gloria's other boy, stationed himself by the cart with the sterile gowns and started tossing them out. I saw one of the nurses at the desk lean over it and look down the hallway, her frown shooting disapproval. But I didn't want to dampen the ebullient spirits. Their actions gently pulled me back to normal. To ordinary.

Judy tugged on my arm, then turned me around and untied the ribbons of my gown. "C'mon. You look like you could use a cup of tea."

"Anneke wants to go to the playroom." I was torn between talking to an adult from the outside world and taking care of my other child's needs.

"I'll take her." Tabitha reached out for her. "I can see Nicholas later."

I relinquished Anneke's damp, sticky hand with some reluctance as Judy took my arm and ushered me down the hallway toward the stairs.

A few moments later, my hands cradled a paper cup filled with warm tea. We sat by a window. Still daylight. In Nicholas's room, time melted and turned into the shape of hands on a clock, the movement and routine of doctors rounds and shift changes.

Through a space in the buildings, I could see blue sky, puffy white clouds. *He covers the sky with clouds, he supplies the earth with rain.*

My attention shifted gently from hospital and illness as I turned back to Judy. "How are things going for you?"

"Fine. But I'm not here to talk about me." She reached across the table and laid her hand on my arm. "I want you to know that we're praying for Nicholas. I know that might not mean much to you..." She let the sentence hang, and I wanted to tell her that it meant more than she could know. But I was new at this God thing and at this family thing and wasn't sure of the proper protocol when people said they are praying for me. So I muttered a quick thanks and spun my plastic stir stick in my tea.

"So, what have the doctors been saying?"

"They're doing the vague doctor-speak. I know that they don't know. With meningitis, time can move things in either direction, good or bad." I sighed, gave Judy a tired smile, hoping she understood. "You know what? Can we talk about ordinary things right now? My life has been doctors and nurses and hospitals for so long, and I want to know there's a life beyond that right now."

Judy's eyes widened for a split second, then she recovered. Smiled. Nodded.

"Sure. You probably talk enough about Nicholas." But then she was quiet, putting the onus on me to come up with a topic.

I gave my tea another stir, trying to find the ordinary. "I'm guessing I can thank either Wilma or you for keeping things moving smoothly on the home front."

"Mostly you can thank Mom or Gloria. Gloria's also been

watering the garden and flower beds for you."

My lilies were going to survive. My house wasn't going to rot away.

Judy leaned forward. "Look, I know Dan asked us to back off, but you know Mom and Gloria. They can't stay away. As for Gloria, she's not the easiest person to get to know, and I know that sometimes she wears her halo a little tight, but she has a good heart. It comes out a little differently with her than it does with most."

I thought of how, only a few moments ago, I felt I could relax when I saw Anneke's hair all shiny and neat. My out-of-control life was gaining control again, and Gloria and Wilma were giving that to me.

"I know she hasn't always been open to you," Judy continued, "but she wants to try. She just isn't sure how to start."

"There are a lot of qualifiers in that sentence." I picked up my cup of tea. I wasn't ready to relinquish the frustration I had nurtured the past few months. No. The past few years.

"I know. Gloria is one of those capable people who set your teeth on edge but at the same time you want in your corner in a rough spot. She's trying so hard to be like Mom. I keep telling her it's not going to work. Mom isn't one you can easily please."

I felt like I should shake my head. Judy was talking this way about her mother? To me, the Imperfect Heathen?

"You look surprised." Judy laughed. "I know what my mom is like. And she's gotten worse since Dad died. He could always tease her out of her little control fits, get her to relax. Keith?" Judy sighed. "Not such a good match. She's gotten more involved and nosy and controlling. She really needs to be put in her place from time to time."

"I've tried."

Judy gave me a quick stroke with her hand. "I know you have. And that's why there's been tension between you and her. She's not used to someone being so blatant about it."

"So I should learn diplomacy, is what you're saying?" I countered with a quick smile to show her that, in spite of what I was dealing with, I hadn't completely lost my sense of irony.

Judy wrinkled her nose. "No. I think you should keep on doing what you're doing. It's good for her."

I almost choked on my tea.

"Seriously. Mom's always had a hard time with boundaries. I'm sure that's why Keith bailed on her. She likes to be in charge and in control. Of everything. She had Dan's life all planned, down to the girl he was supposed to marry." Judy took a quick sip of her tea and waved her hand as if waving off my curiosity. "The girl doesn't live here anymore, so no worries. But Mom is coming around in her own stubbornly slow way. It helps that you come to church once in a while now. I know why you come and that's good, but I also hope someday it will mean something to you."

I thought of the church service and the Coffee Break program Kathy had told me about. An entire world that I was learning to navigate without too many missteps. I liked control too.

"I think it's starting to happen," was all I could say. I swirled the leftovers of my tea around in the bottom of the cup. "There's a lot to learn, and I've never had any background in faith. Or God." But I didn't want to examine my deeper feelings. I didn't want her to think that I had maybe, perhaps, made any kind of commitment.

I could do qualifiers too.

But even so, I knew that my initial hesitation to stay here was slowly wearing away, and I was willing to give our stay a bit more time. See where life took us in the next half year or more.

Judy lifted her shoulder in a careful shrug, as if she didn't dare push too hard either.

"It's a lot to put together." She brushed her cup aside and folded her arms on the table. "But don't let people make it more complicated than it is. God loves you. He's perfect. We aren't.

Jesus came to be the perfect bridge between us and God. Believe that and you're on your way."

He loves me too, he loves me too. The simple words of the children's song came back to me. Not so complicated after all.

"And that's your theology lesson for now." Judy gave a quick laugh. "I also need to tell you that Gloria was pretty impressed with what she saw the other day."

My turn to frown. "What do you mean?" I couldn't imagine doing anything that would impress my very together sister-in-law.

"When Tabitha was in the hospital, and Mrs. Harris came in with a heart attack. She saw a lot of it. Was amazed at how important your job is."

I felt a flush of pride. "I'm surprised she told you."

"About what?"

"Tabitha." And I wondered if she had also told Judy about Dr. Brouwer.

Judy laughed. "I was too. But hey, I'm not going to say too much. Could easily be my Allison in a few years. Or less. Gloria really appreciated the fact that you didn't say anything to anyone about it. Dan didn't even know. Holmes Crossing isn't a big town, and it only takes a spark to get the fire of gossip going." Judy gave me a quick pat on the hand. "Nice to know that if I come in roaring drunk, it won't get put in the *Holmes Crossing Chronicle*."

"Should I be worried?"

"Not yet. Depends on how the next year goes. We've got a major payment coming up, and the government keeps making noises about cutting back our water rights. So it's fight, fight, fight every step of the way."

"But you wouldn't change?" I was testing her commitment.

Judy laughed. "Not on your life. It's not just a job. Farming is a way of life. I like it that Dayton and I are involved in each other's lives. That even though we fight when we do books, we always know where we're at."

Relief flowed through me. "I thought Dan and I were the only ones who squabbled over debits and credits."

"Are you kidding?" Judy looked incredulous. "Dayton and I usually have one major blowout at tax time and a few minor ones along the way. Nothing shock-and-aweish, but close."

"From the looks of things, Dan and I are going to have a few more of these squabbles on our hands. What with Keith demanding money."

Judy held up her hands. "Honey, you have enough on your plate. You don't even need to be sampling that witch's brew." She shrugged. "Besides, I won't blame you if you decide to bail." She held my eyes, her expression suddenly serious. "I mean that, Leslie. Don't feel like you need to hang on longer than you should. I won't blame you if you want to go back to Vancouver and a regular paycheck and get away from us hicks. We can sell the farm and the animals and Mom will be able to manage. But don't feel like you are responsible for us."

I was surprised at the mixture of feelings her comments created. Thankful that I had her blessing to leave. Hurt that she thought I would so easily walk away. Disappointed that she didn't think I could manage.

"I don't mind being on the farm," I said carefully. "And I don't think you're hicks."

Judy pulled a face. "Why not? I do."

I was about to say something more when the sound of hurried footsteps, someone calling my name, sent my heart into over-drive. I pushed away from the table.

Dan appeared in the doorway of the cafeteria, saw me, and called out my name again. "It's Nicholas."

My heart plunged again. *Get up. Get going.*

My hands wouldn't do what my brain told it. I tried to get up, and my knees gave way.

Then Judy arms were around me, holding me up.

"I got you. Let's go."

CHAPTER 19

A machine was breathing for my son. A sudden and unexpected seizure had plunged him further down. The doctor mumbled something about a stroke. I pretended not to hear.

The rash on his legs and arms was still there, cruel patches of ugliness on my son's pale white skin. The disease fought a winning battle in my son's small body, gaining ground inch by precious inch.

Dan stood beside me, watching the lifting and caving in of Nicholas's chest.

"I thought we'd see progress," I murmured. "I thought we were coming ahead."

Dan slipped his arm around me, and once again I turned to him, resting against him.

"We have to keep praying," he said quietly.

"I've been trying," I whispered. "I don't even know how to do it except to say please, please, please."

Dan laid his chin on my head. "If you look at most prayers, that is essentially what they boil down to. That and thank you, thank you, thank you."

I touched Nicholas's face again, trying not to look at the endotracheal tube protruding out of his mouth like an obscenity.

"I'm hoping we can get to the thank you, thank you part."

Dan's arm tightened. "Me, too." His voice broke. The sound cut the ground out from under me. Dan was never weak. He was the one I depended on. He was my strength.

He brushed a kiss over my forehead. "I have a little bit of a thank you. I got a letter from our lawyer in Vancouver yesterday. Lonnie Dansworth settled with his creditors to avoid bankruptcy. We didn't get what he owed, but we got about twenty five cents on the dollar. My lawyer suggested we take it."

I nodded, acknowledging his comment. Lonnie and the money was a part of another world that didn't concern me right now. At one time, I would have been ecstatic, or depressed, depending on my expectations. But now? Nice to know, but unimportant.

We moved closer to the bed, and I caught my foot on a bag of books laying on the floor.

"I brought those. Just in case you might want to read." He gave me a weak smile, his arm still around my shoulder. I bent over and picked up the bag, then sat on the chair beside Nicholas's bed to look through it.

I pulled out the first book, turned it over, and frowned when I saw the faded title.

"The Bible?" I was surprised he would put that in.

"It gives me comfort. Gloria asked me to give it to you. It used to be hers."

I saw the sticky notes bristling out of one side of the book. Just like Dan's. Was this a VandeKeere thing?

Curious now, I turned to one. Psalm 139. I started reading aloud.

"'O Lord you have searched me and you know me. You know when I sit and when I rise; you perceive my thoughts from afar.'" I couldn't help but toss a nervous glance upward. I didn't think

God bothered with perceiving thoughts. What kind of thoughts had He listened in on? I didn't want to contemplate that too much, so I read on. Then stopped and re-read the words: "'If I rise on the wings of the dawn, if I settle on the far side of the sea, even there your hand will guide me, your right hand will hold me fast.'" I lowered the Bible and drew in a long, shaky breath, glancing at Dan. The words touched emotions still tender and raw. For the past few days, fear had been breathing down my neck, hot, hard, and relentless. In the quiet of the early morning, I stood vigil over my son's bed, cocooned by a darkness broken only by the digital readout of the monitors. Utterly and inde-scribably alone. Clinging to trembling hope.

"So the Bible is telling me that no matter where I go, God's hand is there?"

Dan tucked a strand of hair behind my ear in a curiously tender gesture. "That's what the Bible is saying. It's real, Leslie. It really is. I feel like I'm being upheld by the prayers of my family. Like God is nearer to me now than He ever has been." He stopped then and gave me a crooked smile. The self-conscious one he throws out when he feels like what he has said or done has tres-passed some sacred guy code.

I returned his smile but said nothing, giving him the space I knew he needed after such an intimate revelation. I read on.

"'Even the darkness will not be dark to you; the night will shine like the day...I praise you because I am fearfully and wonderfully made...All the days ordained for me were written in your book before one of them came to be.'" Again my eyes slipped to Nicholas. "So how many days has God ordained for Nicholas?" I whispered as my gaze slipped over the array of equipment that kept my son with us. Such a complex organism, the human body, yet so fragile.

Fear gripped me. "Would God take this little boy from me because of things I've thought? Because I haven't paid attention to Him? I've been a bad mother. I've yelled at him. Spanked him.

Does God care enough to let us keep him?" Was this punishment for my foolish dalliance with Dr. John?

"You don't have to fear God." He took the Bible from me, skimmed a moment, and read. "'Search me, O God, and know my heart; test me and know my anxious thoughts. See if there is any offensive way in me, and lead me in the way everlasting.'" As Dan read those last words again, I slipped my hand over Nicholas's tiny one. It fluttered beneath my touch. A faint connection.

Dan's quiet voice washed over me as he finished reading, flipped through the Bible, and read another Psalm. This one was full of praise to a God who took care of nature. Who supplied the earth with rain and made grass grow. As Dan read, I looked off into the distance, thinking of the rain and the cows we had put out to pasture and the crop Dan put into the ground. God cared about that, too? I let the words settle, like the rain the Psalm spoke of, into a parched portion of my life that I never knew needed moisture. Until now. This moment when I felt completely helpless and unsure of what to do. When I felt like I had reached the bottom of a place I could no longer find my way out of. I knew how this could end. I had stood at the bedside of enough children, some babies, fighting for a life that slowly slipped out of our hands. Who was I to think that I deserved to have my son's life given back to us?

Tears gathered in the back of my throat as I put my hand on Dan's. "I want to pray, but I don't know how."

"I'm not an expert either, but I think all we have to do is talk. And I think we're getting better at that."

I smiled back at him, grasped his hand, and let him go ahead. He simply asked for healing for Nicholas. For peace for us. For guidance.

Mine was simpler yet. *Please, Lord. Please.* And as I prayed, it was as if my hands, clinging so tightly to our little boy, trying to maintain control, were slowly releasing. Letting go.

He was God's child first. Mine second.

A moment of anxiety gripped me, and I clung tighter to Dan's hand, then released. "Please Lord. Let your will be done."

And slowly, slowly I released control. Gave our child over to God.

* * *

I KNEW I shouldn't expect miracles, but when I woke up the next morning, for the first time since this disaster dropped into my lap, I felt surging hope.

Nicholas still lay flat on his back, arms and legs splayed out, IV tubes still hooked up to him. The hiss and sigh of the respirator breathing for him.

When the doctor came on his rounds, I kept my eyes on his face, waiting for the surprise to come. But he only shook his head and patted me on the shoulder. Nicholas wasn't going down, was all he would tell me.

It was disheartening, to say the least. My major epiphany had resulted in a stall. Yet, yet, in spite of the lack of miraculous results, as I stood by Nicholas's bed, the peace I had felt last night stayed with me. I didn't want to test it too hard, but when I helped the nurses give him a gentle sponge bath, I didn't cringe when I saw the sores on his skin. I didn't cry when we moved him and his head lolled to one side like a doll's. I could feel God standing beside me, whispering in my ear that He knew what I was going through.

Of course. His son had suffered as well.

I read the Bible some more. Skipped Lamentations. The title was a giveaway. I wanted direction and comfort.

I tried to find the piece Dan had read. Couldn't remember exactly where it came from, so I flipped to the back of the book, looked up *love* in the Concordance...and had a *Whoa* moment. Column after column of Bible verses all referencing the word love. I didn't know there were so many. So I started skimming the columns. "According to your unfailing love...Slow to anger, abounding in love...This is my Son, whom I love..."

I glanced at Nicholas. I understood that part.

I continued. "Love your enemies...This is my commandment: love each other... Love one another... Love one another."

I got the hint. Love was obviously an important concept.

I finally found Dan's passage listed. I turned to it, wishing they'd given the page number instead of just the book of the Bible and the verse, but eventually I found it. I started reading, the words filling a yearning in me that had always lay there, restless and unnamed. Until now.

"Love is patient, love is kind. It does not envy, it does not boast, it is not proud. It is not rude, it is not self-seeking..." I stopped there, keeping my finger on the words.

Self-seeking.

I sighed lightly as I looked at Nicholas. I wanted him healthy for myself. For my happiness to be complete.

I wanted a lot of things for myself. My dream home. My family all to myself where I could control them.

Much control I have now. I watched as the respirator expelled Nicholas's air, then gave him another breath. And much control I would have once we left Holmes Crossing.

But as that thought formulated, another one crept alongside on padded feet.

Stay.

I closed my eyes and gave in to the familiar, teasing thought. It had visited me before. I allowed it more time now. Let it play around in my mind for a while. I imagined us on the farm. Our kids growing up in Holmes Crossing.

A bubble of claustrophobic panic burst in me, but soon dissipated, because with Holmes Crossing came Kathy, who took such good care of my kids. Judy, who made me laugh. Gloria, who made me...well, take another look at myself. And Wilma. A mother who loved my husband and loved my kids. A mother who, unlike my own mother, was at least involved. Cared. Did something to help.

Family. Support.

Letting go.

I remembered what Kathy said about farming and control. Could I allow our family to be held hostage to the vagaries of weather and markets and tariffs and import agreements and countervailing duties? Things so far beyond our control we couldn't even face them down and demand accountability?

And yet...and yet...

I laid my head back against the chair, closed my eyes, and let a small prayer rise up in me. I knew I needed some direction. And as I prayed, I felt a light hand on my shoulder.

I looked up into Dan's smiling face and felt his lips brush mine so gently.

I really, really loved this man.

And I really, really knew what I had to do.

CHAPTER 20

*T*he next few days were a slow grind of doctor visits, nurses' maintenance, and family stopping by. Lots of family stopping by. Wilma came almost every day, and though there were times I wished she didn't, I had come to appreciate the long drive she made just to see Nicholas and me. Kathy came, as did a few of the women from church whom I barely knew. Judy and I had a chance to spend more time together.

Gloria came. There was an initial moment of awkwardness, but she kept things cool. I knew we wouldn't be swapping recipes anytime soon, but something important had shifted between us.

With each visit, I felt as if we were being carried along, supported when we could do nothing more for our son ourselves. I looked forward to each visit, each opportunity to talk to a friendly face, to make another connection with people who cared.

And to rethink our decision to leave after a year. We didn't need to be so hasty. We had nothing waiting for us in Vancouver. We could take our time. Get to know the family a bit better.

I didn't mention my idea of putting our plans on temporary hold to Dan. I didn't dare put it into words yet.

Then, improbably, came the day when Nicholas turned a corner. When the rash started subsiding, leaving only angry red marks, an external reminder of the battle he had fought and won. When the last MRI showed no abnormalities, when he sat up in bed and pulled out his catheter and ripped off his oxygen mask, we knew we were on our way out of the dark plain we had been trudging through for the past ten days.

It was a miracle, plain and simple. Undeserved. Grace granted to graceless people.

* * *

As Dan drove the car up the driveway to the house many long, tiring days later, I glanced down at Nicholas on the seat behind us. He had been quiet all the way home from Edmonton, but as Dan parked the car, Nicholas gave me a loopy grin. Did our little boy know we were home?

I unbuckled my seat belt and felt the hard knot inside me loosen and open up. For some inexplicable reason, I couldn't relax until I saw Sasha running toward us and heard the welcome whinny of the horses as we drove along the fence of the pasture. Normal had returned to our home and family.

Dan turned the key in the ignition and released a belly-deep sigh.

"We're home." He brushed a callused finger over my cheek.

I caught his face in my hands, his shaven cheeks smooth beneath my fingers. His face so familiar. So dear. Then I gave him a noisy kiss.

"I like home."

I pulled down the visor to check my makeup and flipped it quickly up again. Time may be a great healer, but it was a lousy beautician. No sense in looking in a mirror until I got my hair cut again and had access to my own makeup.

I got out of the car, taking stock. The yard looked better than

I did. Lawn, neatly mowed. Flower beds, weeded and tidy. Pots of geraniums, a new note of cheerfulness, hung from the porch.

Home.

Stillness encircled my heart and settled there.

As I gently lifted Nicholas out of the car seat, I held him close to me, curling his warm head under mine. The fresh scent of his clothes couldn't mask the smell of hospital that still clung to him.

He shifted away from me, a hint of the old Nicholas, then drooped against me, as if that small rebellion was all he could manage for now.

We had our little boy back.

Before Nicholas's illness, that whole Valley of the Shadow of Death concept sounded melodramatic. Today, with the sun pouring down bright promises, it became real. Spending time in the shadows gave me a vivid appreciation of light and grace.

I knew the situation could have turned out so differently.

Dan set Anneke down and looked over at me. "Here we are." I saw his gaze flit past me to the fields as the wind flowed over the growing grain. The smile on his face lifted my heart.

"They're here!" Judy's voice called out from the house.

She rushed down the same crooked walk Wilma had so sedately come down when we first came here. Gloria was right behind her.

"Welcome home." Judy gave me a quick hug, stroked Nicholas's head. Gloria hugged Dan and turned to me. A moment of awkwardness hung between us. I didn't know whether we had reached the hugging stage in our detente and, if we had, whether I should make the first move.

She solved that for me by lightly slipping one arm around my shoulder and pressing her cheek against mine. "So glad to see you all back." She stroked Nicholas's head. He blinked at her and snuggled in a bit closer.

My boy.

I caught Gloria's arm. "Thanks so much for taking care of the house while I was gone. I was so thankful to know that things were under control here."

"I know how I would feel if I were in your position and my family looked the way they did." She gave me a quick smile. "Dan stopped by on his way home from the hospital, and I felt so bad that you had to see him and Anneke looking like refugees."

Surprise welled up in me. *I'm more like her than I thought.*

"I really appreciated it. Knowing that the house was well taken care of made things easier for me." I looked around then. "Where's Wilma?"

"Mom's inside." Gloria gave me an awkward pat on my shoulder. "She's taking care of dinner."

Gerrit and Dayton joined us, followed by a crowd of kids and noise. The dogs barked, and a delightful chaos reigned as Dan, Anneke, Nicholas, and I were greeted, patted, slapped on the back, and in general drawn back into normalcy.

As I entered the house, the smell of roasting turkey teased my nose with the promise of the comfort of a home-cooked meal.

Wilma was bent over a roasting pan, basting the golden brown bird. She looked up, her face flushed from the heat of the oven, but her makeup impeccable, her hair stylishly cut. Her eyes held mine a moment longer than usual. She gave me a quick smile, then her gaze moved to Nicholas in my arms, and her features melted.

She put her oven mittens down and walked over, holding out her hands for my son.

"Here, let me take him."

I felt my arms involuntarily tighten around Nicholas. I hadn't had nearly enough cuddling time. I wasn't ready to let go.

But my resolve to learn to let go returned, and I loosened my hold on him, moving him toward Wilma.

He frowned and puckered his mouth, pulling back toward me with a whimper.

Oh, how my heart beat high with joy.

This won't last. I gave Wilma a regretful smile. "He's waking up. Not himself yet."

"Of course." She pressed her lips together, then eased out a dubious smile. "I'm glad he's better, and I'm glad you're home again. Or, well, back at the house." Her small amendment caught me by surprise. It was as if she finally acknowledged the temporary nature of our stay.

"It's nice to be home."

Wilma's features softened, her smile deepened. She turned to Dan and Anneke, and they hugged each other. Wilma cooed over Anneke and lovingly stroked Dan's cheek.

As I watched mother and son together, I thought of all she had lost when Dan moved away and stayed away. Thought of my own relationship to Nicholas and how fiercely I wanted him to be mine. All mine.

I didn't agree with her methods, but I felt a connection.

Dan pulled away and came to my side, slipped his arm around me, and gave me a gentle kiss. "I love you." He laid his forehead against mine.

"I love you too," I breathed, the words settling into my heart.

Judy urged me to sit down while the kids set the table. She and Wilma moved with purpose and calm through my kitchen, finishing supper, delegating tasks, all done with the careless casualness of experts.

Half an hour later, we squeezed ourselves around the table, Dan at the head, me at his side. Nicholas still clung to me. I still savored his neediness.

As we all settled in, Dan looked from me to our kids to his family gathered around the table. "This is wonderful." He laughed lightly. "I'm not a speechmaker, so, thanks for coming. For being a support." He paused and cleared his throat. "But I mostly want to thank our Lord for letting us keep Nicholas awhile longer." He looked at me. "We don't know how long anything lasts, but I know Leslie and I have learned to appreciate each day we have together."

Of course my throat choked up, and of course all I could do at that touching moment was give him a silly smile and look around at our family, blinking furiously.

But when Dan started praying, I let the tears flow. Happy tears. Thankful tears.

When he was done, people got caught up in the serious business of taking food out of bowls and passing them around. Conversation ebbed and flowed punctuated by the clink of cutlery on china, and I savored the belonging. I still didn't recognize all the names, and many of the stories were unfamiliar, but this time I didn't mind. In time I would "get" them.

"Judy, did you make trifle for dessert?" Dan leaned back from the table after lingering over second helpings of his favorites.

Judy clapped her hand over her mouth, her eyes two horrified circles above her fingers. "I forgot. It's on the table at home and everything." She rolled her eyes. "Oh well, you know what they say. Brain cells come and go, fat cells stick around."

"Oh no...Aunt Judy...I love your trifle...what about desert...?"

Dan sighed. "What's a good turkey dinner without the promise of chocolate afterward?"

"I could go home..."

"Don't bother, Judy," I said. "That's too far." Part of me hoped she would pooh, pooh the comment and get up anyway. But she shrugged and stayed where she was.

Another thought slipped into my turkey-tired brain. I weighed it, measured it, and thought, well, why not.

"I'll be right back." I ran upstairs and ducked into our cupboard, then came back downstairs carrying my precious cargo.

"If anyone's interested, I have a box of Lindor chocolates. I believe there's about two hundred and eighty-nine here. More than enough for seconds and thirds."

I could see Dan doing some quick calculations. He knew exactly how many I had bought and how many I should still have.

"What can I say?" I flashed him a smile. "Anything worth doing is worth overdoing."

But while I was trying to be smart, the teenagers whipped the box out of my hand and in seconds were inhaling the chocolates like they were air. Minutes later the box returned to me, half full, or half empty, depending on your point of view. It was like watching six months flash before my eyes.

Dan dug into the box and came up with a handful of chocolates as well. "Thursday, Friday, Saturday..." he intoned as he lay them out beside his plate.

"What are you talking about?" Judy's puzzled glance went from Dan to me.

"Tell you some other time." I dug out a handful myself. I could always buy more if I needed to.

If.

* * *

AFTER CHECKING Nicholas for the seventeenth time, I finally settled into bed.

"Are you done now?" Dan gave me a playful grin as I scootched into his arms and wriggled a moment, trying to get the pillow just right.

"For now." I pulled in a long breath and looked up at the ceiling, my eyes flickering over the water spots, barely discernible in the half light of the bedside lamp. I didn't think I would come to a place in my life where I would be happy to see their familiar shape. "Today was a good day."

"Today was a good day."

"I like your family."

"I do too."

"In fact, I love your family. Judy is funny, Gerrit is kind, and

Dayton is one of those solid people you can count on. The kids are nice. When Gloria has her guard down, she's a good person." My exuberance drifted off. What to say about Wilma? Would he notice that I left her off my little mutual admiration society list?

"It's going to be hard to leave," he said quietly.

I drew in a long slow breath. "We don't need to talk about that yet." In the dim light coming in from the hallway, I saw a half smile curve his lips.

"No. But we're going to have to face reality sooner or later."

"We've had our share of reality." I gave him a kiss, slipped my arms around him, and held him close. "Let's live out some fantasies for tonight."

"We could eat some more chocolate," he said suggestively.

"We'll save that for another fantasy." I giggled. Then kissed him again. And again.

CHAPTER 21

"*Y*ou'll be drowning in zucchini come fall." Kathy yanked out another weed and threw it on the pile at the end of the row, then crouched back on her heels. "You'll be able to single-handedly supply the county with the stuff."

"What's zucchini?" I zeroed in on a plant that rose above the rest, drawing attention to itself. Plus it stank. I guessed it was a weed and pulled it out. You'd think that something that wasn't supposed to belong would have some discretion.

"Looks like cucumber, tasteless, and prolific. And my goodness, could you have planted any more pumpkins?"

I looked up at my friend, who was crouched in my garden a few rows down from me, her hair leaping up in glorious disarray. "I thought it would be fun to have some jack o' lanterns at Halloween."

"You have some scary idea of fun. Well, I'm done" Kathy got to her feet and brushed the dirt off her pants. She walked over to Nicholas, who sat quietly in the garden bench on the side of the garden. "Hey, buddy, how are you doing?"

He lifted his hands to her, and she easily swung him up in her arms. He looked pale yet, but each day brought some new improvement. Some small triumph.

"He's going to be all right, isn't he?" The worried note in Kathy's voice resonated with the niggle of concern that lay tucked in a dark corner of my mind.

"The doctors gave him a clean bill of health." I dug out my last weed and looked over the garden. All tidy until the next onslaught. "It's the only decent bill we have in our house these days."

"Tell me about it. We always have more month than money at our place. But we struggle on."

Kathy said this with a sigh of resignation, but at the same time I knew, as Judy had also said, that she wouldn't trade her life for anything. I looked over the yard again and smiled. Each time I left and came back, it was as if tiny tentacles caught and anchored me here. It wasn't paradise, but hey, where was?

Anneke, Carlene, and Cordell joined us just as we headed to the house for some iced tea.

Keith had phoned this morning demanding his money. When Dan had hung up the phone, he told me he had to go to town this afternoon to see the lawyer. I said I would come with him, but all morning the meeting hung over me like a dark cloud. I couldn't sit still, couldn't concentrate, so I went out and weeded the garden. I had no idea what was at stake and how much money would be flowing out of black hole that was the farm's bank account.

Kathy, who had come to babysit, had found me crouched between the peas and the potatoes and pitched in. Nothing like pulling weeds to cement a friendship.

"Wow, look at all the chocolates." She zeroed in on the bowl I had on the table. "You win some kind of prize or something?" She unwrapped one and popped it in her mouth, sighing in bliss. "I love these. My favorite waste of time."

I put the kettle on the stove and laughed. "No. Just call it an experiment that had its day." I turned on the heat and glanced out the window just as Dan drove up the driveway. My heart kicked in my throat. "Hey, Kathy, I've got to go change. Dan is here. We have to go."

"You go make yourself gorgeous for the lawyer. I'll just make a dent in these chocolates. So good." She unwrapped one for Nicholas. "Here buddy, that'll put some hair on your chest."

She nuzzled him, he laughed, and I felt pure joy pierce me at the sound.

I showered in record time, brushed my hair, checked my lipstick, and pulled a face at my hair. Still needed a cut, still hadn't had time. I pulled out the nail scissors and trimmed my bangs so I wouldn't look like a badger had taken residence on my head, double checked the makeup, and retreated from the field of a losing battle.

Dan had changed by the time I came back downstairs and was helping Kathy put a dent in my chocolate stash. He gave me a tired smile as I joined them. I gave him a hug. Me. Supportive wife.

"Let's go." He pushed himself away from the table.

I kissed the kids, waved to Kathy and, as we walked down the sidewalk, petted Sasha's head. The chickens were scratching in the yard, softly clucking to each other, and the horses, sensing our presence, started whinnying.

Our farm, I thought as I got into the car with Dan. Our place.

As we reversed out of the parking spot and headed down the driveway, I glanced back over my shoulder. The house hadn't changed from the first time we arrived. It still needed a coat of paint, but the defects had become familiar. And they could easily be corrected.

With a bit of cash input.

Dan gave me a nervous smile and reached over and squeezed my hand. "How are you doing? Ready to face a new adventure?"

Since we had come back from the hospital, Dan had made noises about making plans for our future, but I kept putting him off. I'd had enough adventure, I kept telling him. We could wait. But now, Keith's last and final phone call had brought us to a turning point. We had to make a decision.

"How much is Keith entitled to anyway?"

"Not as much as he thinks he is, thanks to the assessment we did, but enough that the farm doesn't have the cash on hand to satisfy him."

"That doesn't tell me anything, Dan." I brushed my hand over his hair. I should have gone after him with the nail scissors.

"We'll know for sure once we talk to the lawyer, but for now we're looking at about thirty to forty thousand."

I drew in a careful breath. That was a lot of money. "And how is the farm supposed to come up with that?"

Dan shook his head. "The only way we can is to sell some land. And if we do that, our income goes down, which means the farm can't support two families." He blew out his breath as he stared out the car window. "So we're pretty much looking at selling the whole deal."

My heart pleated at the thought. Until now, Dan and Wilma hadn't told me everything that had happened while Nicholas was in the hospital. They had kept Keith's demanding calls away from me and the bubble that was Nicholas's health.

I was thankful for their consideration, but at the same time, it meant I knew very little actual facts and figures. Until now.

We came to the top of the hill, and I looked back over the valley. Could I leave this now? After all we had been through?

I looked at Dan. Thought of how far we'd come in the months we were here.

We had come here as married strangers, bound by our children and our promises. We had grown. Our marriage, once raveled and fraying, had been strengthened and slowly woven back together. Dan, Nicholas and Anneke were my breath, my blood, my life. Not accessories in a dollhouse that I needed to make my life complete.

The thought that had taken up residence in my mind some time ago hadn't left. Instead, with each day, each experience, it had grown, settled, and taken root.

I wondered if I dared voice the thought. Dared make it real. There would be no turning back if I did.

My mind flashed back to a summer camp. Two guys had dragged me down the pier toward the lake. I wore a new leather coat and brand new blue jeans, both of which I had saved my tip money for, all in an effort to impress the very guys who were now dragging me down the pier to the lake.

When we got to the end, they lifted me up and started swinging. I was still laughing. Then, to my stunned amazement, they let go.

I remember the surprisingly exhilarating feeling of being airborne, hanging in space over the water, stupefied that they had actually done it, yet realizing the inevitability of gravity would soon make itself known.

That was what I felt like now. I was in the grip of fear, but at the same time, the exhilaration of wonder.

"I want to buy Keith's share of the farm out with our house money." I was taking the proverbial plunge. "With the bit we got from Lonnie Dansworth and what I have saved up, I think we have enough."

Dan laughed nervously. "What are you saying?"

"I was speaking English." I gave a feeble laugh, surprised that I had finally spoken the words aloud. "But I'll say it again. I want to use our money to buy out Keith."

Dan slammed his foot on the brakes, pulled to the side of the road, and turned to me. He rested one elbow on the steering wheel, his other draped over the headrest, his expression full of confused wonder. "Are you saying what I think you're saying?"

I threw my hands up in happy exasperation. "I dunno. What do you think I'm saying?"

"The money. You want to use it to pay Keith."

"He can be taught," I announced to the roof of the car. "Yes. Money. Pay Keith. See Leslie. See Leslie use single syllable words so husband understands." I was getting nervous, and when I got nervous, I got flippant.

Dan bit his lip, ran his hands through his hair, and laughed lightly. "You're making a joke, but I sense you're serious about this."

Okay, I have to confess this was very anticlimactic. I expected him to pull me in his arms, sweep me off my feet, and swing me around like they do in the best romance movies. Of course, I could have chosen a better venue than the cramped quarters of a subcompact car.

"But what about the house? All the plans you made?" He still looked surprised.

"I have a house. I have a yard bigger than I could ever have in Vancouver, or any city." I gave him a slow smile. "I have my small family, and in the past few months, I've discovered I have a bigger family."

"It's hardly a dream home." Dan reached for my hand. Excitement and wonder coiled around him even as his words added reality. "It needs work. We'll need new shingles in a couple years. The appliances are old. The water tank is rusting out...."

"I hope you're not trying to change my mind," I said in mock warning.

"No. Just making sure." He shook his head, amazed wonder in his voice. "I can't believe you want to do this. I can't believe you're serious."

"This time I am."

"This is unbelievable! I can't believe it."

"You're repeating yourself." I took refuge in teasing.

He grabbed my face and kissed me solidly on the mouth. Finally. Then pulled back. "Are you sure?"

"I think I'm sure." Hardly words to go striding confidently into the future with, but they would do for now. "We'll have to draw up some kind of agreement."

"Of course."

"And I want to make sure that the money I make from my job is kept separate from the farm."

"Ah, still wanting control." His grin belied the comment.

"Ah, still being smart." I made a fist and bopped him lightly on the chin. Then leaned over and cancelled my reprimand with a kiss. "I know I can learn a lot more about family. About Jesus and God." I gave him a self-conscious smile. I still felt awkward about the whole issue of faith and religion and a relationship with God. It still felt like talking to my mother about sex. It was intimate and real, and I didn't know the right words to share the emotions I had felt during those moments alone. When I had felt the touch of a Father, the love of a Savior, and the breath of the Spirit.

Dan closed his eyes, then slowly drew me into his arms and squeezed and squeezed. "You are the most amazing woman." He cupped my face in his hands. "I wish there were better words to say than *I love you*. Because I know millions of people have used those words, and I feel like I need something unique. Just for you."

"You're unique." I smiled and kissed him again. "Just like everyone else. Now, we'd better go before Keith thinks he needs interest as well."

As we drove, Dan looked at me a couple of times, as if making sure the woman spouting the strange ideas was still his wife.

We made it to the lawyers in record time and were immediately escorted into his office. There we were greeted by a suavely dressed man, whose suit was perfectly aligned on his shoulders. I couldn't help a quick glance at Dan's best corduroy shirt and jeans. He looked better. Way better. My dearest husband.

"Hello, my name is Phil Brinks. I'll be your lawyer."

Finally. After all this time, here was my chance.

"Hello." I glanced at Dan and winked at him, tucking my arm into his, then turned back to Mr. Brinks. "My name is Leslie VandeKeere. And I'm a farmer's wife."

* * *

I HOPE you enjoyed Leslie's story. You will notice that she was writing e-mails to her sister at the end of many of the chapters. And then, nothing. Want to find out what happened to Terra? Read an excerpt here:

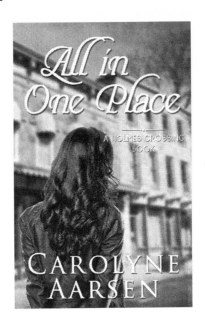

CHAPTER ONE

. . .

BY THE TIME I left British Columbia, I'd stopped looking over my shoulder. When I started heading up the QUE2, my heart quit jumping every time I heard a diesel pickup snarling up the highway behind me.

I was no detective, but near as I could tell, Eric didn't know where I was.

Four days ago, I'd waited until I knew without a doubt that he was at work before packing the new cell phone I had bought and the cash I had slowly accumulated. I slipped out of the condo we shared, withdrew the maximum amount I could out of our joint account, rode the city bus as far as it would take me, and started hitchhiking. Phase one of my master plan could be summed up in three words: Get outta town.

Okay, four words if you want to be precise about it.

Now, as I stood on the crest of a hill overlooking a large, open valley, I was on the cusp of phase two. Again, three words: Connect with Leslie.

I let the backpack slip off my shoulders onto the brown grass in the ditch and sank down beside it in an effort to rest my aching feet and still my fluttering nerves. I was leery of the reception I would get from my sister and not looking forward to what she might have to say. Since August, nine months ago, I'd tapped out two long, rambling e-mails telling her what was happening in my life and laying out endless lists of reasons and excuses. But each time I read the mess of my life laid out in black and white on a backlit screen, guilt and shame kept me from hitting the Send button.

I knew she had a cell phone, and I knew the number, but a text message couldn't begin to cover either apologies or explanations.

So I was showing up after nine months of nothing hoping for a positive reception.

But at the same time my heart felt like a block of ice under my sternum, the chill that radiated out of it competing with the heat pouring down from above.

The click of grasshoppers laid a gentle counterpoint to the sigh that I sucked deep into my chest. I slowly released my breath, searching for calm, reaching into a quiet place as my yoga instructor had been yammering at me to do.

I reached down, tried to picture myself mentally going deeper, deeper.

C'mon. C'mon. Find the quiet place. Anytime now.

The screech of a bird distracted me. Above, in the endless, cloudless sky, a hawk circled lazily, tucked its wings in, and swooped down across the field. With a few heavy beats, it lifted off again, a mouse hanging from its talons.

So much for inner peace. I guess there was a reason I dropped out of yoga class. That and the fact that my friend Amy and I kept chuckling over the intensity of the instructor as she droned on about kleshas and finding the state of non-ego.

The clothes were fun though.

I dug into my backpack and pulled out my "visiting boots," remembering too well how I got them. Eric's remorse over yet another fight that got out of control. On his part, that is. He had come along, urging me to pick out whatever I wanted. I had thought spending over a thousand dollars could erase the pain in my arm, the throbbing in my cheek. But those few hours of shopping had only given me a brief taste of power over him. His abject apologies made me feel, for a few moments, superior. Like I was in charge of the situation and in charge of the emotions that swirled around our apartment. That feeling usually lasted about two months.

Until he hit me again.

I sighed as I stroked the leather of the boot. For now, the boots would give me that all important self-esteem edge I desperately needed to face Leslie.

As I toed off my worn Skechers and slipped on the boots, I did some reconnoitering before my final leg of the journey.

Beyond the bend and in the valley below me, the town of Holmes Crossing waited, secure in the bowl cut by the Athabasca River. For the past three days, I'd been hitching rides from Vancouver, headed toward this place, the place my sister now called home. In a few miles, I'd be there.

I lifted my hair off the back of my neck. Surely it was too hot for May. I didn't expect Alberta, home of mountains and rivers, to be this warm in spring.

In spite of the chill in my chest, my head felt like someone had been drizzling hot oil on it, basting the second thoughts scurrying through my brain.

I should have at least phoned. Texted.

But I'd gone quiet, diving down into my life, staying low. I wasn't sure she'd want to see me after such a long radio silence. I knew Dan wouldn't be thrilled to see me come striding to his door, designer boots or not. Dan, who in his better moments laughed at my lame jokes, and in his worse ones fretted like a father with a teenage daughter about the negative influence he thought I exerted on my little sister. His wife.

Leslie had sent me e-mails about my little nephew Nicholas's stay in ICU and subsequent fight for his life, pleading with me to call to connect. I knew I had messed up royally as an aunt and a sister by not being there. Not being available.

And I'd wanted to be there more than anything in the world. But at the time, I'd been holding onto my life by my raw fingertips and had no strength for anyone else.

You had your own problems. You didn't have time.

But I should have been there for my only sister. I could have tried harder.

The second thoughts were overrun by third thoughts, the mental traffic jam bruising my ego.

I pulled a hairbrush out of my knapsack. Bad enough I was showing up unannounced. I didn't need to look like a hobo. As I worked the brush through the snarl of sweat-dampened curls, I promised myself that someday I was getting my hair cut. I stuffed my brush back into my backpack and brushed the grass off my artfully faded blue jeans, thankful they were still clean. Zipping up my knapsack, I let out one more sigh before I heard the sound of a car coming up over the hill. My low spirits lifted as I turned to see who might rescue me from walking on these stilettos all the way to town.

They did a swan dive all the way down to the heels of my designer boots.

A cop car, bristling with antennas and boasting a no-nonsense light bar across the top, was slowing down as it came alongside me.

Did Eric sic the Mounties on me?

I teetered a bit, wishing I were a praying person. Because if I believed that God cared even one iota about my personal well-being, I'd be reciting the Lord's Prayer, Hail Mary--anything to get His ear right now.

WANT TO FIND OUT MORE? Purchase All In One Place by clicking on the picture below:

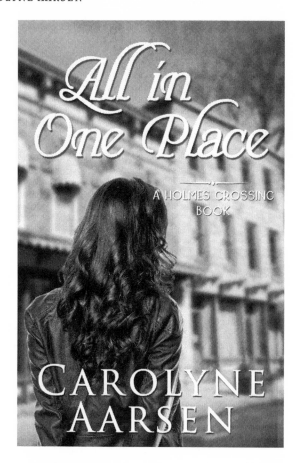

ALL IN ONE PLACE